ELLE GRAY

SHADOWS OF THE FALLS

Shadows of the Falls
Copyright © 2023 by Elle Gray

All rights reserved. Without limiting the rights under copyright reserved above, no part of this publication may be reproduced, stored in or intro-duced into retrieval system, or transmitted, in any form, or by any means (electronic, mechanical, photocopying, recording, or otherwise) without the prior written permission of both the copyright owner and the above publisher of this book.

This is a work of fiction. Names, characters, places, brands, media, and in-cidents are either the products of the author's imagination or are used fic-titiously. The author acknowledges the trademarked status and trademark owners of various products referenced in this work of fiction, which have been used without permission. The publication/use of these trademarks is not authorized, associated with, or sponsored by the trademark owners.

PROLOGUE

"GOD, TONIGHT IS EXACTLY WHAT I NEEDED," ALEXA said.

"Girl, you work too hard. You need to get out and have a little fun now and then. Recharge those batteries," her friend Macy told her. "What you need is a man."

"Yeah, I tried that. Didn't really work out," Alexa replied. "The men I find all seem threatened by the fact that I put my career ahead of everything else. They just don't get it."

"You just haven't found the right guy."

"I'm pretty sure that's because he doesn't exist."

"He exists, hon. You just need to be patient and persistent," Macy insisted.

Alexa sighed and sank into the plush back seat of their rideshare car, feeling pleasantly muzzy after spending the evening having a few drinks and laughs with her friends. It had been far too long since they'd all gotten together and just cut loose and Alexa was realizing how much she missed it. But she was putting in seventy-hour weeks—sometimes more—trying to make her bones at one of the biggest advertising agencies in Seattle.

She'd been with the firm for a few years now but still felt lucky to have landed a gig with such a prestigious agency straight out of college, to begin with. Alexa wanted more than anything to prove she belonged there in the big leagues, sharing the field with the big boys. She knew she had the goods to make a name for herself in the industry. But she needed to prove it to them. It was going to take a few more years of hard, intense work, but she knew she would scale that mountain and put herself on the path where she wanted to be.

"If only it was that easy," Alexa groused. "I have to work twice as long and three times as hard as the men in that firm if I plan on getting anywhere. Most guys don't get that."

Macy grabbed her hand and squeezed it, a sympathetic look on her face. "I hear you. But it's not just guys. We never see you anymore either. Seriously, Lex, we all miss you."

"I miss you guys, too. But I have to pay my dues. It's just the nature of the game," she said. "Besides, it's not like you aren't busy and have your own things going on."

"That's true. But the difference is that I make a point of carving out time to practice a little self-care. I don't run myself ragged like you do," Macy replied.

"Give it a couple more years and I'll be able to throttle back a bit," Alexa said. "It's all part of the grand plan."

"Still with the grand plan, huh?"

Alexa nodded. "Yes indeed, my friend. I have my career arc all mapped out. A couple of years from now, I'm going to be middle management in the firm. A couple of years after that, I'll be sitting in my own office on the executive floor."

Macy laughed. "Is there anything in your life you haven't planned out years in advance?"

Alex pursed her lips and pretended to think about it. "No. Not really."

SHADOWS OF THE FALLS

They shared a laugh together as the Uber driver took a left turn onto Alexa's street. The truth was, Alexa was a planner. She believed in mapping out the important events and plans in her life and putting it all on an ever-evolving vision board. She was a firm believer in the manifestation of your desires, the power of positive thinking, and the laws of attraction. She believed in karma and that what you put out to the universe you got back.

That was why she always took special care to put positive vibes out to the world. She took care to project compassion, kindness, and positivity. And she did her best to always project an aura of confidence and strength. After all, what she put out, she always got back.

"When are we going to see you again, doll?" Macy asked.

"Soon, I hope," she replied. "Let me check my calendar. Maybe we can all get together for brunch or something?"

"I'd love that. There's this cute new bistro I've been dying to try."

"Great. Then I'll get some dates over to you soon and we can work it out."

The car pulled to a stop at the curb in front of the small house Alexa had grown up in. Her parents had died while she was in college when a drunk driver hit them head-on while she was in college and had left the place to her and she just didn't have the heart to sell it. There were too many memories stored within those walls. Alexa planned to always have a swanky condo in downtown Seattle, but she figured that could wait. For a little while, anyway. Once she was ready, she would probably rent the place out or maybe turn it into an Airbnb or something like that. She already knew she'd never be able to bear parting with it.

Financially, it made a lot of sense to live in a house that was already paid for. It would let her save up a nice little nest egg so she could buy her condo outright rather than finance it after she got the promotions she was busting her butt to get. Alexa's vision board mapped out the next few years of her life, but it wasn't set in stone, and she learned long ago the value of being flexible. Plan, but always be adaptable. That was her motto. The condo could wait for a little while.

Alexa pulled Macy into a tight hug and gave her a kiss on the cheek. "I'll call you just as soon as I have some dates," she said. "We are absolutely doing brunch."

"Block out the whole day because we're doing brunch with bottomless mimosas."

"That, my dear, is a plan."

Alexa gave Macy another hug then grabbed her bag and got out of the car, shutting the door behind her. She watched it drive off with a wistful sigh, part of her wishing she could have more free time to have fun with her friends. But that wasn't part of the plan. And though she preached the value of flexibility to herself, she also preached the value of responsibility and maintaining her sterling work ethic. Without hard work, her plans would all be for naught.

She turned back to her house and frowned. The windows in the front room were dark, which they shouldn't have been since they were set on automatic timers that should have turned the lights on a few hours ago. She'd had problems with the timer switch the last few weeks but hadn't gotten around to getting somebody out to fix or replace it just yet. Alexa hated walking into a darkened house.

"Dammit," she muttered to herself.

She headed up the walk then up the three steps to the wooden porch and fished her keys out of her bag. Alexa silently chastised herself for dragging her feet on the repair as she unlocked the door. She stepped inside, quickly flipped on the lights, and dropped her bag on the chair beside the door. Alexa turned and closed the door then made sure to lock it—then double-checked the locks as was her nightly ritual. That done, Alexa headed to the kitchen and poured herself half a glass of white wine.

"Might as well keep the good times rolling for a bit," she said with a smile.

Alexa walked through and into her bedroom, quickly flipping on the lights. She took a drink of her wine, reveling in that slightly tipsy feeling she had. Alexa knew she was wired tight, which is why she enjoyed those rare occasions when she could let go and just float away a little bit. She knew her limits and never let herself get sloppy.

Smiling to herself, Alexa stripped down and threw her clothes into the hamper, noting that she'd need to make a run to the dry cleaner that week. She turned on the Bluetooth speaker and put on one of her playlists. She took another drink then walked into the bathroom and turned on the shower, singing along with "Believer" by Imagine Dragons as she waited for the water to get hot. Once the steam was billowing around her, Alexa set the wine glass down on the back of the toilet and hopped in, letting the heat from the water seep into her muscles.

Alexa took a long, leisurely shower—leaning out a couple of times to finish off her half-glass of wine—before cutting the water and stepping out. She dried off and then wrapped the towel around her body. Alexa used another towel to dry her hair as she walked into the bedroom where she stopped abruptly, a frown creasing her lips. The music had stopped playing. She walked over to the dresser and looked at her phone, a sense of trepidation stealing over her. Her phone hadn't died or been cut out… it had been paused.

A cool breeze washed across her skin and when Alexa turned around, she saw the heavy curtains over her windows stirring. On shaky legs, she walked over and pulled the right curtain aside to find that her window was slightly open. She sometimes cracked the window at night just to get a little fresh air into the room as she slept but Alexa racked her mind and couldn't remember opening it last night—then forgetting to close it again. Being a single woman living alone, she was incredibly safety conscious. She didn't forget to lock doors or close windows. Usually.

"You must be losing your mind," she said with a shake of the head.

It didn't usually happen, but Alexa had forgotten to close the window a few times before. And she'd been so busy and stressed lately that she may have just spaced out and forgot to close the window before she left for work. It wasn't impossible. There was nothing out of place or missing, so she hadn't been robbed. And if somebody was in the house when she got home, she figured they would have made themselves known to her by now.

Silently chastising herself for the second time that night, Alexa quickly closed the window and locked it again then peered outside, half-expecting to see some malevolently smiling person looking back at her from the shadows. There was nobody there, of course, so she pulled the curtains tight. As she did though, the creak of a floorboard behind her sent a dagger of ice straight through her heart. Her entire body began to tremble, and her legs felt like they might give out under her.

Alexa's heart beating wildly inside of her, she slowly turned around and gasped at the large figure filling her bedroom doorway.

"Welcome home, beautiful," he said. "I've been waiting for you."

CHAPTER ONE

"**Y**ou know? I think this is exactly what I needed," Spenser said.

"I thought a little fresh air and outdoor time might do you some good," Ryker replied.

"You were absolutely right. You should be a doctor."

He laughed and hitched his pack up on his broad shoulders. Spenser took a long swallow of water from her bottle before capping it and hooking it to her belt again. She took a moment to catch her breath, nodding to him when she was ready to keep going. Ryker led her up the steep, winding path that circled what felt like a small mountain, cutting in and out of the forest. After another half hour, the trail ended at a plateau atop the hill.

"Wow," Spenser said. "What an incredible view."

"I figured you'd like it."

"You figured right."

Ryker set his pack down and started to empty it as Spenser dropped her pack then stepped to the edge of the plateau and looked out at the town of Sweetwater Falls spread out in the valley below. The sun glinted off the surface of the wide, slow-flowing river that started at the town's namesake waterfall that sat in Stonewood Forest, to the east of the town center. The river meandered through town, basically bisecting it in a serpentine fashion. From her vantage point, Spenser could see all the bridges that connected the two sides of town.

Most of the bigger, older buildings were made of red brick with white peaks and reminded her a lot of the old colonial towns back east. But at the edges of town, Spenser could see all the new construction. Homes, apartment buildings, stores, and more were being built and Sweetwater Falls was growing at a breakneck pace.

"It's so beautiful. Totally picturesque," Spenser said. "I've been working so much that I really haven't had time to get out and appreciate my new hometown."

"For all its flaws, it's a beautiful place to live, that's for sure," he said.

"And for such a small town, it's a lot bigger and more spread out than it looks from the ground level," she added.

"And getting bigger by the day."

"Yeah," she said with a frown. "Here's to progress."

"Here's to something anyway."

Spenser laughed to herself. Ryker was something of a traditionalist and a staunch minimalist. More than that, he was not very good with change. Ryker liked things a certain way and deviating from that certain way tended to throw him for a bit of a loop. He would eventually adapt, but it was a process. He grew up in Sweetwater Falls and had grown accustomed to it just how it had always been, so she knew that watching it grow and evolve over time had been hard for him to accept. But he was getting there.

She turned around to find that he'd spread out a blanket and laid out the food he'd brought along for their picnic. A moment later, Spenser turned and gave a startled jump as Annabelle and Mocha—Spenser's Great Dane and Ryker's Chocolate Lab—burst out of the bushes, barking like mad as they chased each other. They raced around the clearing, taking turns chasing each other. Spenser laughed and shook her head.

"Settle down, you clowns," Ryker called after them.

After a few minutes, they both collapsed in a patch of grass next to their blanket, their breathing heavy, tongues lolling out the side of their mouths, with big doggy smiles on their faces. Spenser walked over and grabbed the bowls out of her pack and poured out some water for them. Both dogs jumped to their feet and happily slurped down the water then looked up at Spenser expectantly. She grinned at them then pulled a couple of the hot dogs she'd brought for them out of her pack and handed them over. Both dogs gave them a quick chew but essentially swallowed them down whole then looked up at her with their big, soulful eyes, trying to silently persuade her to hand over another one. She was unable to resist and handed over another hot dog.

"You're both manipulative little monsters, you know," she said.

"They know. And they think it's one of their better qualities," Ryker said.

"Somebody should tell them they're dead wrong about that."

"I'll leave that to you. You're better at that sort of thing," he replied with a laugh.

Spenser laughed along with him and shook her head. The dogs, sensing they weren't getting another treat for the moment, flopped back down in the grass, content to soak up the sunshine. Spenser sat down on the blanket as Ryker was pouring the wine. He handed her a glass with a smile.

"You thought of everything, didn't you?" she asks.

"It's not a picnic without food and wine."

"You are quite right, Mr. Makawi."

They sat back and sipped their wine as Spenser continued to take in the view. It was breathtaking. She couldn't believe that in all the months she'd been there now, she hadn't once taken this hike and looked at her new hometown from this perspective before. In her defense, she had been rather busy since hitting Sweetwater

Falls. There never seemed to be a shortage of crime. But she was glad she took the day off, not having to think about chasing bad guys, drug dealers, and murderers. She was glad she spent the day taking this hike with Ryker, unplugging, and getting away from it all… if only for a little while.

Spenser looked at him over the rim of her glass, her eyes tracing his strong jawline and the hard angles and planes of his body. His brown eyes sparkled when their gazes met, and the corners of his mouth curled upward in a mischievous grin. Spenser quickly looked away and felt the heat rising in her cheeks. She and Ryker had grown closer over the months she'd been living in one of his cabins and there was an unspoken and undefined "thing" between them that seemed to be growing day by day and week by week.

There was definitely a mutual attraction, and their chemistry was off the charts. But she was still dealing with the fallout from the murder of her husband and Ryker had a whole host of issues that traced back to traumas he suffered over in Afghanistan, so neither of them was really in a good place to spark up a romance. That didn't mean there wasn't some heavy flirting between them. Nor did it keep Spenser from wondering about possibilities. In the future, of course.

Ryker was a beautiful man. Tall, lean, fit, and a body corded with muscle, he had Hollywood leading man good looks. His dark brown hair bordered on black, as did his eyes, and was complemented by his warm, tawny skin. More than his physical attributes, though, Spenser found herself drawn more to Ryker's intelligence, his well-hidden but still razor-sharp wit, and a sense of gallows humor that matched her own.

He projected the image of a crusty, cantankerous, and eccentric hermit—indeed, that was how most of the town saw him. But he wasn't anything like the man people in town thought him to be. Not really. Ryker, however, genuinely didn't care what other people thought of him and was content to let them think whatever they wanted about him. The traumas he suffered overseas made it hard for Ryker to open up to people.

Very few people saw past the image of him as the grumpy old hermit living alone on the hill. Most simply didn't care to try.

SHADOWS OF THE **FALLS**

Spenser's relationship with him had gotten off to a rocky start and she found herself believing he was all those terrible things people said he was. The truth, though, was that Ryker felt things deeply. Probably too deeply for his own good given how profoundly things tended to affect him. He had a deep well of compassion and was incredibly kind. Generous. He had a big heart that nobody ever really saw.

Spenser thought that was a shame and hoped that one day, he'd find a way past the issues that plagued him and that he'd learn to be more comfortable with people. That he'd allow them past the high, thick walls he kept around himself and let others see the amazing man she knew him to be. Spenser gazed into his eyes and felt her heart stutter and the air between them grew thick with expectation. For a moment, Spenser was sure Ryker was going to lean forward and kiss her. And she couldn't say she didn't want him to.

But then he cleared his throat and looked away. They shared an awkward, quiet laugh as the bubble of anticipation between them burst and Spenser felt a hollow pang of disappointment.

"Well," he said. "I guess we should eat before this food gets ruined."

"Yeah, probably. Everything looks incredible, by the way," she replied. "And thank you for putting this entire day together. I appreciate it."

"Of course," he said.

Ryker smiled warmly at her as he handed over a plate then uncovered the fried chicken and all the fixings he'd brought along. They talked about life and everything about it as they ate, tossing pieces of food to the patiently waiting pair of dogs. As the sun warmed her skin and a cool breeze stirred her hair, Spenser smiled. She couldn't recall the last time she'd had such a wonderful day— or enjoyed somebody's company as much as she enjoyed Ryker's.

CHAPTER TWO

SPENSER SAT AT HER DESK RIFLING THROUGH THE SEVERAL files worth of information Blake Wilder, the unit chief for one of the Bureau's rapid response teams, had sent her from the field office in Seattle. There was more information than Spenser thought there would be. A lot more. And coming off such a relaxing day up in the hills with Ryker yesterday, she was having trouble finding the motivation to spend the day sifting through it all. Of course, the silver lining was that it was a quiet day so she could afford to take her time.

"Knock on wood," she muttered to herself.

No sooner had the thought gone through her mind than when a knock sounded on her office door a moment before it opened. Amanda Young, her undersheriff, poked her head in. Her emerald-colored eyes sparked as she flashed Spenser a toothy smile.

"This a bad time, boss?" she asked.

"As good a time as any," Spenser replied. "Come on in."

Young walked in, still grinning like a fool. Though she was twenty-five years old, she looked younger than that. A couple inches shorter than Spenser's five-nine frame, the undersheriff had a cute figure and honey-blonde hair that framed a round, doe-eyed face. A smattering of freckles across the bridge of her nose gave her an all-American, girl-next-door look that made it hard for some of the veteran deputies to take her seriously as their direct superior at first.

Young, as she always did, embraced that challenge and wouldn't let them talk down to or dismiss her. She worked harder than anybody and was probably the smartest person in the entire department. Spenser thought Young even outstripped her, intellectually speaking. What Young didn't know, she made a point of learning, and if Spenser pointed out any weaknesses in her game, the younger woman did everything she could to eliminate that fault. Young asserted herself and demanded their respect and had eventually earned it. Even from some of the most grizzled vets. It had been an impressive process for Spenser to watch play out.

The level of confidence Young had was unusual in somebody her age. She had moments of doubt, of course, but for the most part, she was completely self-assured. She approached that line of cockiness without ever stepping so much as a toe over the line. It was one of the many things that Spenser admired about the younger woman and, in part, why she'd made her the undersheriff. It had taken a little time, but eventually, Young had even won over Maggie Dent, the mayor of Sweetwater Falls, who'd been one of the bigger skeptics of Spenser's decision.

Young was still a work in progress, but both Dent and Spenser were sure that with some more time and experience under her belt, she was going to take over the department, and Sweetwater Falls would be better for it. She was going to make a hell of a sheriff in time. For her part, Young wasn't looking that far ahead, and instead, she was taking nothing for granted and focused on learning everything she could about what it took to be a good cop. She was concentrating on learning the law, inside and out, refining her abilities, and becoming the best she could at her job. It was the right attitude as far as Spenser was concerned.

Young dropped into the chair that sat in front of Spenser's desk and leaned back, casually folding one leg over the other. She looked at Spenser with that goofy grin on her face but remained silent. After a couple of moments, Spenser shifted in her seat and laughed, an awkward tension filling the quiet of her office.

"Why are you staring at me like that, you weirdo?" Spenser asked.

"Are you really going to make me ask you?"

"Ask me what?"

Young rolled her eyes. "About your date with Ryker, of course," she said, sounding almost exasperated. "What else would I be asking about?"

"Oh, I don't know… something work-related, perhaps?"

"I could, but it wouldn't be nearly as interesting as hearing about your date."

"It wasn't a date," Spenser said. "We went hiking."

"And you had a picnic up on Bridger's Flat—the hill above town, right?"

"Well… yeah."

"Was there wine?"

Spenser felt her cheeks flush and she looked away. Young laughed.

"I'll assume by how hard you're blushing there was wine," Young said. "So… date."

"Not a date."

"If you say so," she chirped. "So, how was your not-a-date date?"

Spenser sighed dramatically. "It was a very pleasant day out."

"That's it? That's all you're going to give me?"

"There's nothing else to give," Spenser replied simply. "We hiked with the dogs, had a picnic—and yes, a little wine—then went home."

Young looked at her skeptically for a moment then sat back in her chair. She threw her hands in the air and shook her head.

"When are you two going to give in and take the next step?" she asked.

"Oh, I'm sorry. I wasn't aware we were operating on somebody else's timeline," Spenser replied and chuckled.

"You're not, obviously," she said. "But I, for one, would like to see you happy, Spenser. You and Ryker make each other happy. Everybody who's been around you two can see it."

A gentle smile curled the corners of Spenser's mouth up. "We've both got a lot of baggage we're still sorting through. And neither of us feels the need to rush things or put a label on whatever this is. We're just enjoying it. If it turns into something more down the road, great, and if it doesn't, that's great, too. We're just living in the moment, Amanda."

Young nodded. "That's fair. I get that."

"Good, then can we stop talking about this and move on to something else?"

"If you insist."

"I do."

Young gestured to the mess of papers on my desk. "What's all this?"

"These are all the case files Blake sent me on Alex Ricci," Spenser replied.

"Ricci," Young said. "Any relation to your old partner Derrick Ricci?"

"Younger brother."

"Judging by all that paperwork you're sifting through, it looks like younger brother Ricci has been a pretty busy boy."

"Took his first collar at fifteen years old," Spenser said. "He was a runner for one of the local crime families back in New York—the Sacconi family. Once he did that bid, he cemented his place and gradually started working his way up the ladder. Took a lot of collars but always avoided doing any serious time. The family took care of him."

"So, are you thinking this crime family killed your husband?"

Spenser shook her head. "No. Alex stopped working for the Sacconi family about ten years ago," she said. "After that, there's no paper on him. No more arrests. Not so much as a parking ticket. By all appearances, he got out of the life altogether."

"But you don't believe that."

"Oh, hell no. Like they say, tigers can't change their stripes."

"Okay, so what do you think he's been doing?" Young asked.

Spenser picked up the most recent mugshot of Alex Ricci. It was more than ten years old at that point, but she didn't think he'd changed all that much. Alex had the same flinty blue eyes, sandy blonde hair, square jaw, and patrician nose as his older brother. Despite having four years between them, they looked alike enough that they could have been twins. Alex, though, wore his hair down to his shoulders and had a thin scar that ran from his ear to the point of his chin. According to Derrick, Alex picked up the scar in a jailhouse dispute. Other than those minor things, the Ricci boys were almost identical in appearance.

"I believe Alex has been working for the Arias cartel," Spenser said. "I know that Derrick took money from them to look the other way in cases involving their organization."

"How do you know that?"

"I began to suspect it when I overheard a few phone calls. That suspicion only grew when he made mistakes that were uncharacteristic for him. Those mistakes tanked a few cases we'd built. And all of them involved the Arias cartel," Spenser replied. "So, I started quietly looking into him. I secretly built a case against him and when I had concrete proof that he was on the take, I turned it all over and he was arrested."

A wry grin twisted Young's lips. "I'm sure that made you really popular with the other agents around your field office."

"Yeah, I didn't win any new friends by turning in my partner. The Bureau suffers from a bad case of the blue wall every bit as much as local cops do," Spenser told her. "But the way I see it, corruption is corruption and it's our job to root it out wherever it exists."

Young nodded. "It's a noble thought. Too bad not everybody subscribes to that belief."

"That's what I say."

"So, let me guess, your old bosses pinned your shooting and your husband's murder on your old partner saying it was retaliation for getting him arrested?"

"Give the woman a kewpie doll."

"And now you're thinking that it was Alex Ricci trying to kill you and Trevor so you couldn't testify against his brother," Young continued.

"That and so I couldn't connect Derrick to either him or the cartel," Spenser said. "If he kills me, not only does it make it likelier that Alex's brother walks, it also keeps the Bureau from digging further into it and making a case against his employers."

Young pursed her lips and seemed to be taking it all in. Spenser saw the wheels in the younger woman's head spinning and had a feeling she knew what it was going to land on.

"So… if it was Alex who tried to kill you and not Derrick, you being out here means you're still a threat," Young said, going exactly where Spenser thought she would. "That means there's nothing stopping him from taking another shot at you."

"There's not. But I'm assuming the cartel has people inside the Bureau on their payroll and he knows I've not only left the Bureau, but I've got no plans on testifying for or against his brother," Spenser said. "I'm assuming that since I'm still upright and breathing, they've decided it's best to let sleeping dogs lie."

"That's a big assumption."

Spenser shrugged. "I've been out here for months now, and I've seen neither hide nor hair of Alex Ricci or the Arias Cartel."

"You had a hitman gunning for you when you first got here," Young argued, her tone incredulous. "Or did you forget about that guy?"

"I couldn't forget Dallas Morehead if I tried. But I don't have definitive proof that Morehead was working for the Arias cartel. I ruffled more than a few feathers among the Families back in New York," Spenser said. "And like I said, I'm still upright and breathing, so…"

"Yeah, well, you had better keep your head on a swivel, boss," Young said. "I don't have any real firsthand experience with the cartels, but everything I've read makes them sound like horrible people who are scary as hell."

"They are," Spenser said. "They are definitely horrible and scary."

Young leaned forward, her eyes fixed on the files and papers littering the top of Spenser's desk, concern etched into her features. She was silent for a beat then looked up and met her gaze.

"Is this a hornet's nest you really want to kick?" she asked. "If you keep digging into Alex Ricci and stirring up trouble, they may decide it's worth it to come after you again."

"I want the truth. And I want justice for Trevor. It's like this horribly painful wound that just won't close. And I feel like I won't ever be able to fully move on unless his murderer is rotting in prison for the rest of his miserable life," Spenser said.

"I get that," Young said. "But is it worth getting yourself killed over?"

Spenser met her gaze and held it as she clenched her jaw. The air in her office suddenly grew thick with tension as the anger welled up within her like a dark tide.

"If it means getting justice for my husband and taking his killer down, then yeah," Spenser said, her voice low and cold. "It would be worth it."

The door to her office opened and Alice Jarrett, the department's receptionist, stuck her head in and gave Spenser a small, tight smile.

"Sheriff," Alice said. "Sorry to bother you but you're needed."

Spenser turned to Young. "Well, it's time to go earn our paycheck."

CHAPTER THREE

"**S**HE'S BEEN TRAUMATIZED. BRUTALIZED," MARLEY said.

"What's her name?" Young asked.

"Alexa Beard," Marley replied. "Twenty-six years old, works for a big advertising firm in Seattle, but lives here in town. Her address is over on Felton Street. A friend—Stacy Dobbins—stopped by when Alexa didn't show up for their usual morning run and found her like that. Called an ambulance right away."

Spenser nodded and jotted a couple of notes down in her notebook as Young tapped away at her tablet. She raised her gaze to Spenser and smirked. Spenser shook her head but couldn't stop herself from grinning anyway. Young and her brother Jacob,

Spenser's tech wizard, liked to tease her about being so archaic and her manual notebook being terribly anachronistic. They seemed to take a perverse joy in calling her a Luddite.

"Okay, and did she say anything to you about what happened?" Spenser asked.

Marley shook her head. "Not much. All she said was that he was in her house when she got home. That she never saw him. Not until it was too late. Like I said, she's rattled."

"Understandable," Spenser said.

"Yeah," Marley replied. "I can only give you guys a few minutes with her. We still need to run some more tests and I honestly think she's too shaken to give you much tonight."

"That's fine. I just want to get her initial impressions when they're the freshest," Spenser told her. "We'll circle back with follow-ups later."

"Understood. But really, just a few minutes. She's in pretty rough shape," Marley said.

"Just a few minutes."

"She's in bay four."

"Thanks, Mar."

Spenser led Young over to bay four and they slipped behind the curtain. Alexa Beard was sitting on the bed with her knees drawn up to her chest and her arms wrapped around them. It was strange, but one of the first things Spenser noticed was a citrusy smell—like body wash. And it smelled fresh. Alexa looked up at Spenser. The woman was pale and visibly trembling as she gnawed on her bottom lip with her hair mussed and sticking out in a thousand different directions. The woman's eyes were red and puffy, and her tears left black streaks down her face.

It looked to Spenser like the woman had hastily applied makeup to her face, perhaps trying to obscure the bruises and cuts that marred her skin. Like she had literally tried to hide her shame and embarrassment. Spenser's heart broke for her. Alexa had nothing to be ashamed of or embarrassed about. But she also knew with the state she was in, the woman wasn't going to hear a single word she said. She had to come to it in her own time.

She raised her gaze to Spenser and she could see Alexa was doing her best to control herself and keep from sobbing any longer.

"I'm sorry," Alexa said and winced as she wiped her cheeks.

"You have nothing to be sorry about," Spenser said gently.

It wasn't the smeared and running makeup or her disheveled appearance that drew Spenser's attention the most. It was what had been done to her. Marley hadn't been kidding when she said Alexa Beard had been beaten halfway to hell. Alexa's entire body was a mass of bruises, cuts, welts, and scratches. Whenever she moved, she grimaced in pain. One of her eyes was swollen shut and the other was red from the blood vessels in them bursting. Her bottom lip was crusted with dark blood around the site where it had been split and both cheeks bore deep purple bruises.

There was a shallow cut on her forehead, another on her chin, and a chipped front tooth. It looked to Spenser like she'd had her face driven into a wall.

"Ms. Beard," Spenser started. "We're very sorry you're going through this."

"Just call me Alexa. Or Lex. It's fine," she said, her voice barely more than a whisper.

"Lex," Young said. "Can you tell us what happened to you?"

"I—I was out with some friends last night. I came home and took a shower and was getting ready for bed. When I got out of the shower, I noticed that my music had been turned off and that a window in my bedroom was cracked open," she explained. "I was trying to figure out if I'd accidentally left it open—I'm normally so conscious about my security and all. But I was in a rush that morning and thought maybe I'd forgotten to lock it..."

Alexa's voice trailed off and she looked down, sniffing loudly as her face darkened with emotion. The one eye that was still open shimmered as it welled with tears. Young opened her mouth to ask another question, but Spenser shook her head, choosing instead to give Alexa a couple of moments to gather herself. Young remained silent and looked down at her tablet.

The woman finally raised her face to Spenser. "When I turned around, he was standing in the doorway. He said he'd been waiting for me to come home."

"The man in the doorway," Young said. "Can you describe him?"

"H—he was big. Six-two or three at least," she said. "He was just big all over. He seemed like he worked out a lot."

"Did you get a look at his face?" Young pressed.

She shook her head. "He wore a mask—the kind that only lets you see their eyes."

"A balaclava," Young said.

"I guess. Sure. All I saw was that he had green eyes," she said quietly. "He... he just kept staring into my eyes and wouldn't let me turn away while he... while he..."

Her voice tapered off again, but she didn't need to finish the sentence for Spenser to get the point. He got off on looking into the eyes of a terrified woman as he assaulted her.

"Alexa, could you tell if he was white, black, Hispanic?" Young asked.

"He was white."

"How do you know?" Spenser asked.

"I could see the skin around his eyes," Alexa said. "He looked Caucasian."

"Did he say anything to you, Alexa?" Spenser asked.

She shook her head again. "No... not when he was... not during, no," she whispered. "But afterward, when he was getting dressed, he was singing a song to himself—it was some country song. I recognized it but I can't tell you what it was. I don't listen to country music."

A choked sob burst from her throat and Alexa seemed to draw in on herself as she trembled wildly with tears streaming down her face. The memory of her assault was overwhelming her, and Spenser knew they'd run out of time. They weren't going to be getting anything else out of Alexa. Not for a while. Not until she'd had some time to process it all.

"Alexa, is there anything else you can tell us?" Spenser gently pressed. "Anything he did or anything you might have noticed—"

The woman's face darkened, and Spenser could tell that something else was flashing through her mind. A memory she hadn't shared that she was reliving. And whatever the memory gripping her was, Spenser could see it was shaking Alexa to her very core.

"Alexa?"

"Please—I can't," she gasped. "I can't talk about it right now. I just can't?"

She trembled and cried, pulling her knees to her chest even tighter. Alexa rocked back and forth and was growing more agitated by the second. As if on cue, Marley stuck her head in between the curtains and looked at Spenser with an admonishing gaze. Spenser shrugged, trying to use her eyes to tell Marley she hadn't done anything.

"Sorry, Sheriff," she said quietly. "But your five minutes are up."

"We were just leaving," Spenser said then turned to Alexa. "Thank you for your time and again, we're very sorry for what you've endured. We'll likely have some follow-up questions, but we can talk to you again at another time."

The woman looked up at Spenser, fresh tears spilling down her face. "Please, Sheriff Song, find the animal who did this... and put a bullet in him. Please."

Her voice smoldered with a cold fury that matched the light glimmering in her eyes. Spenser knew the woman meant it.

"We're going to do everything we can to catch this man, Alexa," Spenser said, her tone resolute. "I give you my word."

Marley ushered them out as a nurse stepped into the bay to check on Alexa. Spenser walked down the corridor toward the elevators with Young on one side of her and Marley on the other. None of them had much to say at first. But they stopped on the other side of the nurse's station and turned to each other.

"So, what do you think?" Marley asked.

Spenser shrugged. "Unfortunately, she wasn't able to give us a whole lot to go on other than he's big, has green eyes, and she thinks he's Caucasian."

"Which means he could be Caucasian or perhaps a light-skinned Hispanic," Young offered.

"Right," Spenser said. "We'll need to circle back and talk to her after she's had a little more time to calm down and process everything that happened."

"How long will she be here, Doc?" Young asked.

"A few days probably. Mostly for observation. We think she's got a concussion, possibly some cracked ribs, and a host of bumps and bruises," Marley replied. "Aside from addressing her physical injuries, we'll put her in a private room and have a crisis counselor work with her."

"That's good. Hopefully, that will help start the healing process for her," Spenser said. "That'll also give us some time to process the scene."

"I figured you'd need some time to go through her house," Marley replied.

Spenser flashed her a wry grin. "You're getting pretty good at police procedure."

"Yeah, well, with the uptick in crime around here the last couple of years, I'm learning by necessity," Marley groused. "I remember when the most serious crimes in Sweetwater Falls were bar fights and the occasional domestic violence—"

"And now we've got gangsters, shootings, cartels, drugs, murders, and rapes happening by the bushel," Young finished for her.

"Hey, don't look at me. I've been the canary in the coal mine on this issue," Spenser said. "I've been on the City Council since I got here about funding our department better and getting us the tools we need to do the job right. When a town grows as quickly as Sweetwater Falls is growing, it's going to attract bad people who do bad things. It's as inevitable as the tide."

"But the council is more interested in the optics of it all. They're worried that bulking up and militarizing our department will send the wrong message and make people feel unsafe, which they think will keep people from moving here and hurt the town's bottom line," Young said with a bitter twist to her lips.

"And all the while, innocent people like Alexa Beard are getting caught in the crossfire and getting hurt," Marley said.

"It may be time for some new blood on the council," Spenser said pointedly.

"Yeah, I think you're right. It's probably well past time," Marley said then froze. "Wait. Why are you looking at me like that?"

Young grinned and nodded. "I think you're right, boss. New blood may just do the trick and get this place headed in the right direction again."

"What? No. Absolutely not. I'm neither cut out for politics nor interested in it. Besides, working here keeps me plenty busy already," Marley said.

"It's not like the council meets every single day. In fact, I think they take more days off than they actually work," Spenser noted. "The whole council is made up of working folk. I'm sure you'd be able to work it into your schedule without any problems."

"Spense, I would make a horrible politician," she argued.

"It's not like this is the snake pit DC is," Spenser countered.

"Smaller pit, same snakes," Marley said.

"Mar, wouldn't you like to have some say in how the town's budget dollars are allocated?" Spenser pressed. "Don't you think, maybe, the hospital deserves a little more funding than the damn country club? And before you answer, spoiler alert, I know you do because I've heard you say it."

"Well, of course," she said. "That's just common sense."

"Well, you could have a big say in how those dollars are spent then," Spenser said.

"She's got a good point," Young chimed in. "You're well-liked and very well-respected in town. If you ran, you'd probably be a shoo-in."

"Seriously, I have no desire to run for office," Marley said.

Though she tried to speak those words with conviction, Spenser knew her best friend well enough to hear the slight hint of curiosity in her voice. Marley might not be interested in politics, but she loved the town enough that she might set that disinterest aside if it meant doing good things for the people in it and perhaps, preventing more Alexa Beards.

"We could use a solid ally on the council," Spenser pressed.

"What about Harvey Pace?" Marley asked. "He seems to be on your side."

Spenser shrugged. "The more allies we have, the better," she replied. "Besides, I can't count on Pace. He seems nice and well-intentioned, but I just get a strange hit off him. I've got a feeling his allegiance can shift with the wind. I don't trust him. And I certainly don't trust him the way I trust you."

Marley gnawed on her bottom lip and Spenser could see the wheels in her head turning. She knew her best friend was imagining all the good things she could do for the people of Sweetwater Falls. For as long as she'd known her, thinking about others had always been Marley's default setting. It was one of the things Spenser admired most about her. Having a seat on the council might just give her a broader reach to do that. And Spenser could see by the look on Marley's face that she knew it.

"Just… promise me you'll at least think about it," Spenser commented.

"I'm not making you any promises, but I'll think about it," Marley agreed.

"That's all I ask," Spenser said then turned to Young. "Now, let's get out of here. We've got a crime scene to get to."

CHAPTER FOUR

SPENSER'S FLEDGLING CRIME LAB WAS ALREADY AT THE Beard home when she and Young arrived. Noah Arbery, a forensic technician she'd poached from Seattle PD, was the only full-time member of her crime lab—that was all the council had budgeted for Spenser's department. The other two climbing out of the black van—Vanessa Ortiz and Anthony Price—were students in forensics and criminology at the University of Washington. Spenser had worked some contacts and was able to get her department into a partnership program with their criminology department. In exchange for their service to her department, they got valuable experience as well as course credits.

Ortiz and Price were taking after Arbery in that they were meticulous and thorough. They didn't miss much—if anything. All three were very detail-oriented and very good at the job. She hoped that by the time those two graduated, the City Council would've found a little more funding for her department so she could hire them full-time. The experience they gained as well as the rapport they were building, not just with her but with the rest of the deputies in the department, made them ideal candidates to continue working with them.

"You okay? You look like you just bit into a lemon," Young asked.

She nodded. "Yeah. Just realized I'm starting to think like these political types."

"Yeah, that's a bit off-putting."

Spenser and Young climbed out of the Bronco and headed up the walk to the house—a nice ranch-style home in a middle-class neighborhood. The house, like all the others on the street, was clean and well-kept. It had what looked like a fresh coat of paint and a yard that was nicely landscaped and well-maintained. Like the other houses around it, Alexa's place looked like a nice place to raise a kid.

"Alexa inherited the place," Young read off her tablet. "Her parents—Steve and Katherine—were killed in an accident with a drunk driver some years back. It looks like Alexa was still in college at the time. And she's got no other siblings."

"That's horrible," Spenser said as they mounted the stairs and crossed the porch.

They walked into the house. The inside, like the outside, was clean, organized, and well-maintained. It was tastefully furnished and decorated with photographs of Alexa and her parents displayed prominently all around. Alexa obviously took pride in her home. Equally as obvious was how much she loved and missed her parents.

"We're back here, Sheriff," Arbery called.

Spenser followed Young through the living room and to the back of the house. Arbery and his interns were busy processing the bedroom. They wore dark blue coveralls with "Forensics" stenciled across the back in white, block letters, light blue booties over their shoes, and light blue gloves. As was habit, Spenser pulled a pair of black nitrile gloves from her jacket pocket and snapped them on. Young followed suit.

"We good to come in without booties?" Spenser asked.

"Yeah, you're good," Arbery said. "We've already processed the floor. Not much to find, to be honest. Alexa Beard is a meticulous housekeeper."

"You wouldn't know it by the state of the bedroom," Young remarked.

It was true. Alexa's bedroom had almost literally been turned upside down. Furniture had been turned over, the drawers yanked out and spilled across the floor, shards of broken glass twinkling in the light, and other things smashed to pieces. The violence in the room was so profound Spenser could practically smell it.

"It looks like the Hulk went full-on smash mode in here," Young said.

"Yeah," was Spenser's only reply. "As if Alexa's story wasn't already tragic enough."

Arbery said a few quiet words to Ortiz and Price who continued to process the scene without even looking up. After that, he stepped over to Spenser and Young, removing the protective glasses he wore and tucked them into his breast pocket. He was a small, bookish man, about four inches shorter than Spenser's five-nine frame. She almost felt like she towered over him. He had a head of thick, curly dark hair that was peppered with gray, long, sharp facial features, and eyes that sparkled like chips of obsidian.

"We dusted the window and the ledges all around it for prints. It's clean," Arbery said. "No fibers, no nothing. If he came in that way, he left no trace of it."

"So, he's careful," Young said.

"Or more likely, he's done this before," Spenser said.

"Think so?"

Spenser nodded. "I'd put money on it."

"What leads you to that conclusion, Sheriff?" Arbery asked.

"He's already got his method down. He sneaks in, lays in wait, then uses a little psychological warfare on his victim. Turning off the music, leaving the window cracked, leaving obvious signs somebody's there to increase the sense of tension and fear,"

Spenser explained. "That says to me that this is a practiced and rehearsed scenario. This isn't a guy who happened to see Alexa Beard at the store and decided to follow her home on the spur of the moment."

"But what about the violence? Wouldn't somebody with that kind of experience know to control themselves better?" Young asked.

"Not necessarily. It could be that he's harboring a deep resentment of women. A real hatred. And that hatred makes him act out like this. What he did to Alexa wasn't necessary. He'd gotten what he wanted from her. But it wasn't enough to just degrade her like that. He needed to terrorize her as well. That's why he tore her bedroom apart—to scare her. To make sure she never forgot what happened and would have a harder time moving past it," she said.

"That's an interesting theory, Sheriff Song," Arbery said. "Nothing we've found so far can either buttress that theory or counter it. So, I suppose it's as valid as any other theory."

"I'm glad you think so," Spenser said with a grin.

Arbery remained deadpan. He was very dry, and his sense of humor could be best described as offbeat. He was quirky, very logic-based, and very fact-oriented. If it wasn't something he could see, taste, or touch, Arbery tended to not believe it. While that made him good at his job, of course, it also meant that he wasn't one who put much stock in the soft sciences—he didn't believe in the idea or effectiveness of psychology and profiling.

It made for some interesting theoretical conversations. But Spenser could sometimes get a little frustrated with his lack of imagination and had to remind herself they came at a problem from two very different perspectives. She wasn't the talented or accomplished profiler that Blake Wilder was, but she wasn't half bad at it either.

"Is that what I think it is?" Young asked and gestured to the wall across the room.

Spenser followed her gaze and grimaced. There was an indentation in the wall that looked like it had been caved in with a hard, blunt object. The fantail of blood around it told Spenser what had been used to make it.

"It's an impact site. That's where he slammed Alexa's head into the wall," Spenser said.

"That would be my guess as well," Arbery commented.

"This guy is an animal," Young added, her tone as hard as her eyes.

Thin rivulets the color of rust ran down the white paint on the wall like bloody tears, pooling on the floor, giving it an even more grisly appearance. There were two more impact points in other walls, though neither was nearly as deep as that first one. But it looked like he'd thrown her around the room like a ragdoll in between hammering on her with his fists.

"I guess we see why she was so messed up," Young said.

"Yeah. This attack was brutal," Spenser said.

"Judging by the evidence I see here, it looks like he disabled her by slamming her head into the wall first," Arbery said, pointing to the deepest of the three divots in the walls. "That would have essentially left her too dazed to fight back. The other impact sites were wholly unnecessary. It was nothing but gratuitous violence. Brutality for brutality's sake."

"So, our guy is a sadist," Young said.

"I can't speak to that," Arbery replied. "I'll stick to what the evidence tells me and leave the speculation and psychological profiling to you ladies."

Spenser grinned. "Fair enough," she said. "Noah, did you find anything unusual?"

"I would say what I didn't find was more unusual," he replied.

"What's that?"

"The victim's bedding. It's missing. All of it," he said. "That leads me to surmise the assault took place on the bed and the man who assaulted her took the evidence with him."

Spenser looked at the bed and frowned. The mattress and the box spring had been turned over and were lying in the middle of the floor, slashed in half a dozen different places. With the rest of the bedroom in such shambles it hadn't occurred to her that the bedding was missing.

"We will, of course, process the mattress," Arbery said. "But judging by the pieces of fabric that are missing, I am not hopeful that we will find anything useful."

"Understood. But we can hope we catch a break," Spenser said.

"Yeah, well, there's a first time for everything," Young muttered.

Spenser thanked Arbery and let him get back to his work while she moved around the rest of the bedroom, looking for anything that looked out of place or struck her as odd. Although it was hard to tell, amidst all the wreckage and debris that littered the bedroom, nothing stood out to her.

"Alright, let's let the techs finish processing the scene and wait for their report," Spenser said. "I don't think we're going to find much here on our own."

"I was just thinking that," Young replied.

Spenser followed Young out of the bedroom and back through the house. As they passed some built-in shelves in the hallway, Spenser paused as something caught her eye.

"What is it?" Young asked.

"I'm not sure," Spenser replied. "Maybe nothing."

On the top shelf was a cluster of snow globes—there had to be at least two dozen of them. All of them are from different cities. It seemed an odd thing for a grown woman to be collecting. But then, she knew people sometimes collected strange things. But she had a feeling that this wasn't just a random item to collect but that they held enormous sentimental value for Alexa.

"Snow globes?" Young asked.

"If I had to guess, I'd say these all came from vacations she took with her folks," Spenser said with a nod.

"Okay, what about them?"

Spenser pointed to a gap between the otherwise evenly spaced snow globes. "Looks like one of them is missing."

CHAPTER FIVE

"So, our guy is kind of like an ever sicker, more deranged sport hunter than the ones who like to murder animals for fun," Jacob replied with a grimace. "God knows those freaks are all about taking trophies to memorialize the event."

Jacob sat facing them in his swivel chair, his back to the bank of monitors that lined the wall in his office. Spenser was perched on the edge of the worktable that ran down the middle of the room while Young sat in a chair at the end of the table to her right.

Young shrugged. "Not to be a contrarian or anything—"

"Well, that would be a first," Jacob interrupted.

She rolled her eyes at her brother. "Shut up."

"Children… don't make me put you both in a time out," Spenser said. "Go on, Amanda."

"Anyway, what I was trying to say is I think we're making an awfully big assumption by saying that our guy took that snow globe like it's an indisputable fact," Young countered. "I mean, it could have broken. Alexa might have moved it somewhere else. Or, and here's a thought, maybe there was never one there to begin with. I mean, isn't it possible that the gap between the snow globes has always been there and it only looks like something's missing?"

"She's not wrong," Spenser said.

"Great. As if she wasn't already insufferably smug enough as it is," Jacob groused.

"Deal with it, big brother. Besides, you should probably be used to me always being right by now," Young said with a laugh.

"Of course, it's possible," Spenser said. "It's just not likely."

"I mean, I get what you said about the scene being too clean and too smooth and all. That makes sense," she said. "But—and I really hate to side with Arbery on this—but that's not hard evidence. It's speculation."

"You're right. It is speculation," Spenser said. "But it's also more than a decade in law enforcement and a good portion of those years spent with one of the Bureau's best profilers in Blake Wilder. It's experience and educated speculation."

"Okay, that's fair. And to be even more fair, you're usually right about these sorts of things," Young admitted. "But experience and educated speculation aren't exactly going to hold up in court."

"Sis, your incessant need to always be right is exhausting. And I'm just a spectator here. I can't imagine what it's like to have to defend every word I say," Jacob teased.

"It's all right," Spenser cut in. "Part of the reason I wanted Amanda in this position is because she's not afraid to speak her mind or challenge my theories. The last thing I wanted as an undersheriff was a yes-man. Or yes-woman in this case."

"See?" Young crowed and stuck her tongue out at her brother.

"I *would* like an undersheriff I didn't have to threaten to paddle every five minutes because she can't get along with her brother," Spenser said, drawing a laugh from both of them.

"Don't say I didn't warn you, Sheriff," Jacob said. "She's been this way her whole life. Always needs to be right."

"And she may be right in this case, too," Spenser said. "However, Amanda, did you notice that aside from the carnage in the bedroom, everything else in Alexa's house was perfect? Everything was clean, freshly dusted, organized..."

Young nodded. "I noticed that. Sure."

"More than that, everything in Alexa's house was perfectly placed. Especially in relation to other things," Spenser continued. "Those snow globes on the shelf—they were all perfectly equidistant from one another. I mean, I'm having Arbery do the measurements and all, but I'm positive we're going to find that each globe is the same exact distance from the next one."

"That's a little obsessive-compulsive," Jacob said.

"Exactly. I think Alexa has some OCD tendencies. That would be one of them. Which is why a hole in the snow globe shelf stands out so much," Spenser said. "And that's why I don't think it's an accidental breakage or a hole in the order just because. I don't think Alexa would have been able to stand passing by the shelf and seeing a hole in the middle of her collection. She would have fixed it and gotten them all back into line again."

Young considered Spenser's words. Or more likely, she might've been looking to poke a hole in her theory.

"This is all speculation; you're right about that, Amanda. And the easiest way to get our answer is by asking Alexa herself," Spenser said. "But until she's out of the hospital, on her feet again, and ready to talk to us, we're going to have to speculate and develop leads the old-fashioned way—by using our noodles."

"And why am I getting the sneaking suspicion you've already been developing theories the old-fashioned way?" Young said.

"Because you are a smart woman who knows her job well," Spenser said.

"Can I make a suggestion?"

"Shoot."

"We look at who is in Alexa's life," Young said. "Statistically speaking, women are overwhelmingly more likely to be assaulted by somebody they know than by a stranger."

"I've read the literature, too," Spenser concurred.

"Right. Of course, you have. Sorry," Young replied, a sheepish expression crossing her face.

"Nothing to be sorry about," Spenser said. "Jacob, I need you to comb through Alexa's socials. I need to find out who she's been seeing, anybody she might have broken up with, had a falling out with—anything. Find out who's in her life and we'll start there."

"On it," Jacob said.

"Once you get some names for us to start looking into, I want you to log into VICAP and use the parameters of Alexa's assault and widen the search area," Spenser said. "I want to know if there have been similar assaults in the surrounding towns."

"Will do," Jacob said.

VICAP—the Violent Criminal Apprehension Program—was started by the Bureau back in the mid-80s. The database they put together analyzed and tracked patterns in violent crimes across the country. The program had been a rousing success that led to the capture of a large number of violent criminals as well as allowing agencies to close the books on certain cold cases. The Bureau eventually got around to sharing that information with local law enforcement, finally allowing them access to the database in 2008.

It was an incredibly helpful tool that gave locals a plethora of information about violent crimes in real time. Spenser had always been glad they'd opened it up to local LEOs simply because towns like Sweetwater Falls and others didn't have the resources to put something like that together on their own. As a result, a lot of violent crimes went unsolved. Having access to the database changed the game and allowed smaller agencies to get a leg up on some of the violent crimes that happened in their areas. And a lot of bad people had been put away because of it.

The one downside, though, was that the accuracy of the database relied on locals to enter the information on violent crimes in their region—something many small-town agencies were often slow to do. Most of the time they didn't have the manpower or technical expertise. In some cases, they just didn't give a damn. But the system had far more benefits and uses than not and Spenser had always found it to be incredibly helpful, so she'd trained her entire department to efficiently and effectively navigate the database.

Jacob spun around in his chair. "Okay, well, a quick perusal through her socials shows that Alexa Beard doesn't have much of a social life at all. She was all about work," he said. "Although, it looks like she did try to date a couple of guys about a year ago or so. Lots of flirting and suggestive comments but it doesn't look like they lasted very long. Either of them. Work seems to be her life and those guys didn't seem to dig that."

"She's a driven career woman with goals and aspirations. Nothing wrong with that. Some men can't seem to handle that," Young said.

"Is that why your deal with Billy Toms flamed out, Sis?"

"Shut up," Young snapped. "He was just an insecure little man who couldn't handle the fact that I've got a real career."

"Sounds like there is a lot to unpack there, but we should probably save it for later," Spenser said. "Tell me about Alexa's would-be boyfriends, Jacob."

"Bachelor number one is Dylan Lawrence. Twenty-seven years old and it looks like he works in a bookstore," Jacob reported.

He hit a button and Lawrence's DMV photo popped up on one of Jacob's wall-mounted monitors. With blonde hair and blue eyes, Lawrence had a youthful, clean-cut, and wholesome appearance. At the same time, though, he also had a smug look about him that reminded Spenser of a spoiled, privileged frat boy. And she found the crooked little grin on his face entirely off-putting.

"Lawrence and Alexa only dated a few months—and this was almost a year ago," Jacob went on. "But he still posts about her. Still comments on all her stuff—especially any pictures she posts. He tries to be flirty and smooth, but as far as I can see, she never responds to him."

"And who is lucky bachelor number two?" Young asked.

With a few keystrokes, the screen split, and the image of a second man appeared alongside the photo of Lawrence. The second man had short dark hair and piercing green eyes. He had a strong jawline, a long patrician nose, and had the hard, arrogant look of a man who was used to giving orders—and having them followed.

"Wesley Beal," he replied. "Age thirty, an investment banker in Seattle. Looks like he and Alexa dated about six months ago. As near as I can tell, they only dated a couple of weeks. If that. But like Lawrence, he remained hooked on her."

"Alexa Beard apparently makes an impression," Young remarked.

Spenser nodded. "Apparently. Either that or she has a habit of attracting bad guys."

"Or that. But what I want to know is why she didn't just block these guys on her socials?" Young wondered. "Why let them hang around instead of blocking and moving on when she knew things weren't going to work out with them?"

"Maybe she thought it was rude," Spenser offered.

"Or maybe she liked the ego boost of having these guys chasing her knowing she'd never let them catch her. Maybe she liked playing games like that," Jacob said.

Young looked at Spenser. "My brother might have some personal baggage here."

"But he hides it so well," Spenser replied.

"Right?"

"Not doing so well with the ladies?" Spenser asked.

"Historically, not so much."

"I'm sitting right here, you know," Jacob said.

"Yeah, we know," Spenser teased.

Spenser and Young shared a laugh at Jacob's expense, but he took it in stride and grinned along with them.

"All right, well, this gives us a place to start anyway," Spenser said. "Jacob, please keep digging and run that search through VICAP."

He snapped her a salute. "You got it, boss."

"Amanda, let's go have a chat with these two Romeos and see what we see."

"All right. Let's do it," Young said.

CHAPTER SIX

66 "I'VE LIVED HERE ALL MY LIFE AND EVEN WITH AS MUCH as I read, I can honestly say I've never been to this bookstore," Young said as they pulled to a stop just outside the bookstore. "I never even knew it existed."

"That's because you buy all your books online like a shut-in," Spenser replied. "You're young, Amanda. You need to get out, feel a little sunshine on your face, breathe some fresh air, and like the kids are saying these days, just go and touch some grass."

Young rolled her eyes. "Internet clout chasers and wannabe philosophers are the ones talking about touching grass," she groaned. "They just want to seem deep."

"Still, the point stands," Spenser shrugged. "It's not healthy to be cooped up all the time with nothing but work to keep you going."

"I like my job. Love my job, actually."

"So do I. But I have recently learned the value in getting out and unplugging from it all for a little while," Spenser said.

Young giggled. "You get out and touch grass once in all the time you've been here and all of a sudden, you're a work-life balance guru?"

"Just offering you a little of my hard-won life's wisdom," Spenser said with a proud smile.

"Please. You're like five years older than I am, not some ancient mystic who's been sitting on a mountain for the last fifty years," Young teased. "That being said, I know you're right. I need to be able to get out of my head now and then and I'll make a point of trying to do that—as long as you promise to do the same. You're not much better at it than I am. If we both keep going on this trajectory we're on, we're going to end up living in the same house fifty years from now surrounded by three hundred cats."

Spenser laughed. "Fair point. And it's a deal. I'll do my best to work on that work-life balance thing as well," Spenser said.

"And also, that you'll unpack all that baggage so you and Ryker can be together."

"We'll just take things one step at a time. Work-life balance first," Spenser said, her cheeks flushed. "Now, let's go see what ol' Dylan has to say for himself."

"Fine. Be that way," Young groused.

They climbed out of the Bronco and Spenser put on her sheriff's Stetson then glanced in the side view mirror and adjusted it so it sat right. Even all these months later, she still wasn't fully comfortable wearing it, but she couldn't deny that it had kind of grown on her. Hat fixed, she joined Young on the sidewalk, and they headed to the front doors of Portable Magic Books. Spenser held the door open and let Young walk into the cool, hushed atmosphere first.

An electronic bell chimed in the back as they stepped inside. The floor was covered with a thin but tough industrial carpet that reminded Spenser of gray astroturf—and judging by the grooves worn into it, the carpet had been there for a long while. The walls were all a soft beige color, the rows and rows of shelves a light faux oak, and the overhead lighting was soft. The air was redolent with the smell of lemon cleaner and wood polish. It was all very clean and orderly with not a speck of dust that Spenser could see anywhere.

Portable Magic wasn't an overly large shop, but it held a surprisingly big collection of books. The rows between all the bookcases were narrow to accommodate more and almost every single wall was taken up by floor-to-ceiling shelving. The only exception was the wall to the left of the front door which held a six-foot-long, chest-high counter that held the register and a computer. There were so many bookshelves, all of them crammed with titles, that the interior of the store felt a little claustrophobic.

"Afternoon, Sheriff," Dylan Lawrence greeted them.

Startled, Spenser and Young both turned quickly, their hands immediately dropping to the weapons on their hips. Lawrence held his hands up, an uneasy grin on his face.

"Don't shoot," he said and waggled the book in his right hand. "I'm only armed with a piece of good literature."

Though not as pronounced as it had been in his DMV photo, Lawrence still had that smug, frat-boy look on his face that Spenser found more than a little irritating. Call it profiling, but she just had a feeling he was going to grate on her nerves.

"What were you thinking? Didn't anybody ever teach you it's not smart to sneak up on armed people?" Young snapped.

"Sorry. But I wasn't sneaking. Or at least, I didn't mean to sneak up on you," he said. "These shoes just have real quiet soles."

"Dylan Lawrence?" Spenser asked.

"Yes. Is there something wrong?"

"We just need to have a word with you," Spenser said.

"About?"

"Alexa Beard," Young stated.

Lawrence's face darkened and his jaw flexed as he gritted his teeth. Just hearing her name seemed to strike a nerve. He cleared his throat and motioned for them to follow him, so Spenser led Young over to the counter at the front of the store.

"Just give me one second to finish putting in this special order, please," he said as he walked behind the counter.

Spenser exchanged a glance with Young as Lawrence quickly pecked away at the keys. A moment later, a page slipped out of the printer. He scooped it up and tacked it to a corkboard behind him then turned around and gave them his attention.

"Right. Thanks for your patience," he said. "What can I do for you, Sheriff?"

"We understand you dated Alexa Beard?" Spenser started.

He nodded. "Yeah, we were together for a couple of months."

"She dump you?" Young asked.

His jaw again tightened as his expression darkened. "We came to a mutual decision that we just weren't right for each other."

"Mutual decision, huh?" Young pressed.

"That's right."

"So, why are you still all over her socials begging for her attention?" Young asked. "Kind of makes you seem a little thirsty."

"I'm not begging for her attention," he snapped, then seemed to realize how defensive he sounded and adopted a calmer tone. "Just because we're not together doesn't mean we can't be friends. It was all amicable. I liked her as a person before we ever met."

"How did you meet, by the way?" Spenser asked.

"On Facebook. She's a friend of one of my other friends. We started talking and one thing led to another," he explained.

"And why did she end it?" Young asked.

"I told you, it was a mutual decision—"

Spenser shot a glance at Young. Sometimes, riling up a suspect was a good thing. They were more likely to slip up and make a mistake or admit something they might not have wanted to when they were agitated. And Young had a natural talent for getting under people's skin. But sometimes, it was best to keep the temperature low and the atmosphere cordial and cooperative. Young needed to learn to tell one situation from the other. She needed to teach her.

"Alright, so what led to the split?" Spenser asked. "Why did you two decide it was best to end things with each other… at least, romantically?"

"We're just at two different points in our lives. We wanted different things," he said simply.

"How so?" Young pressed.

"She has a lot going on. Wants to be some big shot ad exec," he said with a shrug. "I prefer my life to be a little more low-key than that."

"So, you didn't like the fact that she had ambition?" Young asked.

"I'm just a lot mellower than her. That's all," he said. "I'm the manager of this bookstore right now, but I'll eventually inherit it—"

"This is a family-owned bookstore?" Young asked.

"It is."

"So, it's not like you had to work for your position."

"I started working here when I was fifteen years old. I started at the bottom and have worked my way up to where I am now," he huffed.

"Yeah, but the point is that your family owns this place so it's not like you had to earn your first position here. Right?" Young kept at him. "Alexa had a drive and ambition that you couldn't relate to. That's why she broke it off with you… because you're content to just sit back and take what's given to you rather than having to hustle and earn what you get."

Lawrence's cheeks flushed and his eyes narrowed. Young was digging at all his nerves that were still clearly exposed in regard to Alexa.

"Like I said, we're just in different places in life and want different things. It made us incompatible," he said, his voice tight.

"And I understand that, but tell me something," Spenser said, trying to reel in the emotions. "Ever since you two parted ways, you've been trying to get her attention. Your comments on her socials can be construed as being… flirtatious. And yet, she's never once replied to you. Not even in a friendly way. It's just been radio silence from her. So, why are you continuing to chase her? It looks a little… desperate."

"What is this all about? Really all about?" he demanded. "Why is my dating life of interest to the sheriff's department?"

"Are you angry that Alexa broke things off?" Young asked.

"Angry? No. People don't always work out together," he said. "And I ask again, why in the hell are you asking me about a relationship I had almost a year ago?"

"Alexa Beard was sexually assaulted last night," Spenser said.

"She was also beaten within an inch of her life," Young added.

Spenser watched him closely as she and Young delivered their lines, looking for the slightest tic or tell in his face. Microexpressions often gave people away when they thought they were controlling their features. Lawrence's face blanched as they told him what happened and the surprise both on his face and in his eyes seemed genuine. He drew in a deep breath and let it out, taking a couple of beats to compose himself.

"That's awful. Horrible," he said. "But I hope you're not suggesting I had anything to do with what happened to her."

"Did you?" Young asked.

"I cared about her—I still care about her," he said. "And yeah, I was disappointed when we split up and was still trying to catch her attention, but I didn't hurt her. I wouldn't hurt her. Never."

Spenser studied him and listened to his words and all she heard was the ring of truth and sincerity in his voice. She didn't detect any guile or evasiveness. Of course not. That would have been far too simple a way to wrap up this case.

"Do you know if she had trouble with anybody else?" Spenser asked.

"As you so astutely pointed out, Alexa didn't talk to me after we split up," he muttered.

He looked at them with a frown on his face, clearly not happy with being reminded of his relationship failings and the woman he couldn't have.

"Dylan, can you tell us where you were last night, say around nine or ten?" Young asked.

"I was here. Doing inventory. I was here until just after two this morning," he said. "You may not think it's overly ambitious, but I am trying to learn how to run a business well. This bookstore has been in my family since the early 70s and I'm not going to be the one who lets it fail."

"And you can prove you were here?" Young asked.

"You can look at the security tapes. You'll see me on them all night."

Spenser nodded to herself. They would, of course, take the security tapes for analysis just for the sake of due diligence. But she was convinced he was telling the truth. She gave Young a subtle nod. They'd gotten what they needed and it was time to move on.

"Thank you for your time, Dylan," Spenser said. "If we have any follow-up questions, we'll get in touch with you."

"You know where to find me," he replied with a shrug.

"We do."

Spenser turned and led Young toward the front door, but Lawrence's voice stopped them and Spenser turned back around.

"Tell Alexa I'm sorry about what happened," he said, his voice calm and thick with sincerity. "And that… that I hope she's okay. Please. If you can."

"I will," Spenser replied.

CHAPTER SEVEN

Spenser dropped the leash on the center island in the kitchen then walked to the refrigerator. As Annabelle noisily slurped away from her water bowl, Spenser grabbed a bottle of cold water and cracked it open. She drank deeply and tried to cool herself down. Sweat slicked her body and beads of perspiration trickled down her face. Her heart was beginning to slow and the fire in her muscles was slowly ebbing. Annabelle had extra energy and made Spenser run harder than normal to keep up with the big, galloping Great Dane today.

After striking out with Dylan Lawrence at the bookstore earlier, she'd dropped Young back at the office then headed home for the day. Annabelle had been eager to get out for her nightly run, barely giving Spenser time to get into her running clothes before practically yanking her out the door. Ryker normally came by at some point to let Annabelle tag along with whatever he and Mocha were doing, but he was out of town for the day, so she hadn't gotten out for her usual bit of sunshine and freedom.

The dog-run attached to her cabin, though large and spacious, didn't compare to running around with Mocha like a maniac in the new park Ryker had built for them. Spenser appreciated that Ryker always made time to let Annabelle run around outside. He told her it was as good for Mocha as it was for Annabelle and that since he didn't have a normal work schedule and made his own hours, he had the time and was happy to do it.

Most of all, though, Spenser appreciated the fact that Annabelle was usually worn out by the time she got home so she didn't normally have to run a marathon at a full sprint after a long day at the office. Of course, on days like today, when Ryker wasn't around, having to race after her giant dog was a stark reminder of just how out of shape she was getting without her nightly runs. She still walked Annabelle at night but that wasn't nearly as physically exerting.

"You're killing me, girl," Spenser said.

Water dripping from her jowls, Annabelle raised her head and seemed to be grinning at Spenser as she turned and walked over to her giant pillow, dropping herself down heavily onto it. The big dog groaned and shifted around, getting comfortable on the pillow, and seemed to fall asleep about three seconds after lying down.

"All right. I'm going to take a shower and we'll see about dinner when I get out, huh?"

Annabelle grunted but didn't so much as open an eye or acknowledge her in any other way. The big dog's batteries seemed to have run out for the night. Not that Spenser was surprised. After a run like the one they'd just taken, she was almost ready to lay down and fall asleep, too. If she hadn't been so sweaty or smelled so bad, she might have. Before she could get to the bedroom, her cell phone rang, drawing a long, loud groan from her. The groan died on her lips, though, when she picked up the phone and saw who was calling. Spenser quickly connected the call and pressed the phone to her ear.

"Caitlyn Boone," she said.

"Spenser Song," came the reply.

"I didn't expect to hear from you for a couple of days."

"What can I say? I'm efficient as hell."

Spenser laughed. "Clearly. That's why they pay you the big bucks."

"Yeah, I wouldn't go that far."

Caitlyn Boone was a friend of Spenser's from the New York Field Office who worked in the Organized Crime Unit. After sifting through everything Blake had sent her on Alex Ricci and not finding anything that moved the needle for her, Spenser had put a call into Caitlyn, hoping that OC had something squirreled away. Specialized units like OC sometimes held back information they kept in what were called red files—that was information not available for public consumption. It kept the most sensitive information under wraps, accessible by very few people, which usually prevented leaks that could derail an investigation or tank an entire case.

"I hear Harris and McTavish flew out there to pay you a visit," Caitlyn said.

"I guess the grapevine is still as chatty as ever back home."

"People talk," she replied. "Did they beg you to come back to the Bureau? Promise you a hefty signing bonus and a boatload of perks?"

Spenser laughed. "Hardly. No, they wanted me to testify against Derrick. They want me to stand up in open court and say that he's the man who murdered Trevor and tried to murder me."

"You don't sound like you're inclined to help them out."

"Because it's not true, Caitlyn," Spenser said hotly. "I've been telling anybody who will listen that he didn't do it. He did not pull the trigger that night and I'm not going to stand up in court and say he did no matter who they send out here to squeeze me."

"Wait, they say all the evidence points to Derrick and his guilt is undeniable. How do you know he didn't?" Caitlyn asked.

"Because I was there," Spenser replied. "And I know my former partner well enough to know how he moves. The man who shot me and Trevor didn't move like Derrick. His body was similar but not the same."

"That's kind of thin, don't you think?"

"You and Hankins have been partners now for what, six years? Seven?"

"Almost eight," Caitlyn said.

"And can you tell me that you wouldn't be able to identify his body type and the way he moves around? Even in the dark?" Spenser pressed.

There was a pause on the line for a moment as Caitlyn seemed to be considering Spenser's words. She used that moment to drain the last of her water bottle.

"I didn't look at it that way before," Caitlyn said. "You're right. We've been partners so long, I probably would be able to identify the way Hankins moved. That's an interesting point."

"Thank you. Finally, somebody gets it."

"I do get it, but that's a long way from proof," Caitlyn said. "And they're moving forward with prosecuting Derrick for the whole truckload."

"With as much concrete proof as I have that it wasn't him."

"McTavish has won circumstantial evidence cases before," she said.

"I sure would like to get my hands on their evidence inventory."

"Afraid I can't help you with that since I'm not privy to the US Attorney's files," she said. "But I would be willing to wager that not only would Derrick's defense attorney have everything he was given in discovery by the prosecutors, they'd also probably love your help in clearing their client of the charges against him."

"Oh, Derrick is definitely guilty of accepting bribes, corruption, and obstruction of justice and he should go to prison for the rest of his life," Spenser said. "The only things he's not guilty of are the charges of murder and the attempted murder of a federal officer he's staring down."

"Can I ask you something without you getting pissed off at me?"

A grin curled the corner of Spenser's mouth up. "I make no promises."

"He's likely going to prison for life anyway because of everything else you mentioned. Does it matter if he's charged with shooting you and Trevor, too? I mean, sentenced to life is sentenced to life," Caitlyn said.

"It does matter because your boss, in all his wisdom, isn't even looking for the real shooter," Spenser said. "I want justice for Trevor, and sending Derrick to prison for a crime he didn't commit, even if it's just tacked on to a laundry list of crimes he did commit, isn't justice. I want the man who murdered my husband and nearly killed me thrown into a hole for the rest of his miserable life."

"Okay. Yeah, I get that. Sorry, I just had to ask," Caitlyn said.

"Sorry, Caitlyn. I don't mean to be snappy. It just touches a very raw nerve for me. Harris and McTavish are more concerned with optics and protecting the Bureau's reputation than they are in finding the truth and putting the right person away."

"No need to apologize to me, Spense. I'm on your side here," she replied. "I just worry that if you keep pressing them on this, or even worse, make them look bad and like they're running a cover-up, you're going to kick up a nasty hornet's nest all over yourself. You know better than most how petty and vindictive those jerks can be."

"Yeah, I remember all too well. But if they want to come after me for trying to get to the truth and put a killer away, so be it. Bring it on."

"There's the Spenser Song I know and love," she said. "So, how can I help?"

"You can give me the red file on Alex Ricci?" Spenser replied hopefully. "I've got copies of the original case files on him from back when he was muscle for the Sacconis—"

"Where on earth did you get copies of the original—you know what? I don't want to know," Caitlyn said. "Believe it or not, we don't have a red file on Alex Ricci."

"How can you not have a red file? Almost every case has a red file."

"Because Alex Ricci has been off the board for a long time, Spense. There are no active investigations, let alone cases on him.

As far as the Bureau is concerned, he's no longer a player worth keeping tabs on and hasn't been for a while," Caitlyn explained.

"But we know he's working for the Arias cartel."

"He's suspected of working for the Arias cartel. But that was looked into a while ago and nobody was able to find anything valid or concrete."

Spenser sighed and shook her head. "Derrick. He scrubbed the investigations and kept his brother's name clean."

"That's a pretty serious charge."

"I also happen to know it's true," Spenser said. "I can't prove it, but I know it's true down in my bones. It's the only way Alex hasn't popped up on somebody's radar. The man is a scumbag whose only talent is killing for even bigger scumbags."

"And you think it's Alex and not Derrick who pulled the trigger that night," Caitlyn said, finally catching on.

"I do. I very much do," Spenser said. "Derrick has been adamant about keeping me from digging into this despite his own problems. I can only think of one person in his life he'd go to the mat to protect and defend—"

"His brother."

"Exactly."

"I wish I could help, Spense. But I promise you, we don't have a red file on Alex," she said. "As far as the Bureau is concerned, he's no longer our problem. If he's even still alive."

"He's alive. That much I'm sure of."

"I'll keep my ear to the ground, but nobody here's even talking about him. He's not on anybody's radar so far as I know. Certainly not in connection with your case."

"I knew it was a long shot, but I appreciate you taking the time."

"Anything for you, Spense," she said. "I mean that."

"Thanks, Caitlyn. I'll talk to you again soon."

"Make sure you do."

Spenser disconnected the call and dropped the phone on the table. She pursed her lips as she folded her arms over her chest and began to pace the room, her mind racing. If she could get a look at the evidence against Derrick, she might be able to deconstruct the prosecution's case against him. She also knew if she did that, she was running the risk of running afoul of ASAC Clark Harris, and Caitlyn hadn't been kidding when she said he was petty and vindictive.

Still... Some risks were worth taking.

CHAPTER EIGHT

"THIS LOOKS LIKE THE PLACE," YOUNG SAID.
"Looks like it."
"That's quite the building."
"It's ... something," Spenser said. "That's for sure."

Spenser pulled into a lot that sat beside a three-story building made of burnished steel and smoked glass. The thoroughly modern, asymmetrical design was cold and sterile. Maybe she was old-fashioned, but Spenser liked more traditional-looking buildings. With a variety of odd angles in the building that made no sense and gave it an overall unflattering shape—at least to her—she supposed it made a statement. What that statement was, Spenser couldn't say for sure. Maybe the people who utilized

Platinum Asset Management's services equated a building like this with success. Who could say for sure?

They climbed out of the Bronco and took a minute to stretch their legs and straighten themselves out. They'd left early that morning to make the commute to Seattle hoping to catch Wesley Beal before he got started for the day. Plus, she thought dropping in unannounced like that might put him back on his heels.

At that time of the morning, the lot was still fairly empty. There were three cars already there but none of them was the vehicle registered to Beal. His investment firm employed thirty-five people and generated millions in annual revenue—Spenser had spent a little time after her call with Caitlyn last night doing her homework on Beal and his firm. Beal himself grew up in Seattle but went back east for his education.

He was a graduate of NYU with a degree in finance and earned a Masters in the same from Wharton at the University of Pennsylvania. He spent a couple of years on Wall Street working for some white shoe firm and had some success. Beal then parlayed that success—and the capital that came along with it—to move back home and hang out his own shingle. And he must be pretty good at what he does because that success he had on Wall Street followed him to Seattle.

"Did you contact Seattle PD and let them know we're here?" Spenser asked.

"I did. I talked to Lieutenant Horan," Young replied. "He thanked us for letting them know and said to call them if we needed help with anything."

"Perfect. Thanks for handling that."

"Hey, it's my job to do the menial tasks you don't want to do," she said with a smile.

"And I'm glad you've finally come to accept that."

Young's laughter was cut off by the sound of squealing tires and the hard-thumping bass of some hip-hop tune blasting out of the open windows of the Range Rover that came screeching into the parking lot. Spenser and Young looked at each other.

"Is that him?" Young asked.

"He parked in Beal's spot so I'm going to say yes."

"How fortuitous."

The music cut off as the dark windows rolled up. Spenser led the way as they crossed the lot and stood beside the silver vehicle. The door opened a moment later and a cloud of smoke came rolling out, filling the air around them with the stench of marijuana, and Beal stumbled out of the Range Rover. He had obviously taken the old saying, dress for success, to heart. His charcoal gray suit was designer and well-tailored, the violet-colored shirt with a white collar and cuffs monogrammed with his initials, and his rich, purple tie made of what looked to be silk. Spenser was sure his wardrobe probably cost more than she made in a year.

When his feet hit the asphalt of the parking lot, he jerked upright, surprise on his face as he seemed to be seeing them standing there for the first time. He quickly dropped the joint in his hand and covered it with one of his thousand-dollar Louboutin loafers, trying to crush it. He gently patted down his expertly styled dark hair and tried to discreetly let the cloud of smoke in his mouth go. He offered them an awkward smile, his green eyes glittering in the early morning sunlight.

"Morning… uhhhh… officers?" he said.

"Sheriff, actually. Sheriff Song," Spenser said. "And this is Undersheriff Young."

Young smiled at him. "Enjoying a little wake and bake this morning, Wesley?"

Beal frowned and his expression darkened as he looked away and tried to find a coherent thought in his pot-hazed mind. He took a moment then looked at Spenser's badge and the patches on her coat sleeves, a slow, smug smirk crossing his face.

"Sweetwater Falls," he said, his tone matching the arrogant grin on his face. "Correct me if I'm wrong, but you country mice are way out of your jurisdiction up here in the big city, aren't you?"

"That's cute. And you're right. We are out of our jurisdiction here," Spenser said. "But if you want to stand here and keep being an idiot, we can certainly get some big city mice out here to haul you in for the weed—"

"I would think a couple of law enforcement officers like yourselves would be up to date with the current laws. Weed's legal in this state, ladies," he said. "Or maybe y'all don't have fancy modern things like the Internet down in Sweetwater Falls?"

"Yes, weed is legal. Driving under the influence of a substance, though, still is not legal. You have two officers here who watched you get out of a vehicle you had just been operating while using. And you are quite obviously impaired," Spenser said. "So, again, we can call SPD down here, but how do you think that's going to go for you, Wesley?"

The smug grin on his face faltered and his expression tightened. Spenser could see his mind spinning as he looked for a way out of his predicament. That was the trouble with smug guys like Wesley Beal—they always thought they had all the answers, had everything all figured out, and couldn't contemplate a scenario where they weren't the smartest guy in the room. They couldn't fathom a world where they couldn't get through any situation with their bluster and bravado. Guys like Beal were so used to bullying everybody around them and having those people capitulate and give in that when somebody pushed back, they didn't know quite how to handle it. They tended to freeze up like deer in headlights.

He returned his gaze to Spenser's and offered her a smile. "Look, I think we got started off on the wrong foot, Sheriff. I'm sorry about smoking that joint while I was on the road, but I was running late and needed to take the edge off before I got here. I've got a high-stress job—"

"Save it. We're not here to hassle you about your weed. That's an issue for the Seattle PD," Spenser said. "Not unless you make us hassle you about it."

"Then... what do you want?" he asked.

"Alexa Beard," Young said.

He screwed up his face and seemed to be trying to place the name. Young rolled her eyes and clenched her jaw as she stared at him. She seemed to be taking the case to heart. Spenser knew Young related to Alexa and recognized it was something she knew she'd have to keep an eye on. Taking a case to heart wasn't a bad thing in and of itself. Having some skin in the game often led you to do your best work. At least, that was how it always was for Spenser.

But the other side of that coin was that it sometimes led you down a path that shouldn't be traveled. Taking a case too personally could lead you to make rash and impulsive decisions you normally wouldn't. Maintaining some sense of objectivity was necessary. And there was some small piece of Spenser that worried about Young being able to maintain hers.

"Don't even try to pretend you don't know her," Young said. "You're all over her socials and I've looked at Alexa's phone records. Guess whose number pops up a lot? Yeah, that would be your number, Wesley. So, let's stop playing games."

He frowned and lowered his gaze to his shoes, looking like he was wishing he could take a big puff off the joint underneath his Louboutin.

"Fine. I know her. We dated for a while," he said. "What about it?"

"Where were you the night before last?" Young pressed.

"Out to dinner with a client. I took them to Brady's Fish House," he said. "You can check my credit card receipts or their security cameras to verify. Why do you ask?"

"So, you weren't at her home in Sweetwater Falls?" Young asked.

He scoffed. "I've never been to Sweetwater Falls in my life."

"But you said you dated her," Spenser chimed in.

"We always spent time together up here," he said. "Please, I wouldn't be caught dead in a cultural wasteland like Sweetwater Falls. No offense. It's just… It's not for me."

"And it's so hard to see why she dumped you," Young said.

He grimaced but said nothing. Beal glanced at his watch and tapped his foot impatiently, glaring at them.

"Are we almost done here?" he asked. "I've got a pretty full day today—"

"We can drag you down to the station in our cultural wasteland and finish questioning you there if you'd prefer. I imagine that would put a crimp in your full day," Young said.

Beal folded his arms over his chest and glared daggers at her. "Fine. Ask your questions. But I really do have a busy day today, so if you could speed it up a little bit, I would greatly appreciate it. Pretty please. With sugar on top."

"We'll do our best. But it's going to take as long as it takes," Young said.

"What is this really all about? What about Alexa?"

"We're curious to know why, after you two split up, you were still trying to get in touch with her so much," Spenser said. "Messages on social media, phone calls, text messages—and she wasn't returning any of them. Why so persistent?"

"You're kidding, right? You've seen her. The girl is smokin' hot. Of course, I was trying to get back on her good side. I never got to seal the deal with her before we split up. I was determined to change that outcome because I've never struck out like that with anybody before," he seethed. "Okay? You've coaxed my biggest shame out of me. Happy now?"

Young looked at him with utter contempt and disgust while Spenser just shook her head. The man was a piece of work. It was no wonder Alexa dropped him so quickly. What Spenser found most perplexing was why any woman would let him into her pants at all. He was classically handsome and obviously wealthy, but his personality was repellent.

"What is this all about? Is she saying I'm harassing her or something?" he asked.

"She was sexually assaulted in her home, Mr. Beal," Spenser told him. "Not just sexually assaulted, she was beaten savagely—"

He put his hands up, palms facing Spenser as he blanched. "Woah, woah, woah," he said. "I never assaulted anybody. I never laid a hand on her. Is she telling you I did? Because if that's what she's telling you, that's a flat-out lie. I don't need to assault anybody. I do just fine on my own—"

"Except for Alexa. She shut you down and wouldn't let you touch her," Young said, her voice tight. "And you were determined to change that outcome… right? You were determined to have what she didn't want to give you."

He shook his head, his face etched with fear. "No way. Not like that. Yeah, I wanted to sleep with her, but I would never rape her. That's not who I am—"

"Really?" Young spat. "Because from what I've seen so far, you're a giant piece of sh—"

"Amanda," Spenser admonished her with a shake of the head.

Beal had given them an alibi that was easy enough to check out. More than that, as repulsive and contemptible a creature as he was, Spenser believed him. She didn't think he assaulted Alexa.

"Check my credit card. Check with the restaurant," he pleaded with them. "You'll see. I was at the restaurant with my clients until midnight. Check."

"Trust me, Mr. Beal, we will," I said. "And if we get even a whiff of anything contradictory to what you told us, we are coming back and we will drag you back to our little backwoods, cultural wasteland of a town."

"I'll clap you in irons and hook you to the back bumper of my cruiser myself," Young said.

"Fine. Check. You'll see. I was nowhere near your town. I swear it," he stammered.

"We'll see," Spenser said ominously. "We'll be in touch, Mr. Beal."

Spenser turned and headed back to the Bronco. Young remained behind for another minute, glaring hard at Beal before she turned and walked back to the truck as well. Beal practically sprinted to the front doors of his building, making Spenser chuckle. She shouldn't encourage Young when she intimidated people like that. It was just sort of amusing to watch a little slip of a thing like Amanda Young put the fear of God into a big, strong guy like Wesley Beal.

"I hate guys like that," Young finally said.

"Really? You hide it so well."

Young's angry demeanor finally cracked, and she offered Spenser a small smile. And just like that, the tension that had surrounded her like San Francisco fog lifted and she was the same young woman Spenser had come to know and adore.

"Come on," Spenser said. "Let's get back to the office and see if we can develop another lead. Hopefully, your brother will have something for us."

"Miracles have been known to happen."

CHAPTER NINE

"She's back here, Sheriff," he said.

"Thanks, Shenn," Spenser replied. "Do me a favor and keep an eye on her. I'll be back to talk to her in a minute."

"You got it, Sheriff."

Spenser stood amidst the destruction that had been wrought in Hannah Bowman's living room. The level of violence on display was eerily reminiscent of Alexa Beard's bedroom just a few nights earlier. Furniture had been turned over and torn to pieces, pictures ripped off the walls and smashed, and holes punched into the walls—and at least one of them looked to be a divot made by slamming a forehead into the drywall. Just like at Alexa's place, the impact site was surrounded by crimson smears.

"Jesus," Young said as she stepped through the front door. "This looks just like Alexa Beard's bedroom did. Like almost identical."

"Yeah, I was just thinking that."

Through the open door, Spenser could see the blue and red strobing lights of the emergency vehicles outside slashing through the darkness of the night. Her deputies were keeping an eye on things outside but some of the neighbors were gathering on the sidewalk outside, undoubtedly curious about what was happening inside the house. No doubt some of them are lining up hoping to get a peek at a body being wheeled out.

If there was one thing people, even in supposedly genteel neighborhoods like this one, could never get enough of, it was drama and murder. The popularity of the literally hundreds of shows dedicated to murders and their investigations was proof of that. Reveling in the pain and misery of others was a constant and one of Spenser's least favorite traits of humanity. It was a trait she could very well do without.

"Find anything outside?" Spenser asked.

"Nothing. I checked all the windows and exterior doors—they're all locked, Spenser," Young said. "I don't know how this guy got in. It's like he walked through a wall."

Spenser shrugged. "Since I don't think anybody has mastered that ability yet and we're not chasing a ghost, I'm going to go ahead and guess that our guy got in through an open door or window and then locked up on his way out."

"Yeah, that's probably more likely," Young replied with a slight grin. "Have you spoken to our victim yet?"

"Not yet. I wanted to get a lay of the land first," Spenser replied. "The scene is fresh. She called it in about an hour ago. An ambulance is on the way so we should probably get in there and have a word with her before they get here."

"Agreed."

Spenser led Young down the hallway, passing a bathroom and two empty rooms before reaching the bedroom at the back of the house. Hannah Bowman sat on the edge of her bed, a thick blanket pulled tightly and protectively around herself. Her black hair was in disarray and her dark eyes were red, puffy, and rheumy. Streaks of mascara, as black as her hair, streaked her face and mixed with the blood, giving her a nightmarish visage.

Like Alexa, she had been beaten savagely. Both of her eyes were swollen and would no doubt blacken by morning. Dark blood had crusted around both nostrils and had spilled liberally down her chin. Her bottom lip had been split and remained swollen. From where she stood in the bedroom doorway, Spenser could see the deep purple marks around her neck left behind by her assailant which were undoubtedly finger marks from choking her. A gash had been opened across her forehead, leaving half her face coated in blood that was drying.

Spenser nodded to Deputy Shenn, thanking and dismissing him. He gave her a nod and a tight smile then departed, leaving Spenser and Young with the shaken woman.

"Ms. Bowman," Spenser said softly. "We're very sorry for what's happened here tonight. I know this isn't the most opportune time, but we need to ask you a few questions. Would that be alright with you?"

The woman was trembling and pulled the blanket around her even tighter even though Spenser was certain her shaking had nothing to do with the temperature. As they stood there, Spenser was sure she could smell a light floral scent. Like body wash. She'd smelled fresh soap when they'd talked to Alexa as well, and at the time, Spenser had written it off since the woman had just gotten out of the shower when she'd been assaulted.

This was different, though. The assault hadn't happened in the bedroom or the shower. By all appearances, Hannah Bowman had been assaulted in her living room. As Spenser processed it, a cold certainty dawned on her that sent a finger of ice sliding up her spine. She believed she knew what it meant and tried to suppress her shudder to focus on the matter at hand. It was something she could deal with later.

The woman stared straight ahead, her face blank and lifeless. It was like she'd gone somewhere far away inside of herself and wasn't even there with them. Spenser couldn't pretend to understand what she was going through or feeling in that moment, and even though it meant little to nothing right then, she had enormous sympathy for her.

"Ms. Bowman?" Young said. "We have an ambulance on the way that will take you to Magnolia General to get checked out—"

"I don't need to go to the hospital," she said numbly.

"I'm afraid we're going to have to insist. You likely have a concussion and possibly some other internal injuries. It's best if you get looked at," Young pressed gently. "But before the bus gets here, we'd like to ask you a few questions. If that's okay."

The woman's lips moved but not a single sound came out of her mouth for a moment. Her eyes were unfocused, her mind far away. Spenser didn't think they were going to get anything out of her until she'd had some time away from this all to decompress and start to get her mind right again. And that might take a minute.

But then Hannah shook her head and her eyes seemed to come back into focus as she raised her gaze, taking in Spenser and Young as they stood beside her bed. She looked confused for a moment as if she was unsure how they'd gotten there.

"I'm sorry," Hannah finally said, her voice scratchy. "Who are you?"

"I'm Sheriff Spenser Song. And this is Undersheriff Amanda Young," she introduced them. "We just wanted to ask you a few questions about tonight if you're up for it."

"Yeah," Hannah said weakly. "Fine. Go ahead."

"Thank you, Ms. Bowman—"

"Just call me Hannah. Please," she whispered.

Spenser pulled her notebook and pen out of her pocket as Young logged into her tablet and got onto a fresh page for her notes.

"Very well. Hannah, can you walk me through what happened here tonight?" Spenser started. "Just a broad overview is fine for now."

"I got home from work about six and was beat, so I ordered some takeout and put something on Netflix and just stretched out on the couch..."

Hannah's voice trailed off and her face darkened as the memories of what had been done to her came flooding back. Fresh tears welled in the corners of her eyes then spilled down her cheeks. Hannah raised the edge of the blanket and wiped them away, wincing as the fabric ran across the cuts and abrasions on her face.

In the distance, Spenser heard the wailing of the sirens on the ambulance that would come to whisk Hannah away. Given the woman's trauma, Spenser didn't want to press her but still needed her to fill in the blank spots while her memory was the freshest.

"Hannah?" Spenser said as gently as she could. "What happened next?"

She sniffed and tried to blink back her tears. "I was just watching TV when I felt somebody behind me. I turned and… and he was just there," she said, her voice thick with horror. "I don't know how he got in or how long he'd even been in my house. He was just there like he materialized out of thin air."

"I can't imagine how much of a shock that must have been," Young said.

If Hannah heard her, she gave no indication. Her eyes were focused on the wall across the room, her face etched with terror and her mind far away from them as she relieved every harrowing moment of what had been done to her.

"He yanked me up by the hair and slammed me headfirst into the wall. Everything after that is kind of hazy, to be honest. But I was still aware of what he was doing to me," she said quietly. "As he tore my clothes off, I tried to fight back, but he just beat me harder. I think I may have blacked out at one point because I don't remember everything."

"Did he say anything to you? Anything at all?" Spenser asked.

She shook her head. "Not that I remember. Not while he was beating me anyway. The next thing I do remember was that after he was—done—he picked me up and put me in the bathtub. That's when he spoke. He told me to wash myself." She paused and gathered herself before another torrent of tears broke loose. "He told me to make sure I scrubbed myself… down there. And as I did, he sat on the toilet watching me, singing some country song to himself."

Spenser knew that was why she'd smelled body wash on Alexa and now on Hannah. He'd forced them to bathe. He'd forced them to wash away trace evidence and any fluids he might have left behind. He was as smart as he was evil, and it turned Spenser's stomach.

"Hannah, is there anything else you can recall? Anything about him that stood out?" Young asked. "The smallest thing might be useful."

She shook her head. "He was massive. Six-three at least. And he wore a mask—you know, the sort that only lets you see their eyes? His were green."

"That's great, Hannah. Anything else?" Young asked.

She looked away, looking as if she was trying to access some deep memory. Spenser gave her a moment, hoping she had remembered some crucial detail. But then Hannah shook her head.

"I thought he had a tattoo on his forearm, but I can't remember what it was—or if he even really had one. I'm not sure if it's something I'm misremembering."

"That's okay. Just let it percolate in your mind and maybe it'll come back to you later," Spenser said encouragingly.

A pair of EMTs from Magnolia General arrived and stepped into the room. The lead, a stout woman named Anne Kane she'd dealt with before, gave Spenser a nod. Just five-three on a good day, Anne projected an image twice that. Larger than life was a fair description. Her dark hair was cut short and shot through with gray, and blue eyes sparkled behind her black-framed glasses. She was usually quick with a joke and had an infectious laugh that was amusingly girlish because it seemed so out of place coming out of Anne's mouth.

"Sheriff," she said.

"Anne."

"You two about done here?" she asked.

Spenser nodded. "Yeah, I think we've gotten what we need for now."

"Good, because I was only asking to be polite. We were taking her to Magnolia to get her checked out whether you were done or not," she said with a quick wink.

Spenser chuffed. "Fair enough," she said, then looked at Hannah. "You're in good hands with Anne. She'll make sure you're stable then get you to the hospital where you can get a thorough exam. We'll have some follow-up questions for you, but we can wait a few days for that. Would that be alright?"

Hannah nodded and she seemed to be slipping backward, drawing into herself again. Her expression was blank, and she had that faraway, not-quite-present-in-the-moment look on her face again. She fell silent and didn't seem to notice anybody around her. Spenser frowned, feeling a wave of pity for the woman wash over her. Anne spoke to Hannah in low, comforting tones, explaining what they were doing and offering her encouraging and supportive words. Spenser didn't know if Hannah was even registering any of it, though.

She gestured to Young then led her out of the room to let Anne and her partner work on Hannah and get her ready for transport. They stood among the wreckage of the living room. It looked like it had been torn apart by a powerfully violent storm. And Spenser supposed in some ways, it had. And she knew if they didn't get a lead on this guy soon, it was a storm that was going to strike over and over again until they did.

As they stood there, Anne and her partner wheeled Hannah out of the bedroom on their gurney, heading for the ambulance. Spenser looked at the woman. She was dazed. Bloodied. Her eyes were unfocused again and she seemed to be completely disassociated from what was happening to and around her and Spenser found herself wondering if Hannah would ever truly be present in the moment and be able to live her life unafraid ever again.

"We need to find this prick," Spenser growled. "And we need to do it quickly."

CHAPTER TEN

"Looks like you were right," Young said.

"About what?" Spenser asked.

"About this not being our guy's first rodeo. And about this only being the beginning," she replied, her tone dripping with disgust.

They stood in the conference room that sat beside Spenser's office. On the whiteboard, Young taped a photo of Hannah up next to Alexa then wrote down her name underneath it. Spenser sat down in the chair at the head of the table and looked at the pictures of the two women, her stomach roiling as she simmered with anger. Very few crimes got under her skin the way sexual assault and crimes against children did. Those sorts of crimes never failed to rile her up.

In both cases, it was somebody exerting their power and control over somebody who wasn't in a position to defend themselves. Rape was never about the sex. It was about power. One person has it and they want to make sure the other person knows they don't. It was, for all intents and purposes, a case of a bully picking on somebody weaker than themselves. Predators, whether they preyed on women or children, were among the lowest forms of life on the planet and deserved to be removed from the population—permanently—as far as Spenser was concerned.

"I'm not sure this is the beginning. Going by what we've seen so far, I'd say he's well into his career already," Spenser said.

"What do we know about him?" Young mused.

"That he's probably six-three. Caucasian. And has a preference for country music," Spenser said. "And is it me, or might he have a preference?"

"What do you mean?"

"Tell me Alexa and Hannah don't bear a resemblance to one another," Spenser said.

Young stepped back and folded her arms over her chest as she studied the side-by-side photos. She took a long minute then turned back to Spenser. She opened her mouth to say something but then closed it again without speaking and instead, stared at Spenser then turned back to the photos, then back to her again.

"What?" Spenser finally asked.

"Well, you're right about Alexa and Hannah looking similar," Young said. "But I can't help but notice that they also bear a striking resemblance to you."

"You need to get your eyes checked," Spenser said with a laugh. "I'm half Korean—"

"Long, dark hair, tall, lean, and athletic," Young noted. "And let's not forget that you're all single, career-oriented women—"

"They both have dark eyes. Mine are green, in case it slipped your notice," Spenser argued. "My skin is a different shade, and my eyes are a different shape entirely."

"I didn't say you were an exact match, but if you put all three of you side by side, there are more similarities than there are differences."

Spenser stared at the photos for a moment and considered what Young had just said, trying to take a step back and look at it objectively. She supposed that, superficially, there were some physical similarities between her and the two victims. Maybe. Not that it meant anything in the grand scheme of things. She turned back to Young and gave her a shrug.

"Even if that were true, what does it matter?" Spenser said.

"I'm just saying, you kind of fit his type. You fall into the preferential category."

"A lot of other women in this town do, too," Spenser said. "So, would you mind if we got back to focusing on them?"

"All right, all right. Cool your jets, boss lady," Young said with a grin. "I was just pointing out a strange little fun fact and didn't mean anything by it."

Spenser scowled, mostly to herself. She didn't know why she'd had such a strong reaction to Young's observation and just chalked it up to the nature of the cases getting under her skin. Not that it excused her for being so abrupt and snappish with her.

"Sorry for biting your head off. I didn't mean to be so short with you," Spenser said.

"No worries. I think we're both riding high emotions here," Young replied.

The door to the conference room opened and Jacob shambled in. He paused and looked from Spenser to his sister then back again as if sensing the awkwardness in the air.

"This a bad time?" he asked.

"Not at all," Spenser replied. "We're just recalibrating."

"Recalibrating. Right. I'm not sure what that means but okay," he said.

"What do you have, Jacob?" Spenser asked.

"I finished running a search through VICAP like you asked me to do, and just to be thorough, I contacted a few people in departments in the surrounding towns to see if they had any cases that matched ours that they hadn't uploaded to the national database yet," he said.

"Gold star for your initiative," Young said dryly.

Jacob ignored her and opened the file in his hand then turned to the whiteboard and paused. He studied the two pictures then turned back to Spenser.

"Hey, did you realize those two kind of look like you?" he asked.

Spenser rolled her eyes and Young snickered. Jacob looked back and forth between them with an expression of confusion on his face, clearly not getting the joke.

"What do you have?" Spenser asked.

"Right. Well, based on what I see on that board, I think we have a pattern," he said ominously.

He took six photos out of his file then taped them to the board with the pictures of Alexa and Hannah. As he worked, Young stepped to the head of the table and stood beside Spenser, and together, they watched Jacob. When he was done, he stepped aside and showed them the fruit of his labors—and Spenser immediately felt sick to her stomach.

"My God," Young said.

"Yeah," Spenser replied.

Jacob had hung up an additional seven DMV photographs of women from surrounding towns and of those pictures, five of them looked like Hannah and Alexa. They were young with long, dark hair, tall, athletic frames, and cool, pale skin. The other two, a blonde and an African-American woman, didn't seem to fit the pattern. But the other five... dead ringers. They looked so similar they could have been related.

"Obviously, we have two that are unlike the others," Jacob said. "The details of their cases don't exactly match but there are some similar markers."

"Like what?" Young asked.

"Both were single women who were assaulted in their homes," Jacob replied. "The level of violence wasn't quite as high, but they both described their attacker as a large man—"

Spenser shook her head. "I think we might be able to exclude them from this case."

"Why's that?" Jacob asked.

"Amanda?" Spenser prompted.

"Because our guy clearly has a type," she explained. "And preferential offenders rarely, if ever, deviate from their preferred type. We've got five women who fit that profile. That makes a pattern and it makes the other two outliers, which means they're outside his preference."

"Wow, Sis. For a minute there, you actually sounded like a real cop," Jacob said.

Young looked down at Spenser. "Would you charge me if I shot him?"

"If you did it in front of me? I think I might have to," Spenser said.

"That's a shame," she replied.

Spenser grinned. "She's right, though. So, for now, let's focus our attention on the obvious pattern," she said. "What can you tell us about the other five?"

"All right, those five attacks occurred over a twelve-month span starting with Jennifer Patterson, age twenty-four," Jacob said, referring to his tablet. "The next victim was Emily Prescott, twenty-five, then Alicia Allen, twenty-three, Bree Wilson was twenty-six, and finally Chanel Brothers, age twenty-four."

"And now Alexa Beard and Hannah Bowman," Young said. "That makes seven assaults over the last twelve to fourteen months."

"Jacob, tell me about the first couple of victims," Spenser said. "Specifically, about the injuries they sustained from their assaults."

He tapped away at his tablet, presumably pulling up the medical reports. "It looks like the first victim, Jennifer Patterson, sustained a black eye and a split lip," he replied. "Emily Prescott, victim number two, had two black eyes and bruising on her cheeks and neck."

"What about the others?" Young asked, already seeming to know where Spenser was going with her questions.

"Alicia Allen had a contusion on her forehead—as if she'd been slammed face-first into a wall. She also had black eyes, cuts and bruises all over her body, and two fractured ribs," he reported. "The other two, Bree Wilson and Chanel Brothers, also had contusions on their foreheads—Bree's forehead had been split open—and more of the same as the others. They were beaten. Like really badly."

Spenser nodded as he confirmed her suspicions. "He's escalating. He's getting bolder. Angrier. His level of violence is increasing with every attack," she said thoughtfully. "Which means it's probably only a matter of time before he kills somebody."

"You think?" Young asked.

"The way I see it, it's a matter of when and not if."

"I don't understand… Why is he getting angrier and more violent?" Jacob asked.

"Probably because he's getting away with it and has for a while now," Young said. "It's probably emboldening him. Making him a little freer to express himself."

"Express himself? Dude should take up painting or photography," Jacob mused.

"These women are all just surrogates, though," Spenser said.

"Surrogates?" Jacob asked.

"His preference was informed by somebody who caused him some sort of emotional trauma. Most likely his mother or some girlfriend he had a particularly tough break up with," Young jumped in. "These women he's assaulting and brutalizing are just stand-ins for the woman he hates. The woman he's picturing when he's doing these horrible things."

"Damn," Jacob said. "But why is he using surrogates? Why not just take his rage out on the woman he hates?"

"That's a good question," Spenser said. "It might be that he's afraid of her. It could be that he just enjoys abusing and degrading these women because he can do it over and over. It feeds into his feelings of power and control. He knows if he goes after the person who is his focus, it's over. That thrill will be gone. It could be any number of things and unfortunately, that's a question only he can answer for us."

"This would be a whole lot easier if we could figure out who his focus is," Young remarked. "Figuring out who she is would help tell us who he is."

"Yeah, but that's like trying to find the proverbial needle in a haystack. Do you know how many tall, athletic brunettes live in the area? And that's even assuming his focus is in the area.

For all we know, he's carried this rage with him from… well… anywhere," Spenser said.

Young frowned. "I mean, that's possible, of course, but I don't think so. I tend to think the inciting event and the person who stoked all this rage in our guy is in the area."

"Why's that?" Spenser asked.

"It's mostly a hunch. But I think this sort of rage is a result of maybe seeing this person—his focus—on a regular basis. If he'd moved here from like, Florida, it would have given him time to cool off. He wouldn't see his focus and that rage would likely peter out," Young explained. "But seeing his focus regularly would build that anger inside of him. It would continue to grow until he couldn't contain it any longer and he lashed out at somebody who reminded him of that focus. In this case, Jennifer Patterson. That might sate his anger temporarily. But it would keep growing the more he saw his focus. And that seems to go along with the increase in the violence of his attacks."

The chair squeaked as Spenser sat back and stroked her chin, pondering her words. Young's argument was well thought out and incredibly well-reasoned. It was so logically sound, not even Jacob had a pithy response. Spenser nodded.

"You may very well be right, Amanda. That's a solid theory. Very solid," Spenser said.

Young beamed with Spenser's praise as Jacob mockingly bowed to her.

"Okay, so, we need to see if we can figure out a way to find out if your theory holds and his focus really is in the area," Spenser said. "In the meantime, we're going to need to interview the other five victims. We need to firmly connect each of these assaults."

"And how are we going to do that?" Young asked.

"Commonalities," Spenser replied. "One thing we know is that our guy is not using a condom with his victims—"

"And how do we know that?" Young asked.

"He makes them bathe. He makes them scrub their bodies—even down there," Spenser said. "He washes away trace evidence and fluids. That suggests to me that he's not using condoms. It also suggests that he is at least conversant with police procedure and forensics."

"Okay, well, aside from adding another layer of creepy and disgusting to this already steaming pile of it, what does that get us?" Young asked.

"Maybe everything. Or maybe nothing," Spenser replied. "'Conversant' doesn't necessarily mean proficient. It's possible there's some DNA in the drain traps in the tub. I'll have Arbery go back and process the Beard and Bowman scenes again. You never know. Maybe we'll get lucky and he'll find something."

"That would be quite a stroke of luck," Jacob said.

"Stranger things have happened," Spenser replied. "In the meantime, let's get out there and start knocking on doors. Liaise with the sheriffs in the towns where these assaults occurred and see if they'll give us their case files. We also need to talk to these other five victims and make sure they're connected to our current cases. I want this all locked down tight."

CHAPTER ELEVEN

Spenser climbed out of the Bronco and settled her gun belt on her hips then put her Stetson on and looked up at the high rise. The Wingate—forty-two floors of luxury living. Spenser had checked it out and the cheapest condo in the building went for half a million. It reminded Spenser of the luxury high rises in Manhattan. Spenser had always felt out of place whenever she'd had to go into one of them. And staring at the building now, looking like she just walked off the set of some show like Longmire only amplified that feeling.

"I should have given this one to Amanda," she muttered to herself.

After they'd interviewed the first two victims—Jennifer Patterson and Emily Prescott—together, Spenser had offered to make the drive to Seattle where Bree Wilson was living. In return, Amanda was going to interview Alicia Allen and Chanel Brothers, who were both still living in the towns surrounding Sweetwater Falls. Once they were done, they'd meet up back at the shop, compare notes, and see what they had and whether their theory held water.

With a sigh of resignation, Spenser hit the button to lock the Bronco and set the alarm then walked out of the lot and around to the front of the building. A doorman in a dark blue uniform with gold braiding and a matching cap held the door open for her. Spenser nodded her thanks as she stepped into the cavernous black and white marble foyer. Soft classical music filled the air and the lobby was filled with lush plants and prints of famous paintings. Everything about the place exudes style, class, and of course, the pungent aroma of money.

"May I help you?"

Spenser turned to find a woman standing behind a marble counter with a black, oval-shaped sign that said "The Wingate" in burnished steel letters. The young, dark-haired woman wore a dark blue uniform like the doorman, though hers was slightly more feminine. She looked like a hotel concierge. Spenser stepped over to the chest-high counter and offered the woman a smile.

"Sheriff Spenser Song," she said. "I'm here to see Bree Wilson."

"Was Ms. Wilson expecting you?" she asked brightly.

"No. She's not. But I'm on official police business and need to speak with her."

The woman frowned and picked up the phone. "I'll need to see if Ms. Wilson is available to see you, Sheriff Song."

"Well, you can tell Ms. Wilson that she can either speak to me now or we can escort her down to my house to have our chat. As I said, I'm on official police business."

Spenser stepped away to give the woman a chance to make the call to Bree. She didn't like having to use the official police business line or threaten to take her down to the station. Bree was a victim, after all, and the last thing Spenser wanted to do was add to her trauma by storming into her place that way. But she believed Bree's attacker was still operating. Still victimizing other women. And she couldn't go back to Sweetwater Falls empty-handed and without getting her story.

"Sheriff?"

Spenser turned and walked back over to the front desk. The woman, her face pinched and expression sour, handed her a small plastic passkey. She looked at Spenser with something bordering on disdain. She didn't like being strongarmed any more than Spenser liked having had to strongarm her in the first place.

"This key will let you access the elevators up to the seventeenth floor. It's specially coded and only good for today," she explained curtly. "Ms. Wilson is in unit number 1742."

"Listen, I'm sorry to have been so abrupt. That's not how I like to do things," Spenser said.

"Of course," she replied, her face softening slightly.

"Thank you," Spenser said as she held up the key.

The woman nodded as Spenser turned away and headed for the elevators. She stepped into the car and paused when she saw there were no buttons marking the different floors. There was a burnished steel place set into the wall beside the door with a slot cut into it that seemed to be the same size as the keycard in her hand.

"Please insert your keycard into the scanner, Guest."

The feminine voice had an English accent as it spoke but also couldn't quite shake that slight hint of the Siri-like robotic tone as it identified Spenser as a guest and not a resident. She assumed the residents had their own keycards that triggered a more personalized greeting unique to them. It was quite the system. Spenser did as she asked and slipped the keycard into the scanner beside the door.

"Seventeenth floor," the voice said. "Please step away from the doors and hold onto the hand railings as we ascend."

Spenser stepped back and put her hand on the stainless-steel railing that ran around the elevator car. The doors slid closed, and the elevator shot up startlingly fast. A moment later, the car slowed then came to a full stop and the doors opened again and let her out onto the seventeenth floor with that feminine yet robotic voice announcing her destination. Spenser walked out and followed the signage to the right place, which, given that every floor only seemed to have three total units, wasn't all that difficult.

As if Bree had been watching for her through the peephole, the door opened before Spenser could even raise her hand to knock. The woman standing before her was about the same height as Spenser with dark, perfectly styled hair. Looking closely at her forehead, Spenser could see a thin, white scar—a remnant of her encounter with her attacker. The woman wore her hair with her bangs brushed over as if she was trying to hide the scar.

Bree wore a fashionable dark blue pantsuit with a pearl-colored blouse beneath her blazer. A red pocket square and a matching scarf gave her a dash of color. And although she was well put together and seemingly composed, Spenser could see the woman was terrified. She hid it well though. Bree's cool, pale complexion seemed to blanch even further, and her wide, jade-colored eyes shimmered with tears that she seemed determined to keep from falling.

She held her hands down at her waist, wringing them together furiously. When she saw Spenser's eyes on her hands, she quickly disentangled them and left them gently clasped together, still and unmoving. It seemed to be a movement she was well-practiced in.

"Ms. Wilson," Spenser said. "I'm Sheriff Song—Spenser. May we talk for a moment?"

"Please, come in," Bree replied. "And it's Mrs. Cohen. Or it will be in a few weeks."

"Oh, well congratulations, Mrs. Cohen," Spenser said as she stepped through the door.

A faint smile that didn't come close to reaching her eyes flickered across the woman's lips that left Spenser wondering if it was her presence causing Bree's obvious discomfort or something deeper in herself or with her relationship. She closed the door behind Spenser then led her down a short hallway and into a living room that looked like it belonged on a television show like *Lifestyles of the Rich and Famous* or whatever people watched. It was a genre of television Spenser had never understood—watching programs that showcased the sort of wealth some people had that the viewers themselves would likely never attain.

High-end, hand-carved furniture sat atop what looked like very expensive Persian rugs, which sat atop genuine marble flooring. The back wall of the living room was made of glass and offered a beautiful, panoramic view of the city beyond it. Pieces of modern art adorned the walls and everything in the room was situated just as her interior designer had obviously set it. It was gorgeous without being gaudy. Tasteful. It was the sort of room that showed off their wealth while simultaneously trying to make them appear humble and like they were downplaying the fact that they were filthy rich.

With her arms crossed over her chest, Bree walked over to the wall of glass and stared out at the city. Her entire body was rigid, and the air was thick with tension.

"You have a lovely home," Spenser said, trying to break the ice.

"It belongs to my fiancé," she replied stiffly.

"Are you still working at the museum?" Spenser asked. "You're a curator, right?"

"I know why you're here. I knew it the moment Ashley called and said the sheriff of Sweetwater Falls was here to see me. Although you weren't the sheriff I was expecting," she said without turning around. "But I have to tell you now that I can't testify. I won't testify. So, I'm sorry, but it seems like you've wasted your time coming here."

She finally turned around and Spenser could see the haunted look in the woman's eyes. Her face was drawn and pale and she suddenly looked twenty years older, as if the emotional burden she'd been carrying was taking a tremendous physical toll on her.

"Daniel—my fiancé—he doesn't know what happened to me back home. He can't know," she said, almost pleading. "The only reason I let you in is because he's out of town and I felt like I needed to tell you that I'm not interested in pursuing this case face to face. It's over for me. It's in the past. And that is where I want to leave it."

"I think there's been a misunderstanding, Mrs. Cohen," Spenser said. "I'm not here to ask you to testify—"

"Then why are you here, Sheriff?"

"Because we believe the man who assaulted you has assaulted others. Two women over the last few days," Spenser said. "In all, we believe he's assaulted seven women over the past eighteen or nineteen months."

She licked her lips but looked away, seemingly unable to hold Spenser's gaze any longer. Even from across the room, Spenser could see the guilt and the pain of the memories that lingered inside of her like malevolent spirits etched into her features.

"That's terrible. Awful," she said. "But I don't see what that has to do with me."

"Mrs. Cohen, I just need you to tell me what happened that night—"

"I already told the other sheriff—Hinton, I think his name was," she said with a snort of disgust. "He didn't seem all that interested in my story. In fact, he said some things that made it sound like he was blaming me for what happened."

Spenser wasn't entirely surprised to hear that. From everything she'd heard and seen with her own two eyes, her predecessor, Howard Hinton, hadn't been overly effective in his post. More than that, he was sexist. Spenser had no trouble believing that he'd victim blame an assault survivor. That seemed to be very on-brand for him.

"I understand that, but I'm not Sheriff Hinton," Spenser said. "I want to find the man who did this to you—to all the others. I want to get justice for you all."

"There is no justice for us, Sheriff Song. There's only the pain that lingers within us. It's a pain that flares up when those old ghosts are stirred up by people like you."

"Bree, that pain will never fully subside. And it will on occasion flare up even without people like me turning up in your life," Spenser said gently. "Bringing the man who did this to you to justice and making him pay for what he's done will help tamp down that pain. And knowing you helped bring him down—that will help turn your pain into strength."

"Have you ever been assaulted, Sheriff?"

"No. I haven't."

"Then what do you know?"

"I have worked with survivors... many survivors. I saw more than my fair share of assault cases when I was with the Bureau," Spenser replied. "And I've seen the strength it takes to survive first hand. I've seen what it takes for some women to not only survive but to not let this horrible event define them or turn them cold. I've seen women take their pain—the exact pain you're feeling right now—and turn it into armor. And I've seen them go on to do some incredible things."

Bree sank down onto the couch and buried her face in her hands, her entire body shaking as she sobbed wildly. Spenser gently sat down beside her and awkwardly put her arm around Bree's shoulder, just trying to let the woman know she wasn't alone. She leaned into Spenser and sobbed until it seemed like she'd run out of tears. She sat up and blotted her eyes with the cuff of her blazer and looked away, an expression of mortification on her face.

"I need your help, Bree. All the victims need your help."

"I told you, I can't testify. Daniel can't know what happened to me."

She sounded terrified of her fiancé, and although Spenser wanted to give her opinion on that, as well as about men who don't seem able to support their partners through traumatic events, she bit her tongue. That wasn't going to accomplish anything productive. Nor was it any of her business.

"That's a long way off and not something I'm even thinking about right now, Bree," Spenser offered. "I just... I need to know what happened. I need to know if the man who assaulted you is the same man we're looking for right now."

Bree was silent for so long, Spenser didn't think she was going to answer her. But then she sat up straight and dabbed at her eyes with the cuff of her blazer again. She turned to Spenser, and instead of fear burning behind her eyes, Spenser saw the fires of anger. Of hate.

"Daniel can never know," she said, her voice firm. "And I will not testify."

"I see no reason to tell Daniel anything," Spenser replied.

Spenser had to stop short of promising that she wouldn't return and ask Bree to testify at some point in the future, after they'd arrested their rapist. But that was a bridge she would have to cross when she came to it. For the moment, she just needed to hear Bree's story. Needed to know if this was confirmation of their theory or just another blind alley.

Bree frowned and looked away for a moment, seeming to take a moment to gather herself. When she was ready, she turned back to Spenser and told her story. It was every bit as harrowing as it was heartbreaking and Spenser felt not just pity for Bree, but the fires of her own anger burning ever higher and hotter. She was determined to bring this monster down no matter the cost.

CHAPTER TWELVE

"**W**HAT TIME DID YOU GET HERE?" SPENSER ASKED as she stepped into the conference room.

"About an hour ago," Young replied. "I wanted to get in and start working on our timeline."

Spenser set the cups of coffee and two boxes of pastries she brought in down on the conference table. Young snatched up a cup of coffee as the deputies on the morning shift shuffled in to raid the boxes of pastries, everybody eager for that early morning sugar fix. They all thanked Spenser for the treat then headed back out to see to their duties. It had become something of a morning ritual and seemed to have helped improve relations between

Spenser and some of her deputies. Sure, it was bribery, but it worked.

Young had brought in a second whiteboard and started putting the pictures of the seven victims up in order of their assaults. She was writing their names and dates below the photos. Looking at them all was just another stark reminder of the damage path this UNSUB was tearing through the women in the area.

"How did things go with Bree Wilson?" Young asked.

"About as well as it could have, I suppose."

Spenser grabbed a donut from the box and sat down in her chair at the head of the table. She took a bite of the chocolate cake with sprinkles then washed it down with a swallow of the rich, dark coffee she'd picked up for herself at Ryker's shop. It was her little treat for herself.

"Does she fit the pattern?" Young asked.

"She does," Spenser replied. "He'd gotten into her place without her knowing how he'd gotten in. She said it was like he just materialized out of thin air."

"Did the other details match?"

Spenser nodded. "He blitzed her, slammed her head into the wall—she's still got the scar on her forehead," she said. "He assaulted her, made her bathe and wash herself out, all the while, he was singing a country song to himself."

"I don't suppose she got a look at him?"

"Yeah, we're not that lucky. Same basic description, though—green eyes, wore a balaclava, massively built, Caucasian man," Spenser said. "What about the two you talked to?"

"More of the same. Alicia Allen and Chanel Brothers had the same experience as the other five. The only thing that's different in all this is the increasing level of violence in the attacks."

"Not to be too graphic, but did Alicia or Chanel mention that their attacker didn't use a condom?" Spenser asked.

"Yeah. They both said he didn't use one."

Spenser ran a hand over her face and sighed. "There have to be others. Victims that predate even Jennifer Paterson. He didn't start this bold or this proficient. This is something that he had to work himself up to."

"Jacob said he searched the surrounding areas and didn't find any other attacks that fit the parameters."

"And I'm sure there aren't. I trust Jacob. If he says there are none, there are none," Spenser said. "But I tend to think there are attacks that don't match the parameters. His first assaults."

Young paced back and forth in front of the board, her eyes pinned to the seven pictures on the board. She finally stopped and turned to Spenser.

"Well, what you said about him being conversant with forensic procedures might account for his proficiency with manipulating crime scenes," Young said.

Spenser shook her head. "Even somebody proficient with forensics is likely going to make some mistakes early on. No early crime scene is going to be clean. These monsters get better over time. It's as true for serial killers as it is for serial rapists."

"So, how do we go about finding these early assaults?"

"That's a good question," Spenser groused.

The door to the conference room opened and Jacob bustled in, giving them both a smile of greeting before grabbing the last apple fritter out of the box and claiming a seat at the table. He took a bite of the fritter followed by a long swallow of his coffee then slumped back in his chair.

"Sorry I'm late," he said. "I overslept this morning."

"Up too late nerding out over something completely dorky, no doubt," Young said.

"Actually, I was up late working," he said.

"On what, your next *Dungeons and Dragons* game?"

"For your information, I was doing some digging on our guy," he said. "Based on what you guys were talking about—and using your unusually astute theory, Sis—I started pulling up cases from around the area that maybe didn't quite fit the parameters I plugged into VICAP and expanded the search looking for earlier cases."

Spenser and Young exchanged a look with each other, earning them a strange expression from Jacob.

"What?" he asked.

"We were just talking about that," Young said. "Right before you walked in."

Jacob turned and gave his sister a smirk. "Looks like you're not the only one who might be getting pretty good at this police stuff, huh?"

"You both get gold stars," Spenser said. "So, what did you find, Jacob?"

"Nothing definitive just yet," he replied. "But I called some contacts I have in the departments in surrounding towns. I've asked them to pull sexual assault records that haven't been plugged into VICAP going back ten years that involve a white male over six feet tall. It's probably going to take a few days to get all those records in, but it's in the works."

"That's good, Jacob. That's really good. I'm impressed, big brother," Young said.

"We're going to have to take time to separate the wheat from the chaff when we get the files in, so it's going to be a little labor intensive," he said. "But it may get us closer to figuring out who this guy is."

"That's great initiative, Jacob."

He smiled wide, soaking in the praise. Young just rolled her eyes but laughed to herself. Spenser grinned and took a sip of her coffee, amused by the siblings. They were the closest thing she had to a younger brother and sister, and she enjoyed watching them interact. More than that, she enjoyed interacting with them because, in some ways, they made her feel accepted. Made her feel like part of their family.

Spenser's eyes drifted to the whiteboard. She looked at the photos Young had taped to it, taking in the progression of the assaults. The faces of the women burned in Spenser's mind, and thinking about the trauma they'd endured at the hands of this monster made the anger in her belly bubble like a bitter acid. Spenser frowned, the similarity in their appearance more than a little eerie. But she sat up in her seat as it triggered a thought.

"Jacob, there's something else I need you to do for me," she said.

"Name it."

"I need you to dig through the financial and phone records of these seven victims," Spenser said. "Tap every ATM card, credit card, store receipt, and anything else you can think of—"

"And what is it we're looking for?" he asked.

"Nexus points," Spenser said. "I want to know if there are any points of commonality between them. Did they go to the same yoga studios, eat at the same restaurants, shop at the same stores... anything? I want to know if there's a place where their paths all crossed—a place where they might have drawn the eye of their attacker."

"That's a great thought," Young said.

"I'll get right on it, boss," he said.

"Good. Good. Hopefully, that will yield something useful," Spenser replied.

Her eyes drifted back to the board again and to the faces of the women looking back at her, seeming to silently plead with her to get justice for them. Spenser gritted her teeth and vowed to herself that she would do it if it was the last thing she did.

CHAPTER THIRTEEN

It had been more than a week and Spenser was still waiting on the other police departments to get their case files over to Jacob. She didn't think they were deliberately stonewalling them. She just knew smaller departments didn't always have an overabundance of staff, nor the best and most organized record-keeping systems around. She had Jacob squeezing them as hard as he could, but it was a fine line to walk. If they squeezed too hard, those contacts he had would get pissed off and likely not help them out of spite. And so, they were forced to wait.

Of course, the problem with waiting was it gave their UNSUB more time to wreak havoc. Spenser knew he was out there lurking. He was like a hurricane out somewhere over the ocean and she knew that like a hurricane, he was slowly moving closer to shore. Gaining strength. Speed. Power. Like a hurricane, he was just waiting to come ashore to inflict destruction and bitter pain on all those caught in his path. And all Spenser could do was sit, wait, watch all the chaos unfold, then help try to pick up all the wreckage and rebuild after it had gone.

"You okay, boss?"

Young's voice snapped Spenser out of her reverie, and she looked up. "Yeah. I'm good."

"Okay, well, she's inside."

"Yeah," Spenser said. "I'll be right in."

Young gave her a curious look but nodded then turned and headed into the apartment building. Spenser took a minute to clear her head and get focused. The red and blue lights of the emergency vehicles parked at the curb slashed through the night, splashing onto the faces of the people behind the tape line jostling with one another to get a better position to see what was happening inside the building.

Spenser shook her head, disgusted by people's need to revel in the misery of others, then headed up the walk. She passed through the front doors of the building and looked around at the U-shaped complex that surrounded a large pool and jacuzzi area. Though upgraded and refurbished over the years, the design of the building dated back to the 70s made Spenser think it may have even started life as a hotel.

Spenser headed up one of the two staircases that sat on either side of the front doors and followed the trail of deputies to the front door of Stacy Trask's apartment. Deputy Jerry Krueger was on the door and gave her a nod as she stepped through.

"Evenin', Sheriff," he said.

"Evenin', Jerry."

The front room of the apartment was small but tidy with off-white walls and a dark brown carpet. Framed pictures of what Spenser assumed were Stacy Trask's family and friends hung on the walls along with large block letters that spelled out "JOY" running down the narrow wall that led to the dining room/kitchen area.

"Not a lot of joy in here tonight," Spenser muttered.

A low entertainment center was centered on the wall across the room from the sofa and a large flatscreen television sat atop that. More framed pictures of Stacy and her friends took up spots on the entertainment center as well. They all looked so young. So happy. Stacy had a wide, electric smile in those photos, completely unaware that her life was going to change forever.

The fabric on the sofa, the blanket that hung on the back, and the pillows that adorned it were all shades of pink and purple. In fact, most everything in the place that Spenser could see was light, pastel colors. The front room of the apartment had such a feeling of optimism. Of, like the letters spelled out, joy. Spenser felt the vibrancy and boundless energy of youth within those walls and reminded her of a girl's dorm room rather than a grown woman's apartment.

From the back of the apartment, Spenser heard a woman softly crying and Young's voice murmuring to her comfortingly. She drew in a deep breath and held it, silently counting to ten before letting it out as she gathered herself. Spenser walked through the doorway beside the sofa. In front of her were the two doors to what she assumed was the linen closet, to her immediate left was a bathroom, and to her right was the doorway to the bedroom. The air was redolent with a thick, citrusy smell she assumed was body wash.

The first thing Spenser noticed when she stepped into the bedroom was the deep, bloody divot in the wall beside the closet. Young sat beside a woman—barely more than a girl, really—with long, dark hair that was wet and clung to her alabaster-colored cheeks and dark eyes. The resemblance to the rest of the victims was striking. It was just one more link in the chain that connected one woman to the next. Stacy Trask sat wrapped in a blanket, her head down, her body shaking. Young sat beside her, holding her hand. She looked up when Spenser walked in, an expression of helplessness on her face.

Spenser noticed the crimson dots on the light-colored blanket she was wrapped in and when the girl looked up, Spenser nearly gasped. Her eyes were swollen—one almost completely shut. The blood vessels inside of them had burst, coloring them both red. Both of her lips were split, and even from where she stood, Spenser could see that both of her top front teeth and one lower were broken, leaving nothing but jagged, white shards.

Her cheeks were a deep purple, almost black, and she continued bleeding from the nose and the gash on her forehead. Bruises on her neck and wrists matched the color of the bruises on her face. Her earlobes were bloody and ragged from having her earrings torn out. Stacy Trask was a bloody, beaten mess. Her injuries were the worst Spenser had seen among the string of victims yet and she sat amid a bedroom that had been utterly destroyed. Furniture had been broken, mirrors and picture frames shattered, and clothing had been pulled from drawers and the closet then sliced to ribbons. It looked as if a violent hurricane had passed through.

"Stacy," Spenser said. "We are so sorry for what you've endured tonight."

Even as she spoke the words, Spenser cringed. She had been saying the same thing so frequently lately that they felt like they'd lost meaning and felt wooden coming out of her mouth. She kept saying them over and over, but hadn't stopped the monster from preying on these innocent women. And they kept being victimized. Brutalized. Those words almost felt like nothing more than a worthless platitude anymore.

"An ambulance should be here soon to take you to Magnolia General to get you checked out," Spenser said softly.

Stacy nodded but didn't say a word. Tears spilled from her eyes and mixed with the blood on her face, sending streaks of pink down her cheeks before splashing onto the blanket she had pulled tight around herself.

"Stacy, would it be alright if I ask you a couple of questions before the paramedics arrive?" Spenser asked.

"Sure," she said, her voice thick and hoarse.

"Did you happen to get a look at the face of the man who attacked you?" Spenser asked.

She weakly shook her head, wincing at the pain the effort caused her. "He wore a mask," she croaked. "All I could see were his eyes. They were green."

"All right. That's good," Spenser said. "Did you happen to notice any other distinguishing features? Scars? Tattoos? Anything at all?"

She opened her mouth to reply but paused and looked away as if she was trying to remember something. It took a moment, but she looked back at Spenser.

"At some point, I saw his forearm. He had a tattoo on his forearm," she said thickly. "It was… a skull. Yeah, I saw a skull and there were two bullets… They were crisscrossed behind the skull with an American flag behind that. And there was fire behind it all."

Spenser felt her stomach lurch. It was the first tangible lead they'd gotten since this whole thing began. She didn't recognize her description of the tat—and judging by the look on Young's face, she didn't either—but it gave them a starting point. There were only so many tattoo parlors in Sweetwater Falls. Surely, somebody would recognize it.

"He watched me bathe," Stacy said, her tone dripping with horror. "He just sang some stupid song to himself as he watched me bathe. He gave me instructions. Told me how to… how to clean myself properly."

Her words were unprompted, and her eyes were far away, but Spenser had no trouble seeing the pain and the outrage in them as she remembered the assault. As she relived every horrifying moment of it. But for some reason, for Stacy, the creep watching her bathe seemed to hold an especially traumatic space inside of her. It was as if that was the most terribly violating moment of the entire encounter for her. As if that was the most terrible memory. Not that Spenser was going to judge or question. She had no idea what was going on in Stacy's heart or mind and couldn't relate to what she'd been through.

Maybe after having been assaulted, having your attacker watching you as he forced you to scrub away any and all traces of himself was that horrifying. Was that violating? Maybe it was the cavalier way he sang to himself as she scrubbed away the residue of his assault. Like it was something fun. Something he'd enjoyed. Spenser couldn't say. As terrible as it sounded, even to herself, Spenser was grateful that she'd never had to experience and endure the sort of pain and horror that came with—and after—surviving a sexual assault.

Tears rolled down her cheeks and her body shook wildly as she began to sob. Anne Kane and her partner came in and dropped their bags on the floor next to the bed. She glanced up at Spenser, her face tight, her expression angry.

"We've got it from here, Sheriff Song," Anne said.

All at once, Stacy stopped crying. She looked up and her face paled even more as she stared Spenser in the eye.

"Sheriff?" she asked. "Sheriff Spenser Song?"

"Yes, that's me," Spenser replied.

"He… he wanted me to give you a message," she said, her voice quaking.

"A message," Spenser said. "For me?"

She nodded weakly, her body shaking violently. Anne looked up at Spenser, silently urging with her eyes to get this over with so they could get Stacy to the hospital.

"Okay," Spenser said. "What was the message?"

Spenser's stomach churned and she tasted bile in the back of her throat. That he'd given this poor girl he'd just brutalized and stripped of her innocence a message for her made this far more personal for her. It hit her on a deeper level and made the fires inside of her burn even hotter.

"He wanted… he wanted me to tell you hi and that he was thinking about you," Stacy said, her voice barely more than a whisper.

CHAPTER FOURTEEN

Her lungs and legs burned but Spenser pushed herself harder, refusing to stop running while there was still so much bouncing around in her head. She crossed through a shallow stream and up a slight rise. The sun was quickly slipping toward the horizon, setting the sky ablaze in vivid shades of red and orange and a cool breeze stirred the branches of the trees and bushes all around her. Annabelle loped alongside Spenser, staying close by. Whenever Spenser was upset or stressed out, the big dog seemed to pick up on it, and rather than race ahead like she normally did, she stayed protectively by her side.

They came around a bend in the trail and Spenser found herself in the clearing where Ryker had built the private park for their dogs. It had been a few days since she'd seen it and he'd gotten quite a bit more work done. For all intents and purposes, the park was finished, but being the perfectionist he was—and being in dire need of things to keep himself busy—Ryker was continuing to add small flourishes to it. She could see that he had added a picnic bench area beneath the wide limbs of the pine trees that stood outside the fence.

Spenser slowed down and Annabelle was already stamping her feet and wagging her tail, anxious to get inside. Laughing to herself, Spenser walked to the gate and opened it. Annabelle raced in, was spotted by Mocha, and together, they raced around the park, barking at one another, big doggy smiles on both their faces. Spenser made sure to close and lock the gate behind her then made her way over to where Ryker stood, completely focused on the black metal control box he'd mounted to a steel pole.

Spenser heard two loud splashes and turned to see both dogs dove into the pond. They dashed through water that almost came up to their chests, kicking up liquid plumes as they took turns chasing one another.

"I swear this place is like Disneyland to them," Spenser said with a laugh.

Ryker gave her a grin. "That's the point. They need a good, safe place to play."

"You could probably charge admission fees to this place," Spenser said.

"Nah. This is for them," he replied then gestured to the picnic bench area. "And for us."

"I can see that. You've been busy these last few days."

He shrugged. "Coffee beans aren't ready to harvest just yet. Don't have any new plants going in and Kelli insists things run smoother down at Higher Grounds when I'm not there. And, she banished me from the store, so it's not like I didn't have the time."

"Well, Kelli is usually right about these things."

Ryker chuckled. "She usually is."

Kelli Butler was the general manager at Ryker's coffee house and one of the only other people on the planet that Spenser knew of who got him the way she did. Kelli was a friend and confidant to Ryker and had been for a while. Spenser liked her enormously and because of that connection they both had with Ryker, they too had become fast friends.

Spenser looked around and saw that in addition to the sod he'd laid down under the picnic bench, Ryker had also spread soft sand around most of the park. He'd told her it would be easier on the dogs' feet when they were running around like maniacs. She turned back to him and cocked her head as she watched him working.

"What are you doing?" she asked.

"Finishing up the pond's filtration system," he said. "We don't want the water getting stagnant, so I put in a pump to circulate. Fresh water in, old water out to be filtered."

"You have gone all out on this park."

"It's good for me," he said. "Except, I'm running out of things to do here."

"What's your next big project?"

He shook his head. "I don't know."

His tone was heavy, and he sounded concerned. Ryker knew that having idle time was a bad thing for him. If he wasn't busy doing something, it gave him too much time to think, and spending a lot of time inside his head was never a good idea for him. He tended to spiral. Even with his regular appointments with his therapist, Ryker hadn't gotten to that point yet where he could be trusted to be alone without anything to do.

Constant motion and always having a project on tap had been his therapist's idea to begin with. And it had been a successful idea. The thought was that having distractions and something to occupy his mind would be good for Ryker as they worked through his issues, and hopefully, were able to eventually put him on level ground again.

"I'll find something to keep myself busy. Don't worry," he said with a half-smile. "Maybe I'll build a roast house and do all the bean roasting here rather than drag it all down to the shop to do."

"Hey, that's not a bad idea," Spenser agreed.

"That'll do it," Ryker said.

He flipped a switch and green lights lit up the board inside the utility box. Together, they watched the water in the pond, and Spenser saw the water churn and bubble in the far corner. Ryker nodded to himself then closed the box and put a padlock on it. They didn't get people out on his land very often, but Ryker was a cautious man by nature. And after Spenser had a couple of people show up and take shots at her he'd gotten even more cautious—almost paranoid really—and had installed a battery of security equipment. Her cabin and the grounds around it felt more secure than a military base.

Ryker silently led her over to the picnic table, and together, they sat down across from each other. They watched the dogs playing in the pond, chasing and wrestling each other with unbridled enthusiasm and joy. It warmed Spenser's heart.

"You're tense," Ryker said.

"How can you tell?"

"Your body language," he replied. "But you also showed up here red in the face, sweating in buckets, and as out of breath as if you'd just run a marathon. You usually only push yourself that hard when something's eating at you."

A wry grin twisted Spenser's lips. "You know me well."

His gaze found hers and Spenser felt her heart skip a beat as his caramel-colored eyes bore into hers with an intensity that nearly stole her breath. Their gazes lingered on each other for a long moment, the air between them crackling with electricity. And just for a moment, Spenser seemed able to forget about the problems plaguing her. She was able to step away from the job and the complicated emotions it stirred within her completely and lose herself in the moment with him.

"I know you about as well as you know me," he said. "And yet, that's not to say that you don't continue to surprise me."

"That goes both ways, mister."

"That's a good thing."

"I think that's a very good thing," she replied as her cheeks flared with heat. She quickly looked away—and immediately regretted it. Rather than remaining wrapped in that bubble of warmth, the reality of the world came rushing back into her head, snuffing out the flickering flames of flirtation. Her smile ebbed and her heart felt heavy again.

"It's these assaults weighing on you, isn't it?" Ryker asked.

"Give the man a kewpie doll."

"Talk to me. What has you so rattled?"

Spenser ran a hand through her thick, dark hair and sighed. She knew she shouldn't be discussing the details of the case with anybody. But she also knew she could trust Ryker. She knew that he would take her secrets with him to the grave. Literally. He had become her go-to when she needed some insight or perspective. Or just a swift kick to the backside to get her head on straight. His experiences in life had given him hard-earned wisdom and a unique way of seeing things that she valued. Plus, he didn't sugarcoat things. If she had her head up her butt, he'd tell her, which, strangely enough, was also something she valued. When Spenser had told Young she wanted straight shooters and not yes-men surrounding her a while ago, she'd meant it. And if there were two words she could use to describe Ryker Makawi, it was straight shooter.

"He called me out, Ryker," she said. "By name."

"What do you mean?"

"This isn't going to be in the papers—and I know I don't have to tell you to keep it under your hat—but the rapist told his latest victim to deliver a message to me. Personally."

"What did he say?"

"He told her to tell me hi and that he'd been thinking about me."

Ryker sat up a little straighter, a look of displeasure crossed his face. He suddenly looked angrily protective. Ryker cleared his throat and leaned forward, clasping his hands together atop the picnic table.

"Well, he obviously wants your attention," he said, his voice low and husky.

"And now he has it," Spenser replied. "The question I have is why? Why does he want my attention so badly he'd do something like that?"

"That's the question. And unfortunately, that's not one I can answer for you."

"But you're supposed to have all the answers."

He laughed softly. "I wish it was that simple."

Spenser growled and scrubbed her face with her hands. "Okay, what I need to figure out is whether this is personal—as in, this guy knows me. Or if this is just some creep who gets his rocks off doing terrible things then taunting law enforcement."

"Like the Zodiac Killer. Or the Son of Sam. Or Jack the Ripper," Ryker offered.

"Right. Exactly. Like those guys. Thank God our guy isn't racking up the body count those guys did," Spenser replied. "But with the escalation in violence and now his open taunts, I fear that's only a when and not if situation. And I'd like to get ahead of him before he crosses that line. God knows he's doing enough damage as it is."

"What do you know about him?"

Spenser shook her head. "Not much. He's big and white. He apparently loves country music and he's disturbingly familiar with police and forensic procedure," Spenser said. "Oh, and he's also got a tattoo that might be distinctive that I wanted to run by you."

Spenser described to Ryker the tattoo Stacy Trask had seen. He pursed his lips and looked away, seeming to mull it over.

"The way she described it makes me think it was a military tattoo," Spenser said.

"Not one I'm familiar with. But there are a lot of unit insignias I've never seen," he replied. "I'll ask around the VA and a couple of vet bars quietly. See if anybody's familiar with it."

"I'd appreciate that, Ryker."

He gave her a gentle smile. "You know there's not much I won't do for you."

"And I'm grateful."

"Now, that being said, do not let this guy get into your head, Spense."

"It's hard not to when he's calling me out by name."

Ryker shook his head. "That's what he wants. And if you let him into your head, he wins. It very well may be what you said—he's getting off on taunting you because you happen to be the sheriff. Nothing more and nothing less."

"Yeah, maybe. I mean, it's probably likely. But it just feels... personal."

"And he wants you thinking that way. It keeps you off balance," Ryker said. "And if you're off balance, you're not seeing things clearly. Don't give him that power. Don't let him cloud your vision or get under your skin."

"I'm trying. But I'd be lying if I said this didn't stir up some strong emotions in me."

"Of course, it does. How could it not? But use those emotions. Don't let them use you," he said. "I've never seen somebody do the job you're doing better than you, Spenser. And I have a feeling this guy just gets a charge out of challenging you. So, step up to the challenge, and don't beat yourself by letting him into your head. Try to relax, clear, and focus your mind, then roll it back to square one and get back to basics. You'll find the answers. I guarantee it."

Spenser fell quiet for a moment, taking in everything he'd said. Then she raised her eyes to his and felt the smile tugging at the corners of her mouth.

"This is why I come to you with these things," she said. "You have a way of hitting a reset button that I can't. Thank you."

He reached across the table and took her hand in his, caressing the back of her knuckles with his thumb as he stared into her eyes. That familiar current of electricity flowed between them and Spenser felt her heart flutter as her face warmed.

"You're welcome," he replied softly. "Like I said, there's not much I won't do for you, Spenser Song."

"And I am grateful for you, too, Ryker Makawi."

CHAPTER FIFTEEN

THE SUN WAS BARELY OVER THE HORIZON IN THE EAST when Young walked into the conference room. She paused and looked at Spenser sitting at the head of the table already.

"What? I get in a little early and now you're trying to beat me in?" Young asked with a grin.

Spenser laughed. "Don't flatter yourself. I woke up early and couldn't get back to sleep so I figured I'd get to work early."

Young set her things down then poked around in the boxes of pastries with a frown. "Day-old goodies, huh?"

"We were lucky to get those," Spenser said. "They'd just started to open up and were still in the middle of making the fresh stuff. But I figured if I showed up here without goodies, the troops would all revolt."

"Well, beggars can't be choosers," she said with a shrug.

"No, they cannot."

"And I, for one, am grateful for this daily infusion of sugar."

Spenser laughed. "You're welcome."

Young settled for a chocolate croissant, setting it on a napkin, then sat down and took a bite of it then washed it down with a swallow of her coffee. With a smile on her face, she sighed and sat back in her chair.

"Sugar and caffeine, all is right with the world," she said.

Spenser laughed. "It's all about the simple pleasures."

"Yes, it is."

Spenser nibbled at her scone then took a drink of her coffee, her eyes scanning the computer screen in front of her.

"And what had you so restless that you had to come in so early?" Young asked.

"I was thinking about the tat Stacy Trask described. The bullets and the flag and all made me think military," Spenser said.

"I had the same thought."

"So, I talked to Ryker about it already and he's going to talk to his military friends—see if they recognize it," Spenser said. "In the meantime, I've been looking through a database of military unit patches to see if I come up with it before he does."

"And how is that going for you?"

Spenser shook her head. "Not very good so far. I don't think I realized just how many different units all the different branches of the military had."

"And that's not even half of it. What you're seeing are the official unit insignias," Young said. "There are twice as many unofficial insignias. Some units make up their own—get them as tats or patches for their civilian clothes. That's why Ryker's probably going to have more luck running it down then we will. You need somebody with access."

Spenser looked at her in surprise. "You seem to know a lot about this kind of thing."

"I've had a couple of boyfriends who were in the service," she replied.

"Did you now? I had no idea."

"I was young and dumb—"

"Now she's a few years older but just as dumb."

Spenser turned to see Jacob coming through the conference room door with a wide grin on his face. Without missing a beat, Young launched a pen that bounced off the side of his head, drawing a laugh from her brother.

"What are you even doing here so early?" Young snarled.

"My job, strangely enough," Jacob replied.

"I guess there's a first time for everything," Young quipped.

"Children," Spenser said.

Jacob put his things down then rifled around in the box, coming away with his usual apple fritter. He was the only one in the department who seemed to like them, so Spenser always made sure there was at least one in there for him. Jacob sat down and dug into his fritter, munching away for a moment as he got his computer setup. After he'd washed it down with some coffee, he turned to Spenser.

"So, what's up with the bad guy calling you out, boss?" Jacob asked. "Do you think that he knows you?"

"Maybe. I don't know," Spenser replied, feeling a stab of guilt. "It might be that he just likes taunting law enforcement."

"He wouldn't be the first bad guy in history to do that," Young offered.

"No, he wouldn't," Spenser replied.

Spenser chewed on a piece of her scone as Stacy Trask's words echoed through her mind. *Tell Spenser I said hi and I've been thinking about her.* The more she thought about it, the more personal that message felt. The more she started to think that this wasn't about taunting law enforcement but putting her on notice. He was taunting her specifically. She had no evidence to base that on and nothing to back that up. It was a feeling. Her gut told her she knew who this man was, and Spenser had learned to rely on her gut a long time ago.

"So, where are we at?" Jacob asked.

"I'm currently trying to find a match to the tattoo Stacy described in the unit patch database I found online," Spenser said.

"Good luck with that," Jacob replied. "My sister worked her way through half of Lewis-McChord when she was back in high school—"

Young squealed with laughter and hurled another pen at her brother. "I dated two guys from the base. Two," she cried. "And both were incredibly short-lived. Like a week. Maybe. Oh my God, I hate you so much right now."

"Two soldiers, half the base… same thing," Jacob said with a mischievous grin. "Anyway, as she probably already told you, there are official patches then unofficial patches. And unfortunately, there is no database for those."

"That's what she was just telling me," Spenser replied. "But you seem pretty knowledgeable about it. Did you date half the base, too?"

Young snorted and laughed as Jacob's grin widened. "No, I didn't date anybody on the base," he said. "But I did sell weed to a lot of guys who were stationed there."

"Yeah, I don't need to be hearing about that," Spenser said.

"You asked."

"And I'm sorry I did."

Jacob shrugged. "I've got some contacts who still work at the base. Let me ask around and I'll see what I can find. Do we have a mockup drawing I can show them for reference?"

"I'll have Dalton mock it up for you," Spenser said. "And Jacob, do me a favor?"

"Name it."

"Don't go selling weed to anybody on the base."

He laughed. "I've been out of the ganja business for quite a while, boss. No worries."

"And by quite a while, he means ever since he started working here," Young said.

"Time is a relative thing, my dear sister."

Spenser shook her head as she took a sip of her coffee. She set her cup down and looked at the unit patches again, realizing they were right. She could probably look through the official insignias for the next ten years and never come up with the right one. As they sat in silence, each of them lost in their thoughts, the undersheriff broke the peace.

"I spoke with Arbery last night," Young said, snapping Spenser back to the moment. "He said he went back through our three crime scenes and didn't find any DNA in the drain traps. No fingerprints, no useful fibers… he's left nothing useful behind."

"This guy is like a ghost," Jacob said.

"I hate to say it, but it kind of seems like this guy is getting away with the perfect crimes. I mean, he's left us nothing to go on," Young said.

"There's no such thing as the perfect crime. There is always something for us to go on," Spenser said. "It's just a matter of shifting our thinking and perspective to find it."

"We're twisting ourselves into pretzels trying to shift our thinking and we're still coming up empty. I honestly don't know what else we can do," Young said.

"Well, we can't just sit back and wait for him to attack again and hope he makes a mistake this time," Spenser said a little more brusquely than she intended to.

"No, of course not," Young replied. "I'm just… frustrated. I want to get justice for Alexa—for all these women—and I don't even know where to start. It feels like we haven't made a single bit of progress and we're still stuck on square one."

"I know it feels that way. Just stay the course and keep working like we are and when that progress comes, it's going to come in a rush. We just need to be patient and do our jobs," she said. "Speaking of which, Jacob, how are you doing with finding a nexus between our victims?"

He shook his head then tapped a few keys on his laptop. The large screen he'd fixed to the wall flared to life and showed a map of Sweetwater Falls and some of the surrounding towns. With another few taps on his keyboard, the map was suddenly overlaid with a web of crisscrossing lines of different colors.

"Each color represents one of our victims," Jacob said. "I've used their financials and phone records to trace their steps. Not surprisingly, most of them have a routine and frequent the same spots regularly. There's usually not a lot of deviation in their day-to-day life."

Spenser's eyes roamed the network of lines on the map, unsurprised by the lack of deviation in their routines. These were single, career-oriented women who, by their own accounts, didn't date much and didn't have much of a social life.

"And unfortunately, as you can see, there isn't much overlap between them," Jacob continued. "A couple of them frequented the same coffee shop, a few of them shopped at the same stores, but there isn't one location I've found that all of them went to. There's just not one singular point of commonality to them all."

"Of course, there isn't," Young groused.

"All right, well, that's a bump in the road but not completely unexpected," Spenser said. "These women don't know each other so it stands to reason that they probably wouldn't hang out in the same places either."

"After all, the universe can't make things too easy on us," Young said.

"Where would the fun in that be?" Spenser replied dryly.

Spenser sat back in her seat and stared at the computer screen on the wall, her eyes tracing all those colored lines, trying to figure out the nexus between them all. Though outwardly calm, Spenser was every bit as frustrated as Young. She had no idea who this monster was, nor how to go about finding him, or whether he already had another woman in his crosshairs.

But the worst bit of it all, Spenser didn't know why he'd called her out by name. Didn't know his connection to her. And whether that connection was the reason these women were being brutalized. She couldn't help but feel she'd done something that had lit the fuse that had started this horrible chain of events. Or had at least exacerbated it.

Spenser frowned. She knew she was internalizing this case and taking it all incredibly personally. She was doing exactly what she'd cautioned Young against. The burden of guilt pressing down on her was so heavy, though, Spenser felt like she was starting to suffocate.

CHAPTER SIXTEEN

Spenser sat at the table in the conference room with the crime scene photos neatly piled in stacks in front of her. She picked up the first stack and slowly flipped through each photo, studying the scene as it had been found. Once again, Spenser was taken by the sheer destruction in the rooms where the assault occurred. The rage on display was breathtaking. And frightening. Spenser couldn't imagine what it must have been like to bear witness to it in person.

Spenser used a magnifying glass, slowly and meticulously studying every photo in the Jennifer Patterson stack. After that, she moved to the stack of photos from Emily Prescott's crime scene—and on down the line until she'd finished with the photos from their latest victim, Stacy Trask. Every crime scene was consistent in its violent brutality. In the complete destruction of the rooms he assaulted the women in.

"What are you still doing here?" Young asked as she walked into the conference room.

Spenser sat back in her chair and rubbed her eyes, which were red and burning. She'd been squinting and staring at the hundreds of pictures far too long and had strained her eyes. She glanced at her watch, saw it was getting late, and stifled a yawn.

"Going blind," Spenser said. "What about you?"

She shook her head. "I've been going over Jacob's maps again looking for some point of commonality between the women that we might have missed."

"And did you find anything?"

"Nah. He was right. There's nothing there," Young said, then gestured to the stacks of photos. "Find anything interesting in all those pictures? Anything we haven't seen?"

"Not really. Nothing stands out in all that wreckage," Spenser said. "They unfortunately don't look any different than they did before."

Young walked over and picked up the picture sitting on top of the pile of Alexa Beard's crime scene photos and looked at it for a moment. Her expression darkened and Spenser could see the guilt and sorrow in her eyes. She could relate to how hard Young was taking it.

"Why did he trash the rooms like that?" Young wondered. "It just seems like overkill. Like it serves no real purpose. Like he was just having a tantrum or something."

"He wanted to intimidate them. Scare them," Spenser corrected.

"Yeah, because beating and raping them wasn't quite enough to do the job."

"No, our guy gets off on the fear. He can't perform without it," Spenser said. "Sadists derive peak pleasure from the suffering and fear they cause in their victims. That's why our guy enjoys showing up like a ghost then taking his time smashing everything around his victim to pieces before he rapes them. And once sexual gratification has been achieved, he prolongs that fear by making the women bathe—and watching them."

"I thought that was to wash away DNA and trace evidence."

Spenser nodded. "It is. But it serves a dual purpose—instilling fear as well as the practicality of destroying evidence."

"I don't see how watching them bathe gets him off," Young said.

"It's power. Control. It's prolonging that fear he's making them feel," Spenser said. "Think about how vulnerable they must feel as they sit in the tub naked, being forced to do what this monster tells them to do. I can't think of a situation where you'd feel more vulnerable."

Young sat down and seemed to think about what Spenser had just said then nodded to herself, that look of sorrow on her face growing even deeper.

"This man is a monster," Young finally said.

"He's worse than a monster."

They sat at the table in silence for a long moment. Spenser stifled another yawn. She was bone weary and wanted nothing more than to crawl into bed and sleep for the next three days. She had been burning the candle at both ends since the start of this case and there didn't seem to be an end to the long days anytime soon.

"Oh, before I forget, did you finish talking to the rest of the victims about the items missing from their houses?" Spenser asked.

Young nodded and looked at her tablet. "I did. And you were right. They were all missing something personal after their attacks," she said. "The snow globe, some jewelry, a silk hair tie… small, inconsequential trinkets. But they all had sentimental value."

"Of course," Spenser said. "That lets him relive the rush he got during the assault every time he looks at or touches those items. And knowing he has those personal, sentimental items also forces those women to relive the trauma they suffered as they were being assaulted. It's just another way of prolonging the fear. It's control and power again."

"This is getting deep," Young said.

"It usually does."

Young frowned and looked down at the table. "Are you sure we're not just overthinking this?" she asked. "I mean, are we overcomplicating the situation?"

"How do you mean?"

"Just... all these theories about motivations and psychological underpinnings. Is it possible we're clouding the issue with all this extraneous stuff and it's maybe keeping us from seeing the bigger picture? Keeping us from finding this guy faster?"

"Do I think it's keeping us from seeing the bigger picture? No. Not at all. I don't think any of this is extraneous. It's necessary. Understanding this man is the key to finding him," Spenser said. "I think getting into his mind and understanding why he does the things he does expands the picture for us. And I think that will ultimately help us catch him."

Young leaned back in her chair and scrubbed her face with her hands. "I'm sorry. I don't mean to doubt or second-guess you. I'm just... frustrated."

"I know," Spenser said sympathetically. "Go home, Amanda. Get some sleep and don't be back here before eight tomorrow morning."

"As long as that applies to you as well," she said.

A wan smile touched Spenser's lips. "Deal," she said. "I was thinking about heading out already. I'm beat."

"Great. Then I'll see you back here at say... eight-thirty?"

"Make it nine," Spenser said.

"Sold."

"Thank you," Spenser said.

"Thank you, Sheriff," the woman behind the counter replied. "Good to see you and we'll see you again very soon."

"Yes, I'm sure you will," Spenser said with a smile.

Spenser picked her bag up off the counter and inhaled deeply, the savory aromas coming from her containers making her mouth water and stomach rumble. She was so tired, she almost didn't realize how hungry she was. But she needed to get some food in her belly, so she decided to eat first, then get some sleep. Spenser stopped off at the Jade Panda and picked up some takeout from the only Chinese food joint in town.

Spenser loved Chinese cuisine and considered herself something of a snob about it. She was skeptical the first time she ate there, but they'd quickly won her over. She thought they had the best Chinese food she'd had outside of New York, which was a good thing, too, because if their food had been crap, Spenser didn't know what she would have done.

She walked out of the restaurant and out to the parking lot. Spenser hit the button on the fob that unlocked the Bronco with a chirp. As she opened the door and set her bag of food on the driver's side seat, the hair on the back of her neck stood up, her stomach churned, and goosebumps marched up and down her body. It felt like somebody was breathing frosty air on her skin. Spenser knew the feeling all too well. It was the feeling of being watched.

Moving slowly, Spenser turned around and scanned the street behind her. Cars passed by, heading in both directions but none of them were slowing or revealing suspicious behavior. But still, that feeling of being watched persisted. She didn't see anything as she scanned the street and was ready to climb into the Bronco and head home when she saw him. Her stomach lurched and it suddenly felt like frigid ice water was flowing through her veins.

Wreathed in shadows, a man in a black, long-sleeved shirt, black jeans, and a black balaclava, was standing at the mouth of an alley between a bakery and an antique shop across the street from her. He was massive. He was at least six-three and seemingly as wide as he was tall. The man was too far away for her to see the color of his eyes, but she knew they were green—and they were fixed directly on her.

As Spenser watched the man, he raised his hand and wiggled his fingers in a gross mockery of a wave. She felt her heart slamming against the inside of her chest with such force, Spenser was half-afraid it was going to burst straight out of her body. Reacting on instinct, Spenser pulled her weapon and dashed across the street. The man was already gone by the time she got to the mouth of the alley, and although she knew the smart play was to call for backup, her anger took control and a feeling like lightning crackling through her body pushed the ice-cold fear out of her veins.

Her weapon at the ready, Spenser plunged heedlessly into the alley. She moved slowly, doing her best to keep her back to the wall at all times as she walked past the dumpster, boxes, and shadowy doorways. Spenser's heart raced and her stomach churned, expecting that mountain of a man to leap out of the darkness and snatch her up. But she made it all the way to the other end of the alley without being attacked.

"What the hell?" she muttered to herself.

She stood on the next street over, cars whizzing past and light foot traffic passing by on the sidewalk. But the giant man who'd been watching her from the alley was gone. Spenser looked up one side of the street and down the other but didn't see him anywhere among the few people she saw on the sidewalk. Spenser didn't know how it was possible, but it was like he'd vanished into thin air. Like a puff of smoke wafting on a breeze, he was just gone.

Spenser holstered her weapon and walked back down the alley, her mind racing. Her skin felt cold, and her pulse had only just started to slow by the time she got back to the Bronco. The driver's side door was still open, and her bag of Chinese food still sat on the seat where she'd left it… though she doubted she was going to be able to eat. When she picked up the bag to move it over to the passenger's seat, the adrenaline that had ebbed came flooding back and Spenser's body hummed with that familiar electricity again as her heart thundered inside of her.

Sitting on the seat was Alexa Beard's missing snow globe.

CHAPTER SEVENTEEN

"They're not going to find anything on the snow globe," Spenser groused. "He's too careful to have left prints or DNA behind on it."

"They probably won't," Ryker said.

"He wants to scare me. Intimidate me."

"Is it working?"

Spenser cast a dark look at him. "You're damn right it's working. I'd be a fool to not be worried. You should have seen him, Ryker, the guy is massive," she said. "More than just being massive, though, the guy is quick. Nimble. He moves a lot faster than a guy that size should be able to move. But am I going to let that stop me from doing my job? Hell no."

"I figured it wouldn't. You've never been one to back down from a fight," he remarked.

She tossed a chunk of char siu pork to Annabelle who snatched it out of midair and swallowed it down whole then looked at Spenser with big, hopeful eyes and a big runner of drool hanging from her bottom lip. Spenser gave in like she always did and tossed her another piece of pork. As Annabelle snacked on the tasty treat, Spenser picked up her chopsticks, took some noodles out of the carton then popped them into her mouth. Lost in her own head, she chewed thoughtfully, replaying the events of the evening for what felt like the ten-thousandth time.

She'd more or less lost her appetite by the time she got home, but she knew her body needed fuel as much as it needed rest. But she also wanted company. At least until the adrenaline and the case of the willies that were gripping her tight had time to subside. So, she'd called Ryker, inviting him to eat with her. As if he'd been reading her mind, he brought a nice bottle of bourbon along with him and they sat at the kitchen island, eating, drinking, and Spenser told him everything that had happened. And he sat on the other side of the kitchen island, listening to her as they ate, the expression on his face growing somber and more disturbed with every word she spoke.

Ryker wiped his hands on his napkin then picked up the plastic evidence bag she'd deposited the snow globe into. The interior scene was a miniaturized version of Park City, Utah. Alexa Beard had told them the globe was special to her because it was the last vacation they'd taken as a family before her parents were killed in that car wreck. Spenser could tell Alexa was heartbroken about the globe being taken and she idly wondered, given what happened to her, if she'd ever be able to see it the same way again. If it would ever conjure the same fond feelings and cherished memories for her again. Or if every time she saw it, she would only be able to think of the dark and terrible things done to her the night it went missing.

Ryker turned the bag over in his hands, studying it from every angle. She didn't know why he was looking at it so closely or what he hoped to find. If he was looking for answers to this madness, Spenser could have told him that the snow globe held none. He finally set the bag down and looked up at her. Ryker held her gaze with his vivid green eyes, an intensely dark and worried expression on his face.

"Spenser, he's taking this to a whole new level. This is getting dangerous," he said. "The fact that he's gone from having his victims convey his messages to stalking you now?"

"I know. But this is the job. This is, in fact, what I signed up for," she replied.

"I don't like this."

"Neither do I, Ryker," she said. "But if him fixating on me takes his attention off other women he might have been hunting, then I call that something of a win."

"You have got a very screwed up barometer of success."

"That too, is part of the job, my friend," Spenser countered with a sardonic smirk.

They both fell silent as they picked at their food and sipped on their bourbon. Spenser didn't like feeling afraid, but she couldn't deny that she did. She hated that this monster had any bit of power over her, but after seeing what he did to those women and seeing the obvious joy he took in brutalizing them, she would have been an idiot to not be scared.

Spenser was well-trained and could handle herself in a fight. But she wasn't indestructible. She wasn't immortal. She bled and could be killed as easily as anybody else. And seeing what she was up against, live and in the flesh, sent a tremor through her heart.

"Any idea why he's making this so personal?" Ryker asked.

"None. But he clearly wants to get under my skin," she replied.

"That's concerning."

"It is. But—"

"You're not going to let it deter you. Yeah, I know," he said, casting her a rueful grin.

Spenser laughed softly then took a swallow of bourbon. As she refilled her glass, Spenser thought about the way the guy had waggled his fingers at her and felt that chill crawl up her spine all over again. She shuddered.

"You okay?" Ryker asked.

"Yeah, I'm fine," she said and took another swallow. "I'll tell you, though, when I saw him standing there waving at me, I couldn't help but feel there was something familiar about him."

"Familiar?"

She shook her head. "I can't say what it was—or even if it was real. It might have all been in my head. But something just felt familiar about him."

"Is it possible you're so invested in this case and taking it so personally that it's making you feel like that?"

Spenser shrugged. "Sure, it's possible. Like I said, I don't know if that feeling of familiarity was even real. It may be that my investment in this case is making me feel that way."

Ryker drained his glass and as he poured himself a refill, Spenser could see the wheels turning in his head. Knew he had something he wanted to say.

"Might as well spit it out," she said.

"Spit what out?"

"Whatever it is you're choking on over there trying not to say."

A wan smile touched his lips. "That obvious, huh?"

"It's because I know you," she replied. "So… out with it."

He swallowed down the last of his drink as if he needed the liquid courage, which told Spenser she wasn't going to like what he had to say.

A look of uncertainty crossed his face. "Now, I want you to keep an open mind—"

"Oh, God," Spenser groaned.

"Open mind, Song."

"Fine, fine, all right. I'll try to keep an open mind."

"Do better than try and take this in the spirit it's meant," he said. "I'm looking out for you."

Spenser chuckled. "Fair enough. So, what is it I need to keep an open mind about?"

"I want to hire some security to patrol the grounds out here—"

"Absolutely not," Spenser cut him off.

"What happened to keeping an open mind?"

"Ryker, I appreciate your concern. I do," she said. "But I'm a big girl and I can take care of myself."

"I'm not doubting that in the least. But let's not forget that people have showed up out here to kill you a couple of times already."

"I haven't forgotten—"

"And if this guy is determined to do—whatever it is he's planning on doing—this cabin is a little bit isolated, Spenser. Not even I'd be able to get down here in time if he showed up."

"I just don't like the idea of strangers roaming around out here, shadowing my every move," Spenser said. "I don't like feeling like somebody's always got eyes on me."

"It's a lot better than the feeling you'd get if this guy gets his hands on you."

Spenser couldn't argue with his logic. He was right. If this guy showed up with bad intentions, although she believed in herself, her training, and her abilities, there was always the chance things could go sideways and he could get the drop on her. But even that fear didn't override her natural resistance to having babysitters shadowing her. She just didn't like the idea of having strangers looking over her shoulder.

"Okay, I can see I'm not going to win this argument," Ryker countered. "So, how about instead of hiring security, you and Annabelle move into the main house until you catch this guy?"

"Move into your house?"

"I've got more than enough rooms. I mean, the place is big enough that we might not even run into each other," he said.

Spenser laughed. "Your house isn't quite that big."

"Maybe not," he replied with a smile. "But I do have a lot of guns and a state-of-the-art security system. Nobody would be able to get the drop on us. Ever. Plus, it would have the added benefit of making me feel better about the situation. If you don't want strangers watching over you, then let me do it."

Spenser opened her mouth to respond but closed it again without speaking. It wasn't a bad alternative. Ryker was very physically capable, and he was right—he had a lot of guns in that house. Plus, he wasn't joking about his security system. Breaking into his house would be about as easy as breaking into Fort Knox. If there was one place she could feel safe and not weird about somebody keeping watch over her, it would be Ryker's house.

The other side of that coin, though, was that she wondered what message it might send if she moved into his place. Even temporarily. Would that constitute an evolution in their relationship? Would that constitute a step forward... a step neither of them seemed ready for? Ryker's offer was innocent enough. It was generous. But it was also fraught with unspoken implications and Spenser wasn't sure if she was ready to grapple with them just yet.

Ryker raised his hand, palm facing her. "I can already see what's going through your mind and I assure you, there's no ulterior motives. There's no subtext or hidden meanings to my suggestion," he said. "I only made the suggestion because I'm worried about you, Spenser. I'm worried this guy can show up at any moment and take you away from me..."

His voice trailed off and he looked away. Spenser could see the fear for her in his eyes and hear the ring of sincerity in his voice. He finally returned his gaze to hers and she knew instantly by the lost and haunted look on his face that he was thinking about his fiancée who had been murdered. Seeing the pain in his eyes broke Spenser's heart.

"It's been a long time since I was worried about losing somebody I cared about, Spenser," he said. "Don't put me in that position. Please."

"Okay," she said softly. "We'll come stay at the main house."

CHAPTER EIGHTEEN

SPENSER FELT THE WEIGHT OF THE SCENE SETTLE DOWN over her the moment she walked through the door. There was a dark bleakness that squeezed her heart. Through an archway to her right a man sat in a recliner, his face buried in his hands, his body shaking wildly as he sobbed. Deputy Lane Summers stood beside him, a comforting hand on his shoulder. Two black, hardshell rolling suitcases and a dark blue duffel bag sat next to the door. Spenser noted the tags on the cases all said "MIA" in big, black letters—the airport code for the Miami International Airport.

Young stood at the end of a long hallway in front of Spenser, waiting for her, a grim look on her face. Spenser glanced around the front rooms of the small house. It was neat and orderly. Tastefully furnished. There was nothing high-end in the home but nothing that looked like she'd picked it up at a flea market either. It was a solidly middle-class home. Spenser surveyed the photos on the wall but didn't see the man sitting in the recliner in any of them. In fact, other than an older man she assumed was their victim's father, she didn't see a man in any of them.

She looked at him again, but he hadn't moved. He remained sitting in the recliner, his face still buried, continuing to sob. Summers looked at Spenser helplessly. She didn't know what to do for or about the crying man. Spenser gestured to just stay put. Clearly, she was going to need to get her deputies some training that might help them deal with emotional victims in crisis situations. She turned then headed down the hall to where Young waited.

"You were right," Young said, her tone as grim as her face. "It was only a matter of time."

The bedroom, like all the others, looked like a wrecking ball had gone through it. It seemed like everything fragile had been smashed to pieces and littered the floor of the bedroom. It looked like the other scenes they'd been to, but Spenser felt a strange energy. She wasn't sure what it was, but it felt like a new and disturbing level of darkness and violence in the wreckage all around her.

"She's in here," Young said quietly.

A frown creasing her lips, Spenser turned and walked into the bathroom that was attached to the bedroom. The moment she stepped through the door, a lance of guilt pierced her heart. Victoria Hall lay on her back in the bathtub, one leg slung over the side, her blue eyes wide open and fixed on some point beyond this world. The glass shower door had been shattered and jagged shards littered the ground, twinkling in the bright lights of the bathroom fluorescents, and crimson rivulets ran down the tile like bloody teardrops.

"My God," Spenser whispered.

Broken glass crunched beneath her boots as Spenser moved deeper into the bathroom and squatted down next to the tub. Her face and body bore the marks of the man's rage—seemingly worse than any of the other women who'd been assaulted—and a puddle of blood pooled beneath her. A pair of nylons had been wrapped around her neck and pulled so tight they'd left shallow cuts in her flesh. Victoria's face still had a bluish tint and her eyes showed petechia, one of the telltale signs of strangulation.

The rest of her body was a mass of cuts and bruises. There was so much blood that Spenser couldn't even see all the wounds. The level of overkill inflicted upon Victoria's body matched the overkill in the destruction of her bedroom. Was it a coincidence that this man's rage was seemingly stoked higher than it had ever been only after he'd taunted her on the street? Spenser didn't know. But the possibility that he had done this because of her somehow tore at her insides.

"It looks like she was beaten almost to death before he choked the life out of her. Why? Why would he kill her?" Young said.

Spenser tried to push away the guilt that clung to her like thick cobwebs. Tried to get her head back on straight and look at the scene with a logical investigator's eye. Tried to see it the way she would if she wasn't as emotionally tied to the case as she was and as if she were profiling it like any other case. It wasn't easy. This wasn't any other case and Spenser knew it.

She cleared her throat. "If I had to guess, I'd say that she fought back."

She pointed to the cuts, bruises, and broken nails on the dead woman's fingers. Young squatted down and looked closer, nodding as if she saw and understood what Spenser was pointing out to her.

"Looks like she fought back hard, and I'd have to assume the fact that she didn't give him the fear he needed to perform lit the fuse," Spenser said. "I think he killed her because she was defiant. Because she stood up to him."

"So, is it possible he didn't sexually assault her?"

Spenser shook her head. "The tub is still wet, and I can smell her body wash. Plus, I can see bruising around her pelvic region," she said. "If I had to guess, he raped her as he was choking the life out of her. Knowing she was going to die would have provoked an uncontrollable fear response—one that would have excited him."

"But if he killed her—"

"I'd have to assume that he washed her body himself. Or at least, it looks to me like he washed his DNA out of her. Hopefully, Arbery and his team will be able to find something he might have missed," Spenser said.

"Geez, you just made my skin crawl," Young muttered.

"Everything about this is making my skin crawl."

Young looked up at her, the look of disgust on her face growing thicker. "Speaking of things that will make your skin crawl, there's something else you need to see."

"Oh, goody."

Young stood up and walked over to the bathroom door and closed it. When Spenser saw the back of the door, her heart lurched and her stomach churned, kicking up the bitter taste of bile in her throat. She got to her feet and looked at the message written on the back of the door—a personal message for her that looked like it had been written in Victoria Hall's blood.

"Jesus," she muttered.

"Spenser Song, feeling superior doesn't make one superior. Hubris does not humble others," Young read the message aloud. "What in the hell is that supposed to mean?"

"He's quoting somebody. Preaching," Spenser said. "He's telling me that because of my own sense of superiority and hubris, this is somehow all my fault."

"He's full of crap."

"I know. But this is how he's justifying it to himself."

Spenser read the words again and suppressed a shudder. There was no question in her mind that this was personal. That she had some connection to the rapist—now murderer. Whether that connection was real or just in his mind, she didn't know. But she was afraid things were about to start getting much worse.

"What is it?" Young asked.

"He has a taste for killing now," Spenser said. "Unless we find and stop him, this is only going to be the first of more to come."

"No pressure," Young muttered.

"Who's the guy in the front room?" Spenser asked.

"He's the one who called it in. Said he's Victoria's fiancé."

"Fiancé?"

"That's what he said."

"That would be a big deviation in our guy's MO," Spenser said. "He's only ever attacked single women before."

"He's never murdered anybody before either," Young noted. "It's like you said… he's evolving. Maybe his choice in targets is, too."

"Yeah. Maybe so," Spenser said. "Let's go talk to the fiancé."

Arbery and his team were already suited up and waiting in the hallway when Spenser and Young walked out.

"It's bad there," Young said.

"I'm sure it's no worse than any other scene I've processed," he said. "But thank you for your concern, Undersheriff Young."

"Make sure you get nail scrapings and swabs for DNA," Spenser said. "His MO changed, and we think he had to bathe the body himself. And she fought back. It's possible he missed something."

"I will be my usual diligent and thorough self, Sheriff," he said with a sniff of indignation.

"Of course."

Spenser turned and headed down the hallway, letting Arbery and his people into the room. Summers looked at her with wide-eyed relief as she stepped through the archway and into the living room. The man sitting in the recliner had stopped crying but had a tumbler clasped between his hands and was staring down into the amber liquid.

"We'll take it from here, Lane," Spenser said softly.

"Thank you, Sheriff."

As the deputy bustled out, Spenser took a seat on the sofa across from the man. Young took a standing position to her left. The man in the recliner was tall… maybe six-one. He had sandy blonde hair that was cut short and neatly styled, his sea green eyes were puffy and rheumy, and his tawny cheeks were splotchy, red, and covered in a few days' worth of stubble. He had the look of a California surfer boy but with a strait-laced corporate edge.

"I'm Sheriff Song," Spenser introduced herself. "And this is Undersheriff Young."

The man didn't raise his head or acknowledge them in any way. He just stared down into his glass. Spenser exchanged a look with Young.

"Sir, can you tell us your name?" Spenser asked.

He drained half the liquid in his glass and finally looked up. "I'm Garrett Amaro."

"Great. Thank you, Mr. Amaro. I understand you're the one who... found Ms. Hall and called it in?" Spenser asked.

He nodded. "Yeah."

"And may I ask what your relationship with Ms. Hall is?"

"I'm her fiancé," he said. "Well... we were engaged. We split up about six months ago when I took a job in Florida..."

His voice trailed off and he looked away as fresh tears started to flow down his face. The glass in his hands shook and his cheeks turned a bright shade of red as he fought to keep himself from crying in front of them.

"If you two split up, what brought you back to the house tonight?" Young asked.

He sniffed loudly and wiped his eyes with the back of a hand. "We've been talking the last few weeks. I missed her and realized I made a mistake in taking that job—in leaving her. So, I've been planning on moving back and finding another job around here. We were going to get back together and give things another try."

He raised his glass and drained the last of it then leaned forward and set it down on the coffee table. Amaro pulled a handkerchief out of his pocket and wiped his eyes.

"Anyway, I came back tonight... We were going to spend the weekend together. We wanted to talk and see about moving forward together," he said, his voice quavering. "I came in and... and I found her like that. Who did this, Sheriff?"

"We're not sure yet, Mr. Amaro. But we're working on it," she answered honestly.

He shook his head. "Who would do something like this? Vic was a good person. She had a good heart. A good soul," he said. "She was the kind of person who would give somebody her last dollar. The shirt off her back if it would help."

"Mr. Amaro, did Ms. Hall ever mention having trouble with anybody? Being afraid of anybody?" Spenser asked. "Did she ever mention anybody following her around? Stalking her?"

He shook his head. "No. She never mentioned anything like that."

"Is that something she would have mentioned to you?" Young asked.

"Absolutely. If she was having trouble with anybody, she would have told me."

As he talked, Spenser looked closely at his hands. It seemed cliché to say the victim's partner was always a suspect. But then, clichés became cliches for a reason. There were a whole lot of men out there who murdered their romantic partners. But Spenser didn't see any cuts or bruises on his hands. Nor any blood on his clothing. Given the savagery inflicted upon Victoria Hall, if Amaro had been the one to do it, he likely would have sustained some injury to his hands or gotten some blood spatter on his clothing when he delivered the beating.

That wasn't conclusive, of course. But his emotional reactions seemed genuine, his grief earnest and sincere. Spenser didn't see any pretense or sense any disingenuousness in his bearing. She was ninety-nine percent sure that he hadn't been involved. She felt certain he was telling the truth about coming in and finding her in that condition.

"I loved her. I never stopped loving her. Not even when we were separated," he said. "I was just getting her back and now… now I've lost her again. Forever this time."

"We're very sorry for your loss, Mr. Amaro," Young said.

"And we're sorry to inconvenience you, but we will need you to stick around town for a little while. We will likely have some follow-up questions and—"

"And you need to make sure I didn't kill her," he said.

"Yes. Not to be too blunt about things. It's standard procedure," Spenser said. "Our techs will need to run some tests."

He frowned. "Fine. If it'll rule me out and let you focus on finding the real killer, then do what you have to do."

"We'll do our best to make it as quick as possible," Spenser said then turned to Young. "Can you go ask Arbery to cut one of his people loose to do what we need to be done here?"

"You got it."

Young walked down the hall to the bedroom, leaving Spenser alone with the grieving man. He stared into his empty glass looking like he wanted nothing more in that moment than to get blackout drunk and forget about everything he'd seen. Spenser knew what it was like to have the last image of the person you loved most in the world to be one of violence and blood. She also knew that no matter how much you drank or how drunk you got, the same images and the flood of emotions that came with it would be there waiting when you sobered up again.

"Please find the man who did this, Sheriff," he whispered.

"We're going to do everything we can, Mr. Amaro. I promise you that."

CHAPTER NINETEEN

"So, we're back at square one," Young said.
"To be fair, I don't think we ever got off square one," Spenser replied dryly.
"Yeah, I suppose not."
Subsequent conversations with Garrett Amaro over the next few days only reinforced Spenser's belief that he'd had nothing to do with Victoria Hall's murder. Fortunately, that belief was finally backed up by some scientific facts. Arbery had found nothing on Amar's clothing or on his body that tied him to the murder. On top of that, Amaro was sticking around Sweetwater Falls until Hall's body was released so he could give her a proper burial. Those didn't seem like the actions of a man who'd murdered his

fiancée. In Spenser's experience, a killer would have looked for a way out of town as quickly as possible.

Spenser pulled into the lot behind Dr. Swift's multi-use office. He owned and operated his family's funeral home, kept his medical practice, and also served as the town's coroner. Swift wasn't Spenser's favorite person on the planet. He was gruff, cantankerous, and felt superior to everybody he came into contact with. Given the intersection between her job and his, theirs was a forced marriage, and she had learned to tolerate him. Most of the time. Not that it was always easy. Spenser shut off the engine and took a moment to steel herself.

"You want me to go in and talk to him?" Young offered.

Spenser chuckled. "I appreciate the offer but I'm a big girl. I can't have you running interference every time we have to deal with him."

"He's going to be in a foul mood. No doubt, having to do a rush autopsy on Victoria Hall cut into his golf time," Young said.

"No doubt," Spenser said. "The way I see it, though, if he doesn't want to do this job, he shouldn't have put his name on the ballot in the first place."

"That makes sense to you and me, but in case you hadn't noticed before, Dr. Swift doesn't always make a lot of sense," Young said. "My understanding is he only ran for the position for the money and prestige."

"Prestige he parlayed into a free membership at the country club?"

"Exactly."

"Why spend your own money when you can play a round on the taxpayers?"

"I hate to admit it, but even though it's incredibly cheap and sleazy, it's kind of smart at the same time," Young said. "I can't say I wouldn't pull the same thing if I had the chance."

"You wouldn't. You're too honest and ethical," Spenser countered. "Now let's get this over with."

They climbed out of the Bronco and headed through the back door of Swift's building and into a small lobby. There was a desk set up in front of them with a door on the right. Three chairs stood against the wall on either side of the room, the walls were all a pale yellow, and cheap linoleum covered the floor. Black and white, picturesque photos of the town hung on the walls behind the chairs in the small waiting area.

The door opened and Swift stepped out. An inch taller than Spenser, he had iron-gray hair, dark eyes, and the golden skin of a man who spent a lot of time outdoors. In Swift's case, working on his golf game. He was fifty-five years old but had a lean, trim physique. He was in good shape and despite his gray hair, probably could have passed for somebody ten years younger. He wore khakis and a white lab coat with his name stitched over the left breast pocket.

Swift had a dark polo shirt underneath the lab coat, telling Spenser he was probably headed to the club once he was done with them. For a guy who wore so many hats in town, he was able to carve out an extraordinary amount of time in his schedule to spend on the golf course. His ability to multitask was impressive.

"Ladies, please step this way," he said.

It always grated on Spenser's nerves that he almost never gave her the respect of using her title. It was always 'ladies' or some derivative of it. He always made sure to sound respectful and never actually crossed that line into misogyny, but he certainly did walk right up to it. Swift didn't seem to be a big believer in women being in positions of authority like the sheriff of a town. He never said anything outright, of course. Expressing those opinions out loud would almost certainly tank his bid for reelection and then, God forbid, he'd have to start paying his own country club membership fees. But his attitude and demeanor said more than enough.

Swift remained silent as they followed him through the door then down the short hallway that led to his autopsy suite. Spenser never failed to feel uncomfortable surrounded by gleaming white tile and stainless steel that gleamed under the harsh and bright fluorescent lights. Or maybe it was the half dozen refrigerated drawers built into the wall on her right that did it.

"I'll do my best to make this quick," Swift said.

"Got a tee time waiting, Doc?" Young asked brightly.

Swift glared at her with a stony expression for a moment before turning to the table in the center of the room. He pulled the sheet down to the top of Victoria Hall's breasts, exposing the stitching of the Y-incision left behind after her autopsy. Her lips were blue, and her skin had the unmistakable pale and waxy sheen of death. The deep purple bruising and shallow abrasions remained around her neck and Spenser observed several puncture wounds marring her flesh in addition to a myriad of other bruises. Though her face looked almost peaceful and serene in death, the traces of tremendous violence inflicted upon the poor woman were undeniable.

The coroner reached up and switched on the adjustable fluorescent lamp above the autopsy table, casting her body in a bright halo of light. Next, he picked up a steel clipboard and quickly consulted his notes.

"Victoria Hall, age twenty-four. Cause of death was asphyxiation by manual strangulation. My best estimate is that she was killed at some point between six and ten p.m. the night of her death. The murder weapon was the pair of nylons you found around her neck. In addition to the strangulation, Ms. Hall suffered seven stab wounds—none of them serious enough to kill straight away, though the totality of those wounds meant death by exsanguination was a possibility if she hadn't been strangled," he recited from his notes. "Also, as you can observe, Ms. Hall's body is covered in bruises and abrasions. She was beaten. Savagely, I might add. And the wounds you see, aside from the ligature strangulation, were inflicted perimortem. If you'd permit me to editorialize, I'd say this unfortunate woman suffered incredibly before her death."

"Thanks, Doc," Young said. "But we kind of guessed that last bit already."

Before Swift could return fire, Spenser jumped in. "Dr. Swift, can you tell me if she was sexually assaulted?"

"I found extensive tearing and bruising around the pelvis and inside the vaginal canal, so I would surmise that yes, she was sexually assaulted," he replied.

"I don't suppose there were any fluids left behind?" Spenser asked.

"Unfortunately, not. No fluids, no lubricants, no fibers— nothing," he said with a frown. "If our suspect washed this body himself, he did a very thorough job of it. He left no trace of himself. As disturbing as it is, he is very, very good at what he does."

"Is there anything else, Doctor?" Spenser asked.

He pointed to Victoria's ring finger and Spenser noted the smooth, white flesh around the digit, paler than the rest of her finger.

"She was still wearing her ring," Spenser said.

"I would say it is very likely she had a ring on at the time of her death," he replied.

"I guess we know what he took this time," Young remarked.

"I have been doing this job for a while, Sheriff Song. I have seen all manner of death and violence," Swift started. "But I have never once in all my years, seen a murder so savage and so brutal. The lack of care for human suffering—no, for human life—is astonishing."

The emotion in the coroner's voice hit Spenser as hard as the fact that he addressed her by her title. Clearly, this case was getting under everybody's skin. Swift looked up and held her gaze for a long moment, his jaw muscles flexing as he clenched his jaw.

"Please, find the man responsible for this act of barbarism," he said softly.

"We're doing everything we can, Doctor Swift. I promise you," Spenser replied.

CHAPTER TWENTY

Spenser sat at the table in their war room studying the pictures on the whiteboard. Her eyes kept drifting from the faces of the victims to the photo of the message their UNSUB had left for her on the bathroom door scrawled in Victoria Hall's blood.

"Spenser Song, feeling superior doesn't make one superior. Hubris does not humble others," she read aloud, pronouncing each word slowly.

Every word was an accusation and the weight of guilt on her shoulders grew heavier with every syllable. Knowing that the monster was out there, taunting her, and using whatever offense she'd caused him as a reason for his actions, jammed that lance of guilt in her heart a little deeper.

It was irrational, she knew. The first rape occurred in a different town and happened just after her arrival in Sweetwater Falls. But Spenser knew their rapist-turned-killer was active before she ever arrived. There was no way he was this slick straight out of the gate. The fact that he was still evolving proved to her that he had to have had practice. There were other victims out there. She just didn't know how to go about finding them. For all she knew they were in another state. But it was just as possible his earliest victims were right there, under her nose. Spenser knew the vast majority of rapes went unreported. Her UNSUB's earliest victims may not have been as brutalized as his later ones and it was entirely possible, if not likely, they hadn't spoken out.

What was twisting her mind and gut into knots was the fact that the attacks had grown fiercer, angrier, and far more violent since she arrived. It might have been part of the natural evolution of this UNSUB. As he continued to grow and evolve, he grew bolder and was able to let his true personality come out. And it was clear he hated women. That might be reflected in how he treated them. But Spenser was starting to think that maybe, she was, as Young had pointed out a while ago, she was the focus. That maybe she was the trigger for his rage. His taunting of her certainly made it seem likely. And it was that uncertainty that tugged at her heart.

"It's a quote by Guy McPherson," Jacob cut into her thoughts.

Spenser gave herself a shake. "Sorry, what did you say?"

"The quote on the door—it's by Guy McPherson."

"Who is that?"

"A scientist. Used to be a professor at a couple of schools," he replied. "He's probably most famous for promoting his theories about human extinction. I seem to remember him being quoted as saying humanity would be extinct by 2026 or something like that."

"There's a rosy outlook on the world," Spenser remarked dryly. "But since we're almost out of time, I guess we better start crossing things off our bucket list then."

"Right?" Jacob said with a laugh.

"How do you know who this Guy McPherson dude is?" Spenser asked. "Are you one of those end-time conspiracy theorists, too?"

"Nah. That's not my thing," he said. "I do have a couple of friends who are preppers. They're devoted to the guy. Personally, I think people quote guys like McPherson when they want to sound more intellectual than they are."

"Wanting to sound more intellectual than they are… that reminds me of you, big brother," Young said as she stepped into the room.

Jacob gave her the finger as Young took her seat at the table. Spenser leaned back in her chair and stroked her chin, thinking about what he'd just said about his prepper friends. It may have added another layer to this UNSUB's personality for her. She knew there was a percentage of former military members who subscribed to the idea of doomsday prepping and living that lifestyle. And that fell in line with the theory behind the quote that was left for her.

"Who's McPherson and what are you guys talking about?" Young asked as she settled in.

Spenser continued to stare at the photo of the quote and think about what Jacob said as he got Young up to speed. She had been trying to put together a comprehensive profile for days now, but her thoughts had been so jumbled, she hadn't been able to nail down anything solid. Spenser knew she was overthinking it. Knew she was only getting in her own way and that was keeping her from seeing things clearly. There were connections there to be made but she was so close to this case, and it was so deep under her skin, that it was keeping her from making them.

"So, is he just a pseudo-intellectual? Or is he a doomsday prepper?" Young asked.

"I'm leaning toward both," Spenser said. "If we're still thinking that tattoo is military, it might lend itself to the idea of a survivalist—"

Young held a finger up. "Let me stop you right there. The tat isn't military after all."

Spenser bit off her next words as she took in that surprising bit of news. She had been operating under the assumption their

UNSUB was former military. Finding out he might not be after all was a curveball she wasn't expecting.

"Okay, so, if it's not military, what is the tat from?" Spenser asked.

Young turned to the door and gestured. Deputy Ricky Sutter walked in, his thumbs tucked into his gun belt, a stony look on his face, which was typical for him. He was a serious young man. He rarely smiled and didn't cut up the way some of the older men in the department did. Sutter's default setting was stone cold serious. In all the months he'd worked for her, Spenser didn't think she'd seen him smile. Not once. Sutter stood at the other end of the table, his eyes on Spenser, waiting for her to prompt him to speak. Unlike some of the others in her department, Sutter didn't seem able to speak without being spoken to first.

At twenty-five, Sutter was one of Spenser's younger deputies, but Spenser thought he had the skills and work ethic to be a good one. He took his job seriously. More importantly, he was eager to learn and dedicated to doing the job the right way. Six-one with a blonde crew cut, cornflower blue eyes, and built like the proverbial brick outhouse, Sutter cut an imposing figure. That hard look he had, though, was belied by his baby face and soft, round cheeks covered in a soft peach fuzz. It was an odd juxtaposition with his demeanor.

"Deputy Sutter? Are you able to shed some light on this subject?" Spenser asked. "Do you know where that tattoo comes from?"

"Yes, ma'am, I do," he said with a crisp nod. "I recognized it when I saw the rendering you've been circulating and came to Undersheriff Young."

Spenser waited for him to finish the statement, but after a long moment of awkward silence, it was clear he wasn't going to. Sutter was a minimalist, only answering those questions he was asked, and nothing more. It was a good thing Spenser wasn't looking for idle chit-chat.

"All right, and where do you know that tattoo from, Deputy Sutter?" Spenser prompted.

"It's the mark of a club within the Full Metal Shooting Range," he replied.

"The Full Metal Shooting Range?" Spenser asked.

"It's a gun club out on the southern edge of town," Young replied. "Opened up a few years back. Gun nuts like to go out there to talk about how big their guns are and shoot things."

"Okay, so that's what, the company's logo or something?" Spenser asked.

Sutter shook his head. "No, the tattoo belongs to a club within the club. They call themselves the Silver Bullets."

Spenser cocked her head. She felt completely thick, but it still wasn't making a lot of sense to her. She turned when Jacob raised his hand and gave her a small smile.

"Think of Full Metal as being like a library. It's where all these gun nuts like to go to hobnob with other gun nuts. To paraphrase the immortal John Bender in *The Breakfast Club*, 'it's sort of social. Demented and sad, but social,'" Jacob explained. "But this club—these Silver Bullets—they're like a book club that operates within the larger context of the library. I assume it's sort of a secret book club and membership isn't open to everybody. Is that about right, Sutter?"

"That would be my understanding, yes," Sutter replied.

"What's the purpose of this club, Deputy Sutter?" Spenser asked.

He shook his head. "I honestly don't know, Sheriff," he said. "I only know of it because my brother belongs to Full Metal and told me about it. But he's not part of the Silver Bullets."

"Sutter, do you happen to know who is part of the Silver Bullets?"

He shook his head again. "I don't. I'm sorry."

"That's all right, Deputy," Spenser said. "That's helpful. I appreciate you coming forward and letting us know."

"Of course, Sheriff."

Sutter gave them a nod then walked briskly out of the conference room. As Jacob went to work on his laptop, Spenser sat back in her chair and absorbed the information Sutter had just delivered. Knowing about the Silver Bullets was one thing. But finding out who belonged to the club was something else entirely. But they had a concrete lead they didn't have ten minutes ago. And that fact alone lit a fire in Spenser's belly.

"The Full Metal Shooting Range is owned and operated by Reggie Coffey, originally born in Eugene, Oregon," Jacob read off his computer screen. "Did two tours in Iraq during the first Persian Gulf war. Honorably discharged with the rank of first lieutenant. Moved to Sweetwater Falls upon discharge where it looks like he got married. His wife, Jenelle, passed away two years ago. Breast cancer. He's clean. No jacket. Not so much as a parking ticket. But he does have twenty-seven guns registered in his name."

"God bless the Second Amendment," Young said.

Spenser shrugged. "It might be a little obsessive and fanatical, but it's his right to own as many guns as he wants."

"I suppose so."

"It also doesn't make him our killer," Spenser said.

"I can confirm that. Coffey is five-nine and black," Jacob said, putting his DMV photo up on the screen on the wall. "About the polar opposite of our suspect."

"Okay, he might not be our guy, but he might know our guy," Young offered.

"Which is why we're going to go have a chat with Mr. Coffey," Spenser said. "Gear up and meet me out at the Bronco in ten minutes."

CHAPTER TWENTY-ONE

THE FULL METAL SHOOTING RANGE WAS LOCATED ON the far, southern edge of town... right where Young said it was. It was in an out of the way spot and hard to find unless you knew what you were looking for. As Spenser parked the Bronco in the lot she turned to her undersheriff.

"You've been here before?" Spenser asked.

Young nodded. "Yeah, I've shot here before. It's how I knew where it was. There are only a couple of ranges in town and this is the cleanest, least creepy one," she said. "And before you ask, no, I didn't know a thing about the Silver Bullets. I just come here to blow off steam every now and then. It's kind of therapeutic."

"I wasn't even going to ask. I know you better than that, Amanda," Spenser replied. "Have you ever met the owner? This... Reggie guy?"

She shook her head. "I haven't. I just come in, plug in some music, shoot some targets, then leave. I don't come here to socialize. I've only been here a handful of times, but I honestly don't think I've ever had a conversation with anybody. Not unless you count the guy at the counter who takes my range fees."

Young looked away, her expression pinched, and her face was clouded over with emotion. Spenser knew what was going through the younger woman's mind. The look of self-recrimination on Young's face was something Spenser knew all too well.

"You know this isn't your fault, right?" Spenser stared. "There's no way you could have known there was a predator here."

"I feel like I should have known. I mean, how did something like the Silver Bullets get by me?" Young asked. "I feel like I should have picked up on... something."

"Amanda, you are a lot of things. Clairvoyant is not one of them. Now, stop beating yourself up because there is no way you could have known, and let's go inside and see if we can start unraveling this thing."

Young offered her a small, thankful smile. Spenser knew from her own experience, though, not even her words were going to allow Young to take herself off the hook. She still felt like she bore some responsibility. Spenser knew that nothing she said was going to fully alleviate that burden no matter how illogical it was. It was because Young was a good cop. She cared. And like Spenser, she sometimes cared too much. Oftentimes, to her own detriment.

"Come on. Let's go talk to this guy," Spenser said.

They climbed out of the Bronco and crossed the lot as the crackle of gunfire echoed all around. The shooting range was housed in a squat, gray, single-story cinder block building. In the center of the wooden front door hung a plastic sign that sported the club's name curled around its circular logo—a pair of crossed weapons, one looked to be a shotgun, the other an AR15 sitting atop a set of crosshairs.

Spenser held the door open and let Young walk in ahead of her. She let the door close behind her as they approached the front counter. Surprisingly enough, the sound of gunfire wasn't audible inside the front office. Apparently, the place had been well soundproofed. In front of them was a long counter that ran nearly the width of the room and to the right of the counter was a door marked "Range Entrance." Guns for sale lined the walls—handguns to the left, long guns to the right. Drawers below the gun racks on the walls contained ammunition for them and racks in the middle of the shop contained shop merchandise—shirts, hats, and jackets mostly.

The shop was surprisingly clean and well-organized. Spenser had been expecting to walk into a building that looked to be on the verge of condemnation and filled with trash. But even despite the prevalent smell of gun oil, it still managed to smell somewhat fresh. A man in jeans, a long-sleeved camouflage shirt, and a dark green cap with the range's name and logo turned around and gave Young a wide, toothy smile—a smile that quickly faltered when he looked at Spenser. He had dirty blonde hair that hung to his shoulders, a patchy and wiry beard, and beady brown eyes that narrowed suspiciously.

"Well, hey there, Amanda," he said.

"Tommy," Young greeted him curtly.

"I didn't know you was a cop. But I guess that explains how you shoot so good," he replied with a chortle.

"Yeah, I don't talk about it because I come here to get away from work," Young replied.

He nodded. "Yeah, okay. That makes sense."

The man behind the counter stood an inch or two taller than Spenser and had a thin, narrow build. His build was all wrong and he obviously wasn't their guy, but his sleeves were pulled down so Spenser couldn't see if he had the same tattoo as the UNSUB. He might not be the man they were looking for, but if he was in the same club, he'd likely know who he was.

"So, anyway, what can I do for you ladies?" he asked.

"Tommy, this is Sheriff Song," Young said. "We need to speak with Reggie."

"He's out on the range right now. He's tryin' out a new Desert Eagle he got in this mornin'. That sucker kicks like a mule," Tommy replied.

"Great," Young replied. "We'll just go talk to him."

"You might want to wait 'till he comes in—"

"Nah. I know my way around out there. It's fine," Young cut him off.

Tommy looked at Spenser as if he thought she might do something to stop Young, but she merely shrugged then followed her through the door to the right of the counter. They stepped into a large room that was set up with tables and chairs that all faced a wall of windows in the back wall that gave anybody in the room a clean view of the shooting range just beyond. Vending machines, a long table with a setup for coffee and pastries, and the classic rock that played over the speakers gave the room the feeling of a social hall.

Three men sat at a table in the corner talking to each other in hushed tones as they cleaned the weapons sitting in front of them. They looked up as Spenser and Young walked in and their expressions dimmed. They all wore short-sleeved shirts and she noted that none of them bore the tattoo on their forearms.

"He's over there in lane eight," Young said. "To the right at the end."

"Lead on," Spenser said.

They walked to a door set on the far right of the room and grabbed a pair of headphones and safety goggles from a rack on the wall. Spenser took her Stetson off and slipped the headphones and goggles on before replacing the hat then followed Young outside. They made their way over to the last lane and stood behind Reggie Coffey as he unloaded a magazine into the target downrange. The weapon in his hand was enormous and every shot—even through their headphones—sounded like a cannon going off. Spenser could see the recoil had a nasty kick, but Coffey seemed to be handling it effortlessly. He obviously had a lot of experience.

He ejected the magazine and set it and the empty weapon down on the counter in front of him then hit the button to bring the target back. It was the standard silhouette target and as it neared, Spenser could see that he'd placed the majority of his shots perfectly center mass. The line stopped and the target rippled in the breeze and that's when Spenser noticed the only shots that weren't center mass were square in the center of the target's face.

As if sensing them standing behind him, Coffey turned around. He was about the same height as Spenser and had a lean, wiry build and warm, umber-colored skin. His dark hair was shot through with gray, cropped close to his skull, and he had dark eyes. Coffey had a thick, bushy beard that was flecked with as much gray as the hair atop his head. He wore blue jeans, black work boots, a black long-sleeved t-shirt, and a black ballcap, both bearing the name and logo of his shooting range.

"There's an awful lot of law sittin' here lookin' at me when I know for a fact I haven't done anythin' wrong," he said.

"No, you haven't done anything wrong, Mr. Coffey," Spenser said. "We just had a few questions we needed to ask you."

"Should I have my lawyer come down and join our little menage-a-trois?" he asked.

Spenser grinned. "If you didn't do anything wrong, why would you need a lawyer?"

He stared at Spenser for a long moment then broke into deep, rolling laughter. "Because I'm a prudent man and know how these things sometimes tend to go."

"We assure you, Mr. Coffey, what we're here for has nothing to do with you," Spenser said. "Not directly anyway."

Coffey looked at her for a moment then turned and quickly took his target down and laid it on the bench over his weapon and the extra ammunition. He turned back to them, his mouth twisting, a considering look on his face.

"All right, so what did you want to ask me about?" he asked.

"We have it on good authority that there is a… social club… that exists within your club," Spenser said delicately. "A group of people who call themselves the Silver Bullets."

Coffey's smile fell away, and a look of irritation crossed his face. He clearly knew who the Silver Bullets were. He folded his arms over his chest and leaned back against the counter in the stall behind him.

"You know who I'm talking about," Spenser said.

"I know there's a group of like-minded people who've formed a social clique, yeah," he said. "Shooting can be a social sport so I'm not overly surprised."

"Then why the look of irritation?" Young asked.

"Because I don't like some of the things I heard this particular social clique talking about," he said. "I'm trying to run a business and provide for my wife and daughter here and I'll be damned if I let the business I built be turned into some sort of fringe fake military headquarters. I served. Most of these clowns didn't, so hearing them talk like they're soldiers makes me sick. They don't know the first thing about service or honor. So, I ran that whole group out of here months ago. Told 'em to take it to some other range where their views might be more acceptable."

"Can you tell us who they are, Mr. Coffey?" Spenser asked.

He shook his head. "Afraid I can't."

"Can't? Or won't?"

"Both," he said. "I can't because I don't know all of 'em. Hell, they were actively recruitin' so there are probably even more of 'em now. Those kinds of groups tend to pull in all the crazies."

"And you won't because... why?"

"Because you and I may find their views disgusting and unpalatable, but they got a right to 'em," he said. "We still have a right to believe what we want in this country. At least for the moment. And upholding that right is one of the reasons I served. It's what I bled for and what I watched my friends die for. I ain't going to betray my beliefs or my oath now."

"We understand and appreciate that," Spenser countered. "But we're looking for a man who is raping and murdering women, sir. And we suspect he belongs to the Silver Bullets. You have a daughter, Mr. Coffey. Surely if, God forbid, something was to ever happen to her, you'd want us to find the man responsible."

He frowned and looked away for a moment. It was a cheap shot and Spenser knew it, but the look on Coffey's face told her she'd hit the mark. If it got him to open up and give them what they needed to find this creep, cheap shot or not, it was worth it.

Spenser exchanged a look with Young then turned to the man again. "Mr. Coffey, all we're asking for is a look at your membership list—"

He immediately shook his head. "I'm sorry, but I'm afraid I can't give that to you without a warrant. The members of my club have an expectation of privacy and I won't betray that."

"It's a shooting club. It's not like we're asking you to out the members of some fetish or swingers' club," Young interjected.

He chuckled. "With the way guns are viewed these days, it might be worse to be associated with a gun club, Undersheriff," he said. "Sheriff Song, I'd like to help you, but I can't. Not that way. My clients put their trust in me, and I won't violate that."

Spenser nodded grudgingly. She frowned and looked down at her boots for a moment then looked up again as an idea struck her.

"I get that. And I respect that," she said. "But maybe you can tell me something."

"Maybe. Depends on what that somethin' is."

"Just… tell me if the man I'm about to describe to you sounds familiar," she said. "The man we're looking for is six-two. Maybe six-three. He looks like he spends hours in the gym every day. He's built. He's got green eyes and will likely be outspoken in his dislike for women. Maybe says things like they're the cause of all his problems or something similar to that. He's going to be white and probably in his mid-thirties."

Coffey pursed his lips and looked away for a moment, a thoughtful expression on his face as he combed his memory banks. He finally turned back to Spenser and shook his head.

"I'm sorry, Sheriff. He don't sound familiar to me. He don't sound like anybody I've ever seen in my club and I'd tell you that if he did," he said. "If he's a member of the Silver Bullets, he didn't join them here, that much I'm sure of. I'd tell you if I recognized him precisely because I've got a daughter, Sheriff."

Spenser heard nothing but the ring of truth in his voice and she felt herself deflate like a balloon as the certainty they were about to get their big break in the case came crashing down in a flaming heap all around her. There was no way any judge in their right mind would ever grant them a warrant for Coffey's membership list. Not with what they had. Or maybe more accurately, not with what they didn't have—probable cause.

This was a dead end. A particularly frustrating one because Spenser had been so sure this was going to bear fruit. But it was like she'd told Ryker... this was the job.

"And there's no way you'd be willing to give us your membership list out of a sense of civic duty?" Spenser pressed.

He offered her a gentle smile. "I'm sorry, but I can't do that. Like I said, whacked out beliefs or not, they've still got the right to believe 'em."

"All right. Well... thank you for your time, Mr. Coffey," Spenser said.

"I'm sorry I can't be of more help."

"Me too."

Spenser led Young back through the club and out to the Bronco, doing her best to keep from blowing a gasket in her frustration. They climbed into the vehicle and Spenser started the engine then pointed them in the direction of the shop. She hated the feeling of coming back empty-handed.

"So?" Young asked. "What now?"

Spenser sighed. "Now we find another lead. Hopefully, before he drops another body."

CHAPTER TWENTY-TWO

"Do you believe him? I mean, do you believe he'd tell you if the guy you described to him sounded familiar?" Ryker asked.

Spenser took a sip of wine and nodded. After a wonderful dinner of salmon, asparagus, and rice pilaf, she and Ryker cleaned up the kitchen and she told him all about what happened down at the shooting range. Spenser honestly never thought she'd be comfortable sharing space with somebody again, but she had to admit that feeling of domesticity between her and Ryker came easy. More than that, it felt... nice. Not that she was ready to chuck it all and move in with him anytime soon, but she took it as a sign that maybe she was healing.

After they finished cleaning up, he poured them a couple glasses of wine as she took over the dining room table. Spenser spread out all her case files, set up her computer, and started going through everything once more, looking for something that would point them in a direction. Any direction. Even running down blind alleys and slamming face-first into the wall was preferable to standing there doing nothing. At least a blind alley could tell you which direction not to run in.

"I do. He's like you—he served and takes things like his honor very seriously."

"As he should. That's not something to screw around with," Ryker said.

"No, it's not," she agreed. "Hey, where are the kids? It's too quiet."

"Crashed out on the couch. They've had a big day," he said.

"Spent most of it playing in the park again?"

He nodded and smiled. "They did. They seem to enjoy having their own space."

"It was kind of you to build for them."

"Yeah, well, it kept me busy for a while. Honestly, it was as much for me as it was for them," he said with a frown. "Now I need to find another project to start working on. Soon."

"You mentioned building your own roast house out on the grounds," she reminded him.

"I did, didn't I? That's a pretty involved project that should keep me busy for a while. That might just work," he said thoughtfully.

Ryker seemed to already be drawing up plans in his head as Spenser shuffled through some of the reports spread out on the table in front of her. As she did, Ryker picked up the photo of the quote the UNSUB had left on the back of the bathroom door. Still holding the photo, he studied it then looked up at Spenser.

"What does this mean?" he asked. "What is he talking about? Your hubris?"

Spenser shook her head. "I'm not entirely sure yet. But it confirms for me that this is personal. That there's some connection between us—at least in his mind. And he seems to think that by punishing these women, he's punishing me."

"And you've got no idea who this guy is?"

"I don't. Nothing's coming to me off the top of my head," Spenser replied. "I mean, I have to assume it's somebody I've locked up. I assume somebody I put away would most likely accuse me of having this hubris he mentioned."

"That makes sense. So, what can you do about that?"

"I have Jacob running the arrest reports for everybody we've put away since I got here whether I personally put the bracelets on them or not," she said. "I have him looking for a size match with our UNSUB."

"That's smart."

"Feels more like a Hail Mary… or at least something close to it," Spenser said. "I just can't stop feeling like this guy is a step ahead of me. Two steps."

"Yeah, maybe. But you've been here before. Yet you always seem to turn it around somehow and get your guy."

Spenser sat back in her chair and took a sip of her wine, her mind spinning. Her eyes drifted over the seemingly endless reports and stacks of crime scene photos as a cold chill wormed its way up her spine, eventually making her shudder.

"I don't know, Ryker. This one… this one seems different somehow," she said softly.

"As far as I can see, the only thing that's different is how personally this is hitting you. How deep under your skin this case is," he said. "You need to find a way to take a step back and see this all from a position of objectivity."

"Easier said than done, I'm afraid."

"But essential."

"Yeah, I know you're right. I'm just having a hard time maintaining a healthy distance here," she said. "And honestly, I don't know why. This isn't the first time an UNSUB has made things personal with me or tried to get under my skin."

"My uninformed, armchair psychologist's opinion from the outside is that you identify with these women. You've told me they're all career-first, driven, passionate, and ambitious women. That describes you to a T," he said and picked up a couple of the DMV photos of the victims. "Then there's the fact that they all kind of look like you. That has to be screwing with your head a little bit."

Spenser looked down and smiled ruefully. She hadn't mentioned the physical similarities between herself and the victims to Ryker, knowing it would only worry him more. And make him more likely to hire a private army to surround her twenty-four hours a day until they bring this creep in and put him away for good. Ryker was far more observant than she gave him credit for—and she should have known that.

"Yeah, well, what it's doing to my head is nothing compared to what he's doing to the women he's attacking," Spenser said. "I'm fine. I'm whole and I'll get through this. I can't say the same for his victims."

"You're going to figure this out. And you will find this guy—"

His words were cut off by the muffled sound of Spenser's phone ringing. She shuffled around through the pile of papers in front of her until she found her phone buried underneath it all. Picking it up, she saw it was from an unknown number and frowned. Spenser exchanged a quick glance with Ryker then hit the button to connect the call while putting it on speaker.

"This is Song," she said.

"Spenser Song. So lovely to hear your voice again."

The man's tinny, robotic voice sent an ice-cold sliver of fear straight through her heart and she shuddered. Whoever was on the other end of the line was using a voice modulator and Spenser knew in an instant that she was speaking with the man she was hunting. Ryker's eyes widened with realization, as his hands squeezed into fists. He looked ready to snatch the phone out of her hand and challenge the guy to a duel at dawn, so she held up her hand, making a "calm down" gesture.

"Again?" Spenser said. "So, we've spoken before."

"You like to think you're so clever, don't you, Sheriff Song?"

"I like to think I'm as clever as the next person, I suppose."

"You think you're so smart. You think you're the smartest person in whatever room you're in," he said. "That sort of arrogance… It's unflattering."

"I'm sorry you feel that way. So, what you're doing to all these women… you think that you're punishing me for what you perceive to be my hubris?"

"I'm showing everybody what a fraud you are. I'm showing everybody that you're not half as smart as you think you are."

"And what makes you think that brutalizing and murdering these innocent women is going to accomplish that?" Spenser asked.

His laughter was low, deep, and even eerier through the modulator he was using. Spenser suppressed a shudder.

"Because it's going to show people you're not even smart enough to see what's right under your nose. What's been under your nose this whole time," he finally said.

"And what is that?" she asked. "What's been under my nose all this time?"

"Me, of course."

"It sounds like your fight is with me," Spenser said. "Why don't you and I settle this? Just you and me, and let's leave the innocents out of this?"

"See, that would be taking the easy way out of things. For you anyway."

"How's that?"

"Because I'd kill you. I'd kill you and then nobody would get to see what a fraud you really are. Nobody would get to see just how stupid you are. And just how unfit you are to wear that badge," he said. "See, people get enamored with the fact that you were FBI, but I don't think that's anything to crow about. Lots of stupid people get into the FBI."

"So, you're smarter than me is what you're saying. And you want the people to see that."

"Obviously."

"And more than my death, you want to ruin my reputation," Spenser continued. "The most important thing to you is showing the world what an idiot I am."

"Now you're getting it," he replied. "Maybe you're not so dumb after all."

"But why? I mean, can you tell me what it is I did to you? How did my arrogance impact your life in such a way that you'd do this?"

That eerie laughter echoed out of the phone again, raising goosebumps across Spenser's entire body. She took a quick swallow of her wine, trying to steady herself. She could hear a low growl emanating from Ryker, his fists looking ready to crush something or someone.

"Don't flatter yourself, Sheriff," he said. "I was doin' what I was doin' long before you showed up here. You just helped give my hobby a little more focus and meaning. That's all. I suppose I should thank you for that."

"Why don't we get together? You can thank me in person—"

"Oh, we'll link up at some point soon. Don't you worry your pretty little head about that, darlin'," he said. "But it ain't going to go the way you think it will. I promise you that."

"Why don't we see about that?"

"Soon. Soon," he said. "But I think this all needs to be a little more personal for you. I don't think this has quite hit home deep enough and before we're done here, I want to make sure it does. I want you to feel it, Spenser."

"I do—"

"Not really. But that's about to change. I promise you. See you soon, Spenser."

Before Spenser could say anything more, he disconnected the call, leaving Spenser sitting there staring at her phone for a long moment. The man's words bounced around in her brain as she tried to put some order to them while extracting any valuable bits of information he might have inadvertently let slip. Eventually, she set her phone down and leaned back in her chair.

"What do you think?" Ryker finally asked after a heaving sigh.

"Any question about there being a personal component in this for him can now be put to bed," Spenser said. "This is personal for him. I've done something to put him on this course."

"You didn't do anything, Spense. This is all him."

She nodded. "I know. I'm just saying that in his mind, I've somehow slighted him. He's taken offense enough to my perceived hubris that it's allowing him to justify what he's doing."

"This has to be somebody you locked up at some point. I can't see anybody else who might be harboring that kind of grudge," Ryker said.

"Yeah, maybe," Spenser said. "Probably."

"Okay, so what are your next steps?"

Spenser felt lost. Like she was wandering around in a fog and had no sense of direction. And for maybe the first time in her career, Spenser doubted herself. She was second-guessing everything she'd done and even worse, everything she was going to do. This man was two steps ahead of her and Spenser had no idea how to go about bridging that gap.

"I honestly don't know," she said quietly.

CHAPTER TWENTY-THREE

"Getting an early jump on the day, are we?" Spenser asked.

"Indeed, I am," he replied. "Indeed, I am."

She walked into their war room to find Jacob already at the table, clacking away at his keyboard. He looked up as she set the box of donuts down then handed him a small white bag that contained his cherished apple fritter. He gave her a wide smile then stuck his nose in the bag and inhaled deeply as a groan that was borderline indecent passed his lips.

"I think you just punched your ticket to heaven," he said.

"I can use all the help I can get," she replied.

Spenser gave him a minute to tear into his fritter as she took a long swallow of coffee and set herself up at the table. She took a few minutes to gather her wits about her. The previous night's conversation with their UNSUB had left her feeling a little more rattled and out of sorts than she cared to admit. Even to herself. But she did wake up angry. And with a sense of determination to catch this guy and put him behind bars forever.

"What are you doing in so early, Jacob?"

"I couldn't sleep so I figured I'd come in to finish up going through all the arrest records you asked me about," he said. "So far, I've got half a dozen guys who fit the physical description who are currently not incarcerated. But none of them were arrested for sexual crimes."

"What were they arrested for?"

"Three for domestic violence, one for assault and battery, and one for theft," he said. "I've taken a peek at their court transcripts and none of them seem like Rhodes Scholars. They can barely string together a coherent sentence. I honestly don't know if any of them are sophisticated enough to be doing what our guy is doing."

Spenser frowned. She thought the man she spoke to last night, while maybe not being the pinnacle of eloquence, displayed an above average intelligence. He was relatively well-spoken, rational, and in his own way, logical. He had a reason for what he was doing and even though Spenser thought it was probably garbage, he was still able to articulate that reason to her clearly and unequivocally. He wasn't a stark, raving, foaming-at-the-mouth lunatic. And to Spenser, that was far scarier and more dangerous than if he had been.

"Well, we'll keep them in the maybe pile for the moment," Spenser said. "We need to cast as wide a net as possible. How many more do you have to go through?"

"A few dozen if we're pulling in the arrest records from our neighboring towns," he said. "But I should be able to separate the wheat from the chaff quickly enough. I'll have you a comprehensive list by the end of the day."

"That's good work. Thank you, Jacob."

'You got it."

Spenser glanced at her watch. "Where's your sister? She's usually here before you."

"Yeah, she likes to show off like that. Damn apple polisher."

Spenser grinned but as Jacob glanced at his watch, his eyes widened, and the corners of his mouth curled downward. It was as if he hadn't realized how late it had gotten. Much later than Young usually got in. He looked at Spenser and gave her a small shrug.

"Maybe she overslept?" he offered.

"Yeah, maybe."

It hadn't happened in all the months Spenser had been there, but there was a first time for everything. Young had been burning the candle at both ends for a while, so she was probably overdue for a late morning. You could only run yourself ragged for so long before your body revolted and decided you needed sleep. Still, with the words from their UNSUB about making things even more personal still echoing around in her mind, Spenser felt a hint of concern make her heart flutter.

"I'm just going to give her a call. Might be she just needs somebody to wake her up."

"What a slacker," he said with a laugh.

"Right?"

A cold and ominous weight settled down over her shoulders and sent a shudder through her. Spenser swallowed hard and thought about her next move. The last thing she wanted to do was worry Jacob... especially if the eerie sense of foreboding gripping her heart turned out to be nothing more than a false alarm. But her gut was tight, and Spenser felt that something bad was coming.

Doing her best to act as if everything was normal, Spenser got to her feet. "I'm going to give Amanda a call then head out on my rounds. Do me a favor and keep hammering away at those case files for me, if you would."

"I'm on it, boss."

Spenser walked briskly out of the war room then stopped by her office to grab her jacket, hat, and the keys to the Bronco. She pulled her phone out of her pocket and hit the button to autodial Young. Her stomach churning and that ominous feeling growing darker, she pressed the phone to her ear as she paced back and forth. The phone rang once. Twice. And on the third ring, it went to Young's voicemail and everything inside Spenser felt like it had turned to ice.

She disconnected the call and dropped the phone back into her pocket then marched out of her office, avoiding eye contact with everyone as she headed for the front doors. She quickly checked out with Alice Jarrett and grabbed a radio from her, making sure it was tuned to the right channel. She gave Alice a smile she hoped didn't look as fake as it felt then turned and headed out of the office and walked swiftly out to the Bronco, saying a silent prayer that she was wrong. With every step, though, her heart pounded harder and the cold certainty of what she was going to find at Young's place only solidified in her mind.

Young lived in one half of a small duplex on the eastern side of town. Spenser opened the gate of the waist-high white picket fence surrounding the front yard of Young's duplex and walked through. She headed up the narrow walk then mounted the four steps to the porch. She turned and looked back at the street. It was a quiet neighborhood filled with neatly tended and well-kempt homes. The yards were all nicely trimmed, the paint on most of the houses looked fresh, and nice cars were parked in the driveways.

The duplex itself was a cute blue and white Craftsman-style home that had been renovated and partitioned into two separate units. White shutters flanked the large picture windows in the front as well as the smaller windows around the house. On the porch, there was a rocking chair and a small table on Young's side. But there was nothing on the other side of the porch, making Spenser think it was vacant… a realization that only made the flutter in her heart speed up as the acrid taste of bile coated the back of her throat.

Young lived in a nice, middle-class neighborhood. People raised families here. It was the sort of neighborhood you would think a violent attack would be noticed and reported. It was a brittle hope, but one Spenser was clinging to fiercely.

"Amanda!" she called out as she knocked on the door.

Spenser waited for a moment then moved over to the large picture window and tried to peer in. The curtains were drawn, blocking her view. She knocked on the door again, a little harder and longer than before.

"Amanda!" she called again.

The longer she stood there with no answer, the deeper and colder the sense of dread filling her belly grew. She licked her lips and tried to control the trembling in her body. She stepped off the porch and walked around to the gate that led to the side yard. Reaching over the fence, Spenser undid the latch, gritting her teeth when the gate squealed sharply as she pulled it open. She moved a brick with the toe of her boot, nudging it under the bottom of the gate to keep it propped open.

Her hand hovering near the Glock on her hip, Spenser moved slowly down the side yard of the house. She tried peering through the windows as she went but the curtains had been drawn tight over them all—something else that set the alarm bells ringing in her head. Spenser made it to the back of the house and froze. Her heart dropped into her wildly churning stomach when she saw the back door standing open a couple of inches.

"Amanda," she muttered.

Spenser forced herself to stop and think. The door had been left open because he wanted her to find it. He wanted her to know he'd been there. He wanted her to fly off the handle and go charging inside, emotionally charged and spinning out. Spenser took a deep breath and let it out slowly, counting to ten as she pulled a pair of black nitrile gloves out of her pocket and snapped them on. The chances of there being any trace evidence were slim, but she wasn't going to screw this up. She had no idea what she was going to find beyond that door but no matter what it was, Spenser was going to do right by Young.

Gloved up and her nerves settled, Spenser pulled her Glock and held it in the ready position as she moved to the back door and gently nudged it open with the toe of her boot. The kitchen lay just beyond the door and was cloaked in thick shadows.

Leading with the barrel of her gun, Spenser moved inside, quickly checking behind the door. Nobody was hiding behind it. Her heart was hammering so hard in her chest, she was sure anybody in the house would be able to hear her coming. She paused and focused her breathing, doing her best to settle herself down.

The interior of Young's house was silent. As silent as a tomb, a dark voice in the back of her mind said with a giggle. Spenser clenched her jaw and tried to banish the voice. She moved through the kitchen and stepped through the rounded archway into the living room, her heart nearly stopping upon seeing the destruction that had been wrought. Just like all the other crime scenes they'd been to since this case landed, everything around her was in ruins. Glass shattered. Pictures pulled off the walls and destroyed. TV and stereo smashed into ten thousand pieces. If it could be broken, it was. But the one thing missing was Young herself.

What sounded like a low groan drifted from the back room and Spenser jumped, feeling a white-hot rush of adrenaline pour into her veins. She moved down the short hallway toward the two bedrooms at the back of the duplex. The door to the guest room was standing wide open. Young had turned it into her home office and even though it too was wreathed in dim shadow, Spenser could see it was intact. A quick check showed there was nobody behind the door or in the closet.

She stepped back into the hallway and faced the closed door in front of her. Young's bedroom. Spenser broke out in a hot sweat and felt like she was going to be sick. Her weapon still positioned in front of her, Spenser reached out with her free hand and turned the doorknob. She used the toe of her boot to push the door open and quickly followed it in. As the door bounced off the wall behind it, she stepped in and swept the room from left to right, clearing it before going any further.

"My God," Spenser whispered.

The bedroom, like the front room, looked like a hurricane had blown through. Everything was in shambles. Young's entire room had been torn apart. It wasn't the massive destruction that nearly stopped Spenser's heart, though. Young lay amidst the wreckage, her body as torn and broken as the room around her.

"Amanda," Spenser croaked.

Quickly holstering her weapon, Spenser fell to her knees beside Young's bloodied and ravaged body, her vision blurred by tears. She reached out and gently stroked the younger woman's cheek, tenderly brushing a thick strand of her long blonde hair away from her deeply bruised and nightmarishly bloody face. As Spenser knelt beside her, the grief bubbling up inside of her dense and colder than a glacier, Young's eyes fluttered then opened halfway.

"Spenser," she whispered, her voice hoarse and cracking.

"Amanda!"

Young took Spenser's hand and gave it a squeeze that was alarmingly weak. Her eyes continued to quiver, and she seemed to be fading quickly. Clinging to Young, Spenser used her free hand to yank her phone out of her pocket and quickly dialed 9-1-1.

"Hang in there, Amanda. Help is coming," Spenser said, her voice thick with emotion. "Just stay with me. Please, stay with me."

The phone pressed to her ear, Spenser's entire body trembled as she waited. It seemed like it took forever but the connection was finally made.

"9-1-1, what is your emergency?" came the operator's voice.

"This is Sheriff Spenser Song," she said as she choked back tears. "I need help."

CHAPTER TWENTY-FOUR

Spenser sat in a chair on one side of Young's hospital bed while Jacob sat on the other. They'd been there all night but neither of them had spoken for hours, their attention focused solely on Young. Jacob and Amanda bickered and fought, but in moments like that, when she saw the pain on his face, Spenser could see just how deeply he loved his sister. He raised his gaze to Spenser.

"She's going to be okay. She's always been tougher than she looks. She used to beat up my bullies when we were kids," he said, his voice hopeful but his smile weak and watery.

Young was hooked up to a battery of machines, all of them flashing or beeping, filling the room with more light and sound than a casino in Vegas. As she looked at all the wires connecting Young to those machines, Spenser had to fight back the tears as she felt assailed by a thousand daggers of guilt, all of them piercing her heart.

"She will be. Amanda is one of the toughest people I know," Spenser said.

Young lay perfectly still in the bed, arms down at her sides, the sheets pulled up to her chest. She was so still and her breathing so soft, she was almost serene. Peaceful. The mass of gashes and bruises on her face, however, told the story of the violence that was visited upon her. The swelling had gone down but both eyes were blackened, and Spenser knew the whites had turned blood red from the burst blood vessels within them. Deep purple fingermarks encircled her throat, and a bandage covered the deep gash on her forehead—the worst of what seemed like a thousand cuts and abrasions that crisscrossed her face.

Spenser knew from Marley that Young had suffered two broken ribs and a punctured lung. She had a fracture in her left wrist and her right shoulder had been dislocated. Her body was covered in bruises that were so deeply purple, they were almost black, cuts, and other abrasions, it looked like a roadmap of the pain she endured. She'd been beaten savagely and stabbed twice during her attack, and she was still incredibly pale from the massive blood loss.

"She's alive," Jacob finally said. "She's alive because you got to her in time."

"She never should have been in that position to begin with—"

"This isn't your fault."

"Isn't it?"

"No, it isn't," Jacob argued. "There's no way you could have known he would go after her."

"I should have. I should have known," Spenser said. "He pretty much told me he was going to when he called me. He said he was going to make it even more personal for me."

"Right, and based on that, you should have immediately jumped to the conclusion that he would go after my sister. I totally get that from that vague threat. Yeah, that makes sense."

Spenser shook her head and fell silent. She leaned forward in her seat, resting her forearms on her thighs and clasped her hands together. She knew Jacob truly didn't blame her for what happened to his sister and that he was trying to let her off the hook. Spenser didn't feel she deserved to be let off. She should have known their UNSUB would do something like this and the fact that she didn't left her choking on her guilt. Maybe he was right. Maybe she was too arrogant. Too blinded by her own hubris to see what was happening.

"This isn't on you, Sheriff," Jacob said. "This isn't your fault."

"I appreciate that, Jacob. I do," Spenser replied. "But it's my job to know that things like this are going to happen and that I didn't—"

"Spenser…"

Spenser whipped her head around to see that Young's eyes were halfway open and she was looking right at her. The woman's voice was scratchy and thick, and she winced like every thought firing through her head caused excruciating pain, but she was awake. Spenser and Jacob both jumped to their feet and stood on opposite sides of the bed looking down at Young with unabashed expressions of relief on their faces. Spenser's vision blurred as tears welled in her eyes.

"Amanda," she said softly.

Young grimaced, her face etched with agony as she tried to sit up but Spenser and Jacob both put a hand on one of her shoulders and gently kept her on her back.

"Don't try to move, Sis. You're pretty banged up," Jacob said softly.

"I'm fine," Young argued.

"Yeah, you look it," he said with a mischievous grin.

"Shut up," Young countered with a laugh then winced in pain.

"Take it easy. I'm glad to see you back with us," Spenser said softly.

Young's features softened but her eyes took on an intensity as she held Spenser's gaze. She frowned, fearing that Young blamed her for what happened to her. Young would be right to blame her, of course. But she valued Young as both her undersheriff and as a friend—and as a member of her chosen family. Young was like the kid sister she never had and knowing that she probably blamed Spenser for the horrific things done to her, that she would likely never forgive her, drove that dagger of guilt and self-recrimination even deeper into her heart.

"Spenser, you know this isn't your fault, don't you?" Young croaked.

"That's what I've been telling her," Jacob said.

"I should have known what he was going to do," Spenser said as she shook her head. "And I'm sorry I didn't. I'm sorry that I failed—"

"You're a lot of things, but clairvoyant isn't one of them," Young cut her off.

A rueful grin touched Spenser's lips and she chuckled softly as Young threw her exact words back in her face. It helped lift some of the burden that pressed down on her heart, but Spenser knew nothing would eliminate it completely until they had the man who'd done this to Young and all the other women dead or in cuffs. And at the moment, she thought dead was the preferable outcome.

"This isn't your fault, Spenser. Stop beating yourself up," Young went on. "This isn't on you. It's on him. He did this. Period."

"He said he was going to make it more personal for me. He was right. I can't think of how he could have made it any more personal. And that's why I should have known," Spenser said.

"We'll get him," Young said.

"No, you will stay here and rest. Heal up," Spenser said.

"I'm fine—"

"You're not fine. You've been beat to hell and you're going to stay here if I have to handcuff you to this bed myself," Spenser said.

"Yeah. What she said," Jacob added.

"I don't think the handcuffs will be necessary. But I will make sure to whack her out on enough drugs that she won't be able to get out of bed until I say so."

Spenser turned and gave her best friend Marley a wide smile. Almost half a foot shorter than Spenser's five-nine frame, the smaller Marley stepped to the side of the bed and looked down

He harrumphed and then scowled at her disapprovingly. "It takes a minute for us to mobilize, Sheriff. I have to call my team to make sure they are available—they are volunteers, if you recall correctly. Coordination and mobilization is not an instantaneous thing. Now, if you had given me a pair of full-time techs—"

"Enough. I get it, Dr. Arbery. It's not your fault and I'm sorry for snapping."

Arbery stood at the far end of the conference table in the war room, his hands clasped behind his back, a prissy expression on his face. Spenser couldn't blame him for being upset with her, after all, she'd just ripped him a new one for something that wasn't his fault. It was entirely her fault. She'd made that fatal, emotionally driven mistake the UNSUB had been counting on her to make and now, it might have cost them everything.

She pinched the bridge of her nose and tried to keep from sighing out loud, lest Arbery take it the wrong way and think it was directed at him. He was tremendously skilled at his job and Spenser was thankful to have him. But he could oftentimes be prickly and sensitive about things. He often took offense to even the smallest things and Spenser had to continually remind herself to make sure she was treating him with kid gloves.

"And you're certain it's all gone?" Spenser asked.

He nodded. "I smelled the bleach and cleaning chemicals the minute we walked through the door, Sheriff. The bedroom where you found Undersheriff Young had been cleaned. There wasn't a drop of blood to be found anywhere—hers or his. Also, we did not find the knife she used to wound her attacker either. He must have taken that as well."

"Son of a..."

Spenser let her voice trail off and clenched her jaw. She was gripping the pencil in her hand so tightly, it snapped. Jacob looked at her with a frown on his face.

"How in the hell did he manage to pull that off?" he asked.

Rather than answer him, Spenser looked up at Arbery instead. "Were you able to pull anything from the scene?"

"Vanessa and Anthony are still processing it, but I wanted to give you an update," he said. "I thought sooner, rather than later would be wise."

Spenser nodded. "Yes. Thank you," she said. "I know you guys are thorough and precise, but I'd like for you and your team to back through the scene one more time and see if there's anything that might have gotten missed or didn't stand out the first time."

"But, Sheriff—"

"Humor me, Dr. Arbery. Please."

He stared at her for a moment, caught somewhere between being offended that she'd question his thoroughness and understanding that she was grasping for straws. Finally, he nodded, wisely choosing to pick his battles and deciding that wasn't a hill he wanted to die on.

"Of course," he said then turned and walked out of the war room.

"Boss, what happened?" Jacob asked again.

Spenser scrubbed her face with her hands and let out a frustrated growl. She opened her mouth to respond but closed it again without saying a word, terrified of telling Jacob that she screwed up maybe the only real lead they had to find the man responsible for what happened to his sister. How could she admit to her colossal failure? How could she not, though? Jacob was looking to her for answers. He was looking for her to deliver justice for his sister. If she couldn't find it within herself to be honest with him, then Spenser knew she was failing them both on all fronts.

"I didn't secure the scene, Jacob," Spenser said through clenched teeth.

"What do you mean?"

"I mean that I called the ambulance to come get Amanda. Instead of waiting for somebody to get there to lock down the scene, I called Arbery and Woods from the hospital," Spenser said. "The scene was open for thirty minutes. The UNSUB obviously came in during that window of time and scoured the scene, washed away any blood evidence, and took the knife."

He didn't say anything for a long moment. And as the silence stretched out, the air in the room suddenly felt heavier. Spenser's stomach fluttered and she felt sick.

"I'm sorry, Jacob," Spenser said quietly. "I screwed up and I am so sorry—"

"You got my sister to the hospital. Like I said, she's alive because of you—because you acted quickly," he said, cutting her off. "Is losing that evidence a setback? Sure. Do you think that means I'm going to rake you over the coals? Absolutely not. The most important thing to me right now is that Amanda is alive. We'll find another way to get this prick, boss."

Spenser felt like a thousand-pound weight had been lifted off her shoulders. It didn't do anything to diminish the rest of the weight her guilt forced her to carry, but she didn't quite feel like she was on the verge of suffocating beneath it anymore.

"Thank you, Jacob."

He shook his head. "You have nothing to thank me for, boss. Like I said—and more importantly, like Amanda said—none of this is your fault. So, let's stop beating this horse now, shall we? It's long dead, Sheriff. Let it rest in peace, huh?"

That drew a smile from Spenser, and she gave him a nod. "Fair enough."

"Okay, so what's our next move?"

Spenser took a sip of her coffee, leaned forward, and tried to shift her mind away from the cloud of self-pity and self-recrimination she'd been laboring under. As she put her mind in gear and tried to focus on the case, tried to call up all the facts and put her mind into gear again, she immediately felt the energy of her determination crackling through her veins like lightning.

"I've been thinking on it—obsessing on it, really—and I know we went through all their financial and phone records. I know we looked for a nexus where all the victims might have shopped or gone to socially," she started.

"Yeah, and we came up with bupkis."

"Right. But one thing we didn't check was whether or not any of them had commonalities in service companies—cable and the like," she said. "It would be really easy for a cable repairman to gain access to somebody's keys—maybe make a copy of the key on the sly. That would account for how he's able to get in and out of the house as smoothly as his victims say he does."

Jacob snapped his fingers. "That is brilliant. Absolutely brilliant."

"I don't know about brilliant. A decent thought maybe," Spenser said. "And even that depends on how it pans out."

"Oh, ye of little faith," he said. "Let me work my magic."

Jacob's fingers flew over the keyboard filling the war room with the tap-tap-tap of the keys. His eyes were narrowed, the tip of his tongue poked out the side of his mouth, and he had a look of grim determination on his face. Spenser knew him well enough by that point to just let him go and do his thing. She sipped her coffee and said a silent word, hoping her hunch bore fruit.

"Yahtzee. Each of our UNSUB's eight victims—nine if you include my sister—use EmComm Cable," he said. "See? It *was* a brilliant thought."

"Hold that pony. It's a tenuous link at best right now. We need—"

"Another link to make it more solid. Yeah, I know," he said. "Being that each of these women is career-driven and very likely Type-A—and because I'm industrious and brilliant myself—I accessed their calendars. Are you ready for this?"

"Tell me something good," Spenser said.

"Each of them had a service call within three days of their attack," he told her.

A slow smile spread across Spenser's face as adrenaline surged through her veins. The flames of hope in her belly, flickering and guttering a moment ago, suddenly burst into a bonfire.

"Looks like I'm going out to EmComm to have a conversation," Spenser said. "And while I'm gone, I need you to do something for me."

CHAPTER TWENTY-SIX

"**J**ESUS," SPENSER MUTTERED. Deputy Lane Summers, first on scene, stood silent and barely moving beside Spenser amidst the wreckage in the bedroom looking positively shellshocked. It was her first murder scene, and she was looking a little pale. Not that Spenser blamed her. For a first murder scene, this was a bad one to have caught. Especially when you weren't expecting to find one. It was just about one of the worst surprises you could walk into.

Summers had been called out for what she thought was a simple wellness check and walked into an act of savagery. Spenser had to credit the young woman, though. She'd kept her head about herself well enough to call Spenser who'd been en route to

EmComm, then call for backup, and finally, to Dr. Arbery and his team. After that, she'd secured the scene. She even kept her wits about her well enough to string up a tape line while she waited for reinforcements. Unlike Spenser, Lane had kept her cool and had done everything right.

"What sort of monster could do this?" she asked.

"That's what we're trying to figure out," Spenser replied.

Stretched out on the floor in front of them was the nude and broken body of Lia Rice. The woman's tawny skin was pale, cold, and had the waxy sheen of death Spenser had seen all too often in her life. Lia's dark eyes were wide open and fixed on some point beyond Spenser's sight, and her long, dark hair was fanned out like a halo.

Lia Rice had been beaten to a pulp. This time, however, rather than with fists, Spenser thought it looked like she'd been beaten with a blunt object. The wounds could have been made by a baseball bat, but her gut told her it was something smaller. She'd have to wait for Arbery to confirm it. The side of Lia's head was literally caved in and split open. Spenser could see the gleaming white bone through the wound.

Blood coated the woman's face and a good portion of her body, grimly reminding Spenser of that movie *Carrie* after her tormentors had dumped a bucket of blood on her at the high school prom. Even through that grisly red sheen, Spenser could see the mass of bruises and cuts that covered Lia's body. There were half a dozen visible stab wounds—deep stab wounds—potentially fatal in their own right. Both of her arms were twisted at unnatural angles, obviously broken, and a jagged shard of bone had burst through the skin of Lia's right arm.

Her body was a wreck. It was more than clear that she had suffered enormously before she'd finally been killed. A thick purple bruise encircled the woman's neck. Obvious strangulation marks, but not those synonymous with hands. He'd used something. A rope? A belt maybe? As Spenser looked around the room, she didn't see anything that stood out to her among the debris. It made her think he brought his tools with him.

If that was true, it constituted another step in his evolution, going from weapons of opportunity to bringing his own. That also meant that he was not going to stop. Not unless and until Spenser stopped him.

"Walk me through it, Lane," Spenser said. "What happened?"

Summers swallowed hard and tried to pull her eyes away from the ravaged body at their feet and focus on Spenser. She pulled off her sheriff's department ballcap and mopped her brow with her sleeve before tugging the hat back on. She blew out a long breath, taking a moment to steady her nerves and stomach. When she was ready, Summers turned to Spenser.

"I got a call out to the house—a neighbor saw the front door standing open and was worried," she explained. "I came out, identified myself, and didn't get a response. I called out a couple more times then announced I was coming in."

Summers took another beat, studiously avoiding looking down at the body, even though her eyes kept drifting down to the dead woman on the ground at their feet. It wasn't until Summers physically turned around to keep her gaze from drifting that some color crept back into her cheeks.

"I feared something was wrong, so I pulled my weapon and searched the house," she said. "It didn't take me long to find her back here in the bedroom. After that, I made my calls and secured the location."

Spenser nodded. "Good work, Lane. You did everything right."

She shook her head. "I mean, I knew this was going on— you've kept us in the loop about everything. But hearing about it and even seeing the pictures and reading the reports can't prepare you for actually seeing it for yourself."

"Nothing can prepare you for seeing something like this with your own two eyes. I've been to more crime scenes than I can count, and I still get shaken up when I see things like this. Don't beat yourself up about it, Lane. You've done well," she said.

"Thank you, Sheriff."

"Let's get out of here and let the techs do their thing."

"Yes, ma'am," Summers said, the look of relief on her face palpable.

Spenser led the young deputy out of the bedroom and away from the body. Arbery and his team were already standing in the living room waiting when they emerged from the back of the house. He looked at Spenser curiously.

"Body number two. And this woman suffered horribly," Spenser said. "I know you guys are always thorough, but please take your time with this one. No detail is too small, Dr. Arbery."

"Of course," he said without any trace of offense.

"Also, it looks like she was strangled with a rope or a belt maybe. I didn't see anything lying around—and honestly, I doubt whatever he used is in there to be found anyway—but just keep your eyes peeled. Just in case we get lucky," Spenser said.

"You have my word, Sheriff."

"Thank you, Dr. Arbery," she said. "And thank you also, Vanessa and Anthony."

"You're welcome, Sheriff," Anthony replied.

"You can thank us if we find something," Vanessa chimed in then headed for the bedroom.

"She takes her job very seriously," Arbery offered.

"And I appreciate that about her," Spenser replied. "You're training them well."

Arbery gave her a nod then picked up his kit and led Anthony to the back of the house. Spenser turned and walked out of the house with Summers right on her heels. They stepped off the porch then onto the yard and both drew a deep breath at the same time then let it out, as if cleansing the stench of death out of their lungs.

"I've never seen something like that before," Summers said. "I mean, I'm a policeman. I know I should expect it and shouldn't be shaken up like this, but—"

"Like I said inside, nothing can prepare you for seeing something like that. This is your first murder scene, Lane. Of course, you're going to be shaken up. What you're feeling is natural."

Spenser pursed her lips and looked away. She'd never thought of herself as very comforting or nurturing and didn't know how to alleviate what Summers was feeling. Coming face to face with evil could shake you to your core. Especially for the first time. Spenser had seen evil enough over the course of her career that she had become somewhat desensitized to it. But she saw the young deputy struggling and wanted to help her through it. If those feelings were allowed to take root and fester, it could leave deep scars. It might also drive Summers away from law enforcement entirely and Spenser thought the young woman had too much potential to allow it to happen.

"Take a moment to clear your head, Lane," Spenser said. "And just keep in mind that days like this are rare. This job isn't always having to face this sort of evil and destruction. We do a lot of good in this community and most days reflect that."

A few of her deputies were manning the tapeline, keeping curious neighbors on the other side of it. Standing front and center was Leigh Hart, a reporter for The Sweetwater Observer, their local daily newspaper—and somebody she had been ducking for days now. Hart was a talented and dogged reporter who was good at her job, which meant she was a thorn in Spenser's backside. Although Spenser had instituted a media blackout about the current case within the department, Hart's presence at the tapeline suggested that she'd tumbled onto it anyway.

She shook her head, looking miserable. "Why would somebody do something like this?"

Spenser thought about the scene inside. Specifically, she thought about the differences between Lia Rice's murder and Victoria Hall's. The level of brutality inflicted upon Lia was even greater than the savagery exacted upon Victoria. More than that, she was left in the middle of her bedroom floor rather than in a bathtub. As she recalled the condition of the body, Spenser realized Lia's hair was dry, suggesting to her that she hadn't been bathed. That realization, in turn, suggested that perhaps, he had either changed his MO—something she didn't think was likely— that he'd made a critical error, or that he hadn't sexually assaulted her.

As she put all these seemingly disparate pieces of the scene together in her mind, she replayed the elements of Lia Rice's scene, analyzing the similarities and differences from the others. From her years of experience, Spenser knew that crime scenes were confessions. They were letters from the perpetrators to law enforcement confessing all their sins. It was up to those whose job it was to analyze the scenes to decipher that confession and interpret what the UNSUB was trying to tell them.

"This was about rage. This was about getting even for his failures with Amanda," Spenser said. "This was our UNSUB sending us a message."

"What was he trying to tell us?"

"That he's not going to stop," Spenser said. "Until we stop him."

CHAPTER TWENTY-SEVEN

SPENSER PULLED INTO THE LOT AND LOOKED FOR A SPOT to park. EmComm Cable was a satellite storefront that sat in a squat, off-white cinderblock building on the edge of the parking lot of a strip mall in a shabby part of town. A small sign with the EmComm name and logo hung on the wall to the right of the glass front doors, but other than that, there was nothing else identifying it. Spenser guessed you just had to know it was there to find it.

Spenser found a spot and parked in front of a discount cigarette shop and a liquor store then climbed out of her Bronco. She looked around as she put her Stetson atop her head. She caught a couple of guys in their twenties standing outside of the smoke shop casting dark, uneasy looks her way as they puffed away on their cigarettes. This wasn't the "rough" side of town, per se, but there wasn't a lot of love lost between some of the people in the area and her deputies and there had been a couple of confrontations.

Spenser gave the two men a nod then turned and walked to the office. She pulled the door open and as she stepped inside, an electronic bell chimed. The interior of the office was as drab and uninspiring as the exterior. The walls were a pale, washed-out yellow and the linoleum underfoot was gray, dingy, and cracked. Three plastic chairs stood to Spenser's left, and EmComm advertising posters had been taped to the walls on both sides of the lobby area.

She stepped to a chest-high counter that stood across from the doors and waited for a couple of minutes. A bunch of literature and pamphlets were scattered across the surface of the counter along with a telephone and a computer terminal. Spenser drummed her fingers on the pamphlets.

"Hello?" she finally called out. "Sheriff's department. Anybody here?"

Country music flowed from an open door to the left in the wall behind the counter. The music was loud, which probably accounted for whoever was back there not hearing her come in. Tired of waiting, Spenser walked behind the counter and walked through the door that led to a hallway. She called out again as she passed a couple of empty offices but still got no response. As Spenser walked toward the open door at the end of the corridor, the music got louder and she caught the distinctive aroma of marijuana.

Spenser stepped through the door and into a service bay. There were several tall racks of shelves loaded up with all manner of parts and equipment needed for service calls. Through a wide roll-up door at the back of the building, she spotted three white panel vans with the EmComm logo on the sides. A man sat at a desk to her right—and obviously he didn't see her.

The man was leaning back in his chair, feet atop the desk, face turned up to the ceiling and Spenser watched as he took a deep drag off the joint pinched between his fingers. As he grooved along with the music, he blew a thick plume of smoke up to the ceiling. He looked like a man in a state of bliss without a care in the world.

"That smells like it was expensive," Spenser said.

He jumped up so quickly the chair clattered loudly to the concrete floor behind him. He dropped the joint in his hand and quickly stomped on it, doing his best to discreetly blow out the smoke he was holding.

"Sheriff," he said, his voice deep and gravelly. "Afternoon."

Spenser's first impression was that the man was massive. He was probably six-two and as wide as he was tall. He obviously spent a lot of time in the gym. The dirty blonde hair atop his head was wild and unkempt and matched the bushy beard that covered the lower half of his face. His eyes were a dazzling shade of green, but what immediately captured Spenser's attention was the large, colorful tattoo on his forearm.

As she gazed at the tattoo, Spenser felt her stomach lurch and a flutter pass through her heart. Could this be the man they were looking for? He matched the physical description, and he had the same tattoo, but Spenser had been in the presence of killers and rapists before and he just wasn't putting off that vibe. She wasn't getting that kind of hit off him. That didn't mean he wasn't their guy, but her gut was telling her that despite the similarities, he wasn't. The tattoo on his forearm, though, meant that he very well might know him.

"H-how can I help you, Sheriff? Need some help with service? I can hook you up with some service down at your office—free of charge, of course," he stammered.

Spenser tried to act casually but let her hand drift closer to her Glock. Since she didn't think this was her UNSUB, she didn't expect there to be any trouble, but she'd been wrong before. It was better to be safe than sorry.

"What's your name?" she asked.

"Dave Peck," he replied. "I'm the manager of the office here."

"Dave, I'm investigating a series of very serious crimes and we've learned that each of the victims in these cases had a service call just a few days prior to the event," Spenser said.

"Are you talking about the rapes and murders I been reading about in the paper?"

"Frankly, yes."

He shook his head. "There's no way any of my guys are good for these, Sheriff."

"I appreciate you wanting to stand by your guys, but I'm going to be making those investigative determinations," Spenser said. "Now, I need to get the names of the service techs—"

He ran a hand through his scraggly hair and shook his head. "Let me stop you right there, Sheriff," he said. "I don't mean to be a problem, but I can't go giving out the personal information of my employees."

"Dave, this is a murder investigation."

"And I'm sympathetic to that, but my corporate policy is clear about giving out the personal details of our employees," he said. "Now, if you'd like the number for somebody up at corporate HQ in Seattle, I'd be happy to give that to you."

"Uh yeah, I don't think you quite understand—"

The man folded his massive arms across his equally massive chest with a frown. He looked like a man preparing to dig in... which wasn't a good sign for Spenser since she knew he was right. She couldn't compel him to turn over private information. Not without a warrant. And she wouldn't get that warrant without probable cause—something she was sorely lacking in. He seemed to know that and was getting a little bolder and more obstinate as a result.

"I do understand, Sheriff. But I also understand my rights," he said, his voice as firm as his posture. "You can't compel me to give you privileged information without a warrant. At least, not according to the Fourth Amendment anyway."

"When did everybody around here become constitutional scholars?" she muttered then decided to switch tracks. "Your tattoo."

"What about it?"

"You belong to a group called the Silver Bullets, right? Used to hang out at the Full Metal Shooting Range?" she asked.

The cocky grin on his face faltered but he quickly tried to hide it. The effect wasn't what he'd intended as his grin looked more sickly than cocky.

"Yeah? So?"

"There is no constitutional protection for social groups," Spenser said. "Our suspect is a member of your group and I'd like to ask him a few questions—"

He shook his head. "I'm afraid I can't tell you what you want to know."

"As I just told you, there is no constitutional protection."

"No, there's not. But I have a moral obligation to protect my brothers from authoritarian overreach. I can't let you persecute one of my brothers in arms."

Spenser stared at him in consternation for a moment. "Brothers in arms? You're not in the military and there is no war going on, Mr. Peck."

"There's always a war going on in this country, Sheriff. A war between those who want to take our freedoms and those of us who want to protect them."

"Mr. Peck, what you're doing isn't as grandiose as you think—"

"But it is, Sheriff. Some of us aren't willing to sit back and do nothing while the government encroaches on our rights and freedoms. Some of us are willing to do something about it."

"So, let me get this straight… you're willing to go to jail to protect a rapist and murderer?"

He looked at her with a perplexed expression on his face. "Jail? What did I do?" he asked. "I didn't do anything."

"Smoking marijuana in public view is a crime, Mr. Peck," Spenser said. "That also gives me probable cause to search this shop. And I have a sneaking suspicion I'm going to find more than the ounce of pot you're legally allowed to possess. What do you think?"

"This is garbage. And this is exactly the type of overreach me and my brothers are fighting against. You're trying to squeeze me with this trumped-up crap to get me to give you what you want," he said, his voice hard. "It ain't going to work, Sheriff."

"All you have to do is give me a name. One name."

SHADOWS OF THE FALLS

He raised his chin, the light of defiance gleaming in his eyes as he remained silent. Spenser knew she might well be giving him what he wanted by making him a martyr for his "cause." Taking him in might be a badge of honor. But she'd known plenty of tough guys like Peck who acted hard outside, but once the cell door closed, they started bawling like babies and singing like canaries. Spenser was hoping against all hope that he was the latter.

"Please put your hands behind your back, Mr. Peck," Spenser said. "You're under arrest."

CHAPTER TWENTY-EIGHT

"I'M GOING TO PICK UP SOME DINNER THEN I NEED TO swing by the cabin to grab a couple of things," Spenser said into her phone. "Any requests for dinner?"

"You're going to laugh."

"I might. But you shouldn't let that deter you."

Ryker laughed on the other end of the line. "Very kind of you."

After getting Dave Peck booked in on possession charges, she'd called it a day. She'd made sure to book him in late enough in the day that a public defender wouldn't be available, forcing him to spend the night in a cell. He remained willful and defiant, refusing to give up the name of his buddy in the Silver Bullets. It was frustrating. Maddening. The fact that his friend was very likely a serial rapist and killer and it didn't move him enough to give her a name made her sick.

His loyalty to his friends and their "cause" might be admirable in any other situation but not this one. Not while women were being assaulted and murdered. Spenser had spoken with the DA and had even called a judge she knew and was friendly with, but they both told her they were sorry, but couldn't sign off on a warrant for the employee records. She didn't have enough to meet the threshold for probable cause.

She knew they were going to say that before she'd even made the calls. But Spenser was hoping they might bend the rules a little bit for her once they knew the details of the case she was trying to make. Now, with their refusal to sign off on a warrant, the only hope she had was to flip Dave Peck and get him to roll on whomever he was protecting. She hoped that a night in a cell and the stark reality of doing some jail time might help to loosen his tongue.

If it didn't, Spenser wasn't sure what she was going to do. She'd had the thought to stake out the cable company and see who came and went, sizing up every single employee to see who matched the physical description and was a potential member of the Silver Bullets. It wasn't a guarantee he worked for Emcomm—the cable company's connection to all the victims was still a theory. But it seemed likely. Knowing that, staking out the company might be the only choice she had.

"Okay, so what are you in the mood for?" she asked.

"I'm craving some of that lo mein and shrimp egg rolls from Jade Panda," he said.

"Oh, well, look who I've made a convert."

"Yeah, I suppose you have."

"Done," Spenser said. "You never have to twist my arm to get Chinese food."

"Good to know. I'll keep that in mind," he replied.

As she walked into the department's parking lot, Spenser switched the phone to her other ear. She unlocked the Bronco then opened the door. She tossed her bag onto the passenger seat and her hat on top of that then turned and leaned against the vehicle as she watched the cars passing by. The sun was setting and the world around her was already thick with gloomy shadows as day gave way to night and edged quickly toward full dark.

"How is Annabelle doing? Did she behave herself today?"

"Of course, she did," Ryker said. "She always does."

"I appreciate you babysitting for me."

"You never have to thank me," he replied. "Having her around does as much for me and Mocha as it helps you out."

A large black pickup rumbled down the street, its engine loud and throaty. As the sound of the truck waned and plunged the world into silence, a strange, foreboding feeling settled down over Spenser's shoulders. Her skin tingled and the hair on the back of her neck stood on end. She turned around, peering through the pools of shadow that surrounded her, positive she'd find somebody staring back at her. She was certain somebody was watching her.

"Spense? You there?"

Ryker's voice cut through the eerie feeling that gripped her and snapped her back to the present. She gave herself a shake but continued searching the shadows around her, unable to dismiss the sensation of having eyes on her.

"Yeah, I'm here," she said slowly. "Anyway, okay, so lo mein and shrimp egg rolls?"

"Yes, please," he said.

"Mongolian beef?"

"If you're so inclined, I wouldn't say no."

"Well, that's good to know," she said with a laugh. "Okay, I'm heading over to pick up the food now and then I'm going to grab a few things. I'll be at your place in thirty?"

"Great. I'll set the table and keep an eye out," he said.

The hair on the back of her neck remained standing on end and her skin tingled like tendrils of electricity were crawling all over it. She kept her eyes moving, trying to search out the source of her unease. But she still found nothing and nobody and started to think that maybe this case was just deep under her skin and making her paranoid.

"Alright. See you soon," she said.

Spenser pulled the Bronco to a stop in front of her cabin then jumped out. Her stomach rumbled as she walked up the stairs to the porch and pulled her keys out to unlock the door. The Bronco was filled with the aroma of the Chinese food she'd picked up. She was hungry and ready to eat. Spenser had just put the key in the lock when she felt the presence behind her. When the wooden tread on the staircase behind her squeaked, a shot of white-hot adrenaline surged through Spenser's veins.

In one fluid motion, Spenser dropped her keyring and spun around. She reached for her Glock but was instead, driven backward, the breath exploding from her lungs as a fist smashed into her belly. Spenser's head bounced off her door as she was slammed into it by the force of the blow. Before she could recover, another hard fist crashed into the side of her face. Her vision wavered, stars burst behind her eyes, and Spenser's mouth filled with the coppery taste of her own blood.

The blow dropped Spenser to her hands and knees. She tried to scramble away but she let out a sharp yelp of pain as a heavy boot was driven into her side. It practically lifted her off the ground and she was driven into the front wall of her cabin again. Spenser lay crumpled in a heap, her vision wavering, wheezing, and gasping for breath. She managed to turn her head enough to see the man standing over her. He was dressed in black from head to toe and all she could see were his eyes. Eyes she knew would be green. They glittered darkly and crinkled up at the corners in a way that told her he was smiling beneath the balaclava.

"You think you're so smart," he said, his voice a harsh whisper.

Even though he was taking pains to disguise his voice—and even though her ears were ringing—there was something familiar about it. She tried racking her mind but was in rough shape and couldn't hold a coherent thought. She rolled onto her side, looking up at the massive man standing over her. He looked down at her and Spenser could practically smell the bloodlust wafting off him as he considered her. As he reveled in the thought of killing her.

As Spenser watched, he reached into one of the deep pockets of his tactical pants and pulled out a length of rope. He'd brought his weapon with him, just like she'd thought. He was evolving. Spenser winced in pain as she drew in a deep breath. She didn't think he'd broken any ribs when he kicked her but she was sure he'd bruised the hell out of them.

"Why are you—"

"Killing you now?" he asked.

She nodded.

"Because it's time to end this game," he said. "I've proven what I needed to prove."

"And what was that?" she asked.

"That I am smarter than you," he said. "And that you are unfit for your office."

He continued to speak in that forced, harsh whisper, still doing his best to disguise his voice. She didn't know why, given that he intended to kill her. But maybe he just wanted to keep his identity a mystery, even all the way to her grave.

"Is that what you think you proved?" Spenser croaked. "From where I am, all you proved is that you're a disgusting piece of filth. A rapist and a murderer."

"I would say you've got time to think about your role in all that, but, well… you don't. This ends tonight because there's no sense in continuing to play this game with you. Not when I've already won."

"You haven't won," Spenser said. "You may kill me, but my people will keep hunting you. And they won't stop until you're either in a cell or in the ground."

His laughter was low and hoarse. It wasn't as ominous sounding as it was when she'd heard his laughter shot through his voice modulator, but it was still a creepy sound.

"They can hunt me all they want, and I'll bury each and every one of them," he replied. "The same way they're going to have to bury you."

"Your arrogance is your weakness."

"Well, it seems as if we share a weakness then," he said. "But, enough of this chit-chat. It's time for you to die since I've got other things to do."

The man knelt down beside her, his eyes gleaming with a murderous light. With each end of the rope wrapped around one of his hands, he reached forward to press it to her throat, intending to strangle her. When he drew close enough, Spenser summoned her strength and threw her head forward as hard as she could. She grunted in satisfaction when she felt his nose buckle and heard him let out a pained yelp. The man stumbled backward, hitting the wooden porch with a thunderous thud when he came down hard on his backside.

Her head still ringing, Spenser jumped to her feet and launched herself forward. She delivered a vicious kick that caught the man in the side of his head. The momentum of the blow knocked the man over, sending him bounding down the steps and sprawling in the dirt of the driveway. Pressing her advantage, Spenser followed him down the steps, ready to deliver another kick, but the man recovered enough that he grabbed her foot with one hand and threw a wild punch that caught her in the side of the knee, drawing a pained scream from her.

Spenser staggered back a few steps, her knee throbbing as badly as her head. The man was back on his feet already and charging at Spenser. For such a large man, he was disturbingly quick and nimble. She caught the dull gleam of the blade in his hand a moment before it was cutting a murderous arc through the air. She jumped backward but felt a line of fire erupt along her belly as the edge of the blade left a shallow furrow across the flesh of her belly. Blood, thick and tacky, spilled down her torso, the pain making her grimace.

She didn't have time to catalog her wounds as the man was already pressing his attack. Spenser dodged it but not quickly enough. The edge of the blade bit into her upper arm, sending another cascade of blood flowing down her skin. Her body sang with pain, and she was growing lightheaded from the agony she was in combined with the blood loss. Spenser knew if she didn't do something to create some separation between them soon, he was going to make good on his promise to kill her.

The man waded in again, the edge of his blade slick and dark with her blood. He cocked his arm back, ready to deliver another wicked slice, this one aimed at her torso again, but Spenser anticipated it. She spun to the side, narrowly avoiding the edge of his knife. His momentum carried him past her. Spenser pistoned her leg out, driving into the side of his knee, making it buckle. The man screamed in surprise and pain as he dropped to the dirt.

Moving as quickly as she could, Spenser stumbled away, creating some distance between them. She pulled her Glock and turned to find the man already getting to his feet again. Her eyes focused on the long, serrated blade in his hand, transfixed by the dark blood coating the edge of it. As the man started toward her again, Spenser raised her weapon and fired. She watched the man's body jerk as the bullet punched into him—she couldn't tell exactly where it hit him, but the man spun around like a top.

Before she could squeeze off another shot, the man cocked his arm back and launched the knife at her. She watched it slicing through the air toward her, turning end over end, hilt over blade. The throw was true, and Spenser had to throw herself to the side to avoid having it pierce her body. She hit the ground with a grunt, the impact of it rocking her and sending a bright, white light of pain coursing through her.

Laying on her side, Spenser raised her Glock and fired off several more shots. They were off the mark. But they did force the man to turn and run as fast as his legs would carry him. She watched as he disappeared into the shadows of the woods that surrounded her cabin. Spenser felt herself wavering, growing more lightheaded with every passing second. Dropping the weapon, she fished into her pocket and pulled out her cell phone.

Her heart racing and her stomach churning, she fumbled with her phone. She finally managed to press the first name that came up in her contacts list then pressed the phone to her ear. She heard the line ring once and then twice. Her eyes were growing heavy, her body felt cold, and she was suddenly feeling exhausted.

"Spense, what's up?" Marley asked on the other end of the line.

"Mar," she gasped. "I need help, Mar."

CHAPTER TWENTY-NINE

"Marley is right, Spenser," Ryker said. "You need to let her take you to the hospital. You need to get a thorough check-up and let her properly tend to your wounds."

Spenser shook her head. "No, just patch me up. I'm fine."

"You're not fine," Marley argued. "Ryker found you face down in the dirt. You're a bloody, cut up mess who's been beat to hell, Spense. You might have a concussion or some other internal injuries I can't diagnose in Ryker's living room."

"I don't have a concussion or any other internal injuries."

"Uh-huh. So, you ran yourself through an MRI machine before I got here? Also, where did you get your medical degree from again?" Marley quipped.

"I've got some bumps and bruises and I'm sore from head to toe, but all things considered, I've had worse beatings," Spenser said lightly.

"Not funny," Marley said. "You were barely conscious when I got here."

Spenser remembered calling Marley, but things got blurry after that. She knew she'd passed out at some point but realized she couldn't have been out for very long. Spenser had woken up in Ryker's place and Marley had arrived shortly after that. She remembered him telling her that when he heard the gunshots, he'd come running and found her where she'd fallen. Her phone was still lying open on the ground and Ryker saw she'd called Marley and had quickly called her back. She was already en route, so he'd told her what happened and to meet at his place.

After she'd gotten to Ryker's, Marley had tended to her wounds. Spenser didn't remember a lot of what happened but knew she'd drifted in and out of consciousness. Her body was a mass of aches and pains, cuts and bruises, and she'd had trouble holding onto a cohesive thought at first. But eventually, the pain dulled slightly. It went from a raging roar to a quiet shout, allowing Spenser to come back to herself and once she'd come back to her senses, she'd fought them about going to the hospital. Spenser knew if she gave in and let them take her to the hospital, she wasn't going to be getting out again for at least a few days… and she didn't have time for that.

"How did this happen?" Marley asked.

"I stopped at the cabin to grab a few things. He was there waiting for me. Got the drop on me," Spenser replied tightly.

She was angry with herself for allowing him to sneak up on her like that. Angry with herself for not being more aware of her surroundings. She preached that simple lesson to all her deputies—always be aware and always keep your eyes moving. Policing was a dangerous business these days, so it was something she told them during roll call almost every single day—stay on your toes and be aware of your surroundings. She always harped on them about it, telling her deputies to never let themselves get complacent. Yet, that's exactly what she'd done.

It embarrassed Spenser that she got caught out not practicing what she preached—or maybe it was because of that specifically—but it somehow made things even more personal for Spenser. She'd gotten complacent and that man had come to her home. He'd tried to kill her at her home. The fires of her determination to find and end him, one way or another, already burning brightly, exploded with a fury she'd seldom known in her life.

"Spenser, I think you need to go to the hospital," Ryker said. "You need to be smart about this. This is your health."

A wry grin curled her lips as she gestured to the IV bags of blood and antibiotics hanging on a stand next to the recliner she was sitting in.

"I don't need to. The hospital came to me," she replied.

"Yeah, well, you get yourself into trouble so often, I've had no choice but to put together a ready bag just in case," Marley said.

"See? All good," Spenser replied.

"No, not all good," Marley said, her tone hard. "This isn't normal, Spense. I'm not a mobile medical clinic and you need treatment in an actual hospital."

"You're the best doctor I know—"

"I'm the only doctor you know," she countered.

"That's not true. I know Dr. Hedges."

"She's your gynecologist."

"Well, the point remains, I trust you to patch me up and get me back into the fight."

Spenser saw Marley exchange a frustrated and worried look with Ryker. He shrugged. There wasn't much he could say because his feelings about hospitals were roughly the same as hers.

"Look, I appreciate your concern. And I appreciate your help," she said. "But the cuts feel like they're pretty superficial and other than that, I took a few punches. I don't need to be in a hospital bed for those to heal up."

"No, but you should stay out of the fight, so they actually do heal up instead of running around and letting whoever did this to you get a crack at finishing the job," she said.

"Marley is a trained professional, Spenser. You should listen to her," Ryker noted.

Marley sighed and shook her head. "Sure, the cuts aren't super deep, but you did still lose a lot of blood. I stitched them up, but they could break open again and if that happens, you're going to be right back in this same boat."

"Okay, tell me this. Are any of my injuries life-threatening right now?"

"Technically not. Not at the moment," she started. "But you never know when—"

"Okay, good. Then there's no need for me to go to the hospital."

Marley let out a frustrated growl. She was always a little overcautious and protective of Spenser. It wasn't that she didn't appreciate it and wasn't thankful for the care she always provided, but she had a job to do.

"Is there any way I can get you to reconsider coming to the hospital with me?" Marley asked.

"I'm sorry, but I've got a killer to catch—a killer who has now attacked both me and Amanda in addition to all the others. And he's not going to stop until I stop him," Spenser replied. "The last time he tried and failed to kill Amanda, he went after another woman and tore her apart. I fear what he's going to do now that he's tried and failed to kill me since, for whatever reason, I'm the actual object of his rage."

"You're not going to be doing anybody any favors if you get yourself killed because you're too banged up to do your job well," Marley said.

"And I'm not going to be doing my job at all if I hide in a hospital either," Spenser argued. "This man is going to kill somebody else if I don't stop him. My wounds getting worse isn't a guarantee. Him murdering another woman is."

Marley frowned. "Spense, you've got an entire department at your disposal—"

"And none of them know this man or this case like I do," Spenser cut her off.

"You need to learn to trust your deputies," Marley argued.

"I do trust them."

"Only to a point—"

"Marley, we're never going to be able to talk her out of this. She's too hard headed to listen to reason and common sense," Ryker said.

She sighed and ran a hand over her face. "Yeah, I'm getting that."

"Good. I'm glad we're finally all on the same page," Spenser said.

"I wouldn't go that far," Marley said.

"We *are* on the same page," Ryker said. "That's why I'm going to be shadowing you."

"Shadowing me?"

"Consider me your new partner," he said.

"Ryker, you're not a deputy—"

"You can deputize me. Or not. It doesn't matter. I'm going where you go," he said. "And if you refuse, then I'll carry you down to the hospital and put you in restraints to keep you there myself. Those are your choices. Decide."

Spenser groaned as she looked from Ryker to Marley. She shrugged and offered Spenser a lopsided grin. She sighed. It wasn't the perfect solution. But it was a solution that would get them off her back. Plus, as much as Spenser hated to admit it, having somebody trained to kill as efficiently as Ryker watching her back would make her feel a bit better. Not that she needed it. Spenser was well-trained and capable of taking care of herself.

"Fine," Spenser said. "Consider yourself my shadow."

CHAPTER THIRTY

Spenser pulled to a stop outside of Victoria Hall's house. It was still taped off as it was still an active crime scene. Her fiancé had taken up residence in one of the hotels in town and had made himself available for questions, although he hadn't provided any new information. He was still an absolute wreck, though he seemed to be holding up better than she'd anticipated he would. He was holding up better than she had after her husband's murder.

She parked the Bronco and got out, taking a couple of moments to look up and down the street as she settled her gun belt on her hips. Spenser carefully eyeballed the cars parked along the street, searching for anybody sitting there watching her. Anybody who looked like they didn't belong. After failing so badly at it, Spenser was making sure to keep an eye on and be aware of her surroundings. She wasn't going to let herself be complacent, nor would she let anybody get the drop on her again. Some lessons were tough to learn. But they were necessary.

Ryker settled his jacket on his shoulders as he walked around the truck and Spenser caught a glimpse of the holster sitting on his hip. She looked at him with an expression of consternation on her face.

"I told you not to come armed," she said. "You're not one of my deputies."

"No, but I do have a concealed carry license," he replied smoothly.

Spenser sighed. "Just… don't pull your gun. Please. You'll create a hell of a lot of paperwork for me if you shoot somebody."

"I make no promises," he said, his expression deadpan.

Spenser eyed him closely. "I can't tell if you're joking right now or not."

"I guess we'll find out," he said.

"Don't make me regret bringing you along."

"You act like you had a choice."

"Fair point," she muttered. "Come on then. Let's get this over with."

Spenser and Ryker headed up the walk. She opened the door and pulled the tape down, allowing Ryker to walk in ahead of her. Her hand on her Glock, Spenser followed him in. She quickly swept the room, looking in all the nooks, crannies, and pockets of shadow, making sure it was clear. It was. She heard Ryker moving through the back of the house. A couple of minutes later, he walked out, slipping his weapon back into his holster.

"The rest of the house is clear," he said.

She hadn't expected it to be otherwise, but Spenser still let out a silent breath of relief as the muscles in her shoulders relaxed.

"So? What are we doing here?" he asked.

"We are here because I'm hoping that Victoria Hall was as Type-A as we all thought she was," Spenser replied.

"What do you mean?"

Spenser briefly filled him in on their working theory about the cable repairman being their rapist and murderer. Dave Peck was still choosing to remain silent on the matter, so she was moving forward with his prosecution on possession charges. She hoped that as the process started to play out, he might have a change of heart, particularly with having found over 40 grams, a felony conviction was a real possibility. At that point, it wasn't looking likely, but she was going to let it run its course one way or the other.

Regardless of whether he talked or not, the bust was righteous, and she was feeling vindictive since he had the chance to help stop a killer and declined. He chose to hide behind his so-called beliefs and his loyalty to his so-called brothers, so Spenser was going to see to it that he did a little time. Let him call it an overreach. Let him call it persecution by the government. Let him say that his arrest and prosecution were proof of his "cause" and justified his beliefs. Spenser no longer cared what happened to him.

Of course, since she hadn't been able to secure Peck's cooperation, that meant she needed to find another way to get the information she needed. It was while she was looking at the accordion file she kept her bills in, though, that she had an idea. Recognizing that like their UNSUB's victims, Spenser had some anal-retentive tendencies of her own, she had the thought that they too might keep their bills well-organized and filed for easy access.

"So, you think they might have kept the service paperwork with the technician's name on it," Ryker said. "That's a brilliant thought."

"It's only brilliant if we find what we're looking for."

"Nah. Whether it works out or not, it's a great idea," he replied. "The question is, where might she have kept her bills?"

"If I were a betting woman, I'd say they're most likely in her home office," Spenser said.

"Let's go take a look," he said.

Ryker followed Spenser to the back of the house and into the spare bedroom she'd converted into her home office. Like the rest of the house, the office was clean and well-organized. A metal-framed, glass-top table sat in the center of the room. It held a computer, a telephone, some papers, a cup filled with pens, and a day planner. A pair of plants suspended from the ceiling flanked her desk, soaking in plenty of sunlight from the large, picture window behind her desk. The walls to the left and the right of the room held a bookcase and two tall, four-drawer metal file cabinets making the room perfectly balanced and symmetrical.

"You take the file cabinets on the left and I take the right?" Spenser asked.

"Sounds good."

"We're looking for her bills," Spenser said. "If I know this victim as well as I do, she's going to have her files marked and probably alphabetized."

"Got it."

"Okay, let's hit it."

Spenser moved to the cabinets on the right as Ryker went left and they silently got to work. The first few drawers Spenser rifled through contained work-related things as well as some personal items. She got through the entire first cabinet without finding anything relevant then moved on to the next cabinet and squatted down, pulling open the bottom drawer first. She methodically worked her way up to the top drawer then grinned.

"Bingo," she said.

"You got something?"

"I do," she said. "Just as I thought, all her bills are perfectly organized."

Ryker stepped over to where she was as Spenser pulled out the file marked "Emcomm." Inside was a collection of bills dating back three years as well as half a dozen sheets of pink papers from service calls over that same period. Spenser pulled out the most recent one and looked at the signature of the technician on the bottom line. It was a scrawling, chicken scratch of a signature that was completely illegible. She'd seen doctors who signed their names more legibly.

"Dammit," Spenser muttered.

"Well, that's real helpful," Ryker said. "It's almost like he signed it that poorly on purpose."

"He's smart. It wouldn't surprise me if he did," she replied.

Spenser studied the signature on the sheet closely for several long moments, gnawing on her bottom lip as she stared at it. Despite it being all but illegible, it still set a few bells ringing in the back of her mind.

"What is it?" Ryker asked.

"The signature… It's familiar," she said. "I know I've seen it before."

"Seen it? Where?"

She shook her head. "I don't know. But I know I've seen it before."

"Are you sure?"

She nodded. "Yeah. I just… I can't remember where."

Spenser racked her brain but couldn't place it and it was driving her nuts. But she knew that if she let it percolate in the back of her mind, she would eventually come to the answer she sought. At least, she hoped that would be the case.

"Come on," Spenser said. "We need to go by the other victims' houses and see about getting their cable service records."

"I'm at your disposal."

Together, they walked through the house then out onto the porch. Spenser took a moment to lock the door and restring the tape across it before they headed back down the walk toward the Bronco. Spenser saw the white panel van a few doors down a moment before she saw the barrel of the rifle extend out the window. A blast of adrenaline flooded her system as her heart raced.

"Gun!" she screamed.

Spenser threw herself into Ryker, driving him to the ground a moment before the thunderous crash of gunfire erupted. Two, three, then four shots cut through the air they'd occupied just a moment before. A pause in the gunfire gave Spenser the time to pull her Glock as she got to a knee. She squeezed off a pair of shots that tore through the side of the van as its tires squealed on the pavement a moment before it rocketed off.

The van tore by them on the street and she only got a glimpse of the man behind the wheel. He was wearing a black balaclava, only allowing her to see his eyes as he sped away. She looked down at Ryker who was just sitting up. It was a bold attack. Bolder than anything he'd done to that point. Firing on them in broad daylight like that meant that she'd rattled him. Had put him back on his heels so much that he was willing to do something desperate to eliminate the threat to him.

"Are you okay?" she asked.

"Yeah, I'm good," he replied. "You?"

"Fine."

"That was a hell of a tackle. If this whole sheriffing thing doesn't work out for you, I think you might have a future as a free safety," he said.

"Yeah, I think I'll stick with this. The money's not as good, but on the plus side, people shoot at me fairly regularly."

"You're a sick woman, Spenser Song," he said.

"It's all part of my charm."

"Or something," he said. "What was that, anyway?"

"That was him sending me another message."

"And what's his message?"

"That we're getting close to him ... too close for his liking."

CHAPTER THIRTY-ONE

S PENSER LOOKED AT THE PAGES IN HER HAND AGAIN AND sighed. She threw them down on the table with a frustrated growl. After the incident out at Victoria Hall's house, she came back to the office, and only after extracting everything but a blood oath that she would call him if she was heading out did Ryker agree to give her a little space. It wasn't that she didn't appreciate his concern. She very much did. But she found it hard to function when somebody was looking over her shoulder.

Applause erupted in the bullpen, drawing Spenser's attention. She stood up from the table in the war room and walked to the door to see Young walking alongside her brother. She was using a crutch and moving slowly, but she was getting along. The rest of the deputies out in the bullpen were cheering her return, patting her on the back as she passed, and shouting their welcome backs. Young's face was bright red and though she looked embarrassed by the attention, the wide smile on her face told Spenser she was enjoying it as well.

Leaning on her crutch, Young made her way through the gauntlet of well-wishers then walked over to the doorway of the war room and stopped, looking Spenser up and down with an expression of concern. Spenser's face still bore the marks of the beating she took at the hands of their UNSUB and Young's look was pointed. Jacob slipped into the war room behind them, preferring to stay out of the middle.

"And just what in the hell do you think you're doing here?" Spenser asked.

"My job," she replied.

"I thought I told you to take some time off."

"Yeah, well, I figured if you could be in the office after taking a beating and almost getting yourself killed, I could, too," Young said. "I mean, you do set the example around here."

"I gave you an order," Spenser said.

"Did you, though?"

"Amanda—"

"Look, I heard what was going on—what happened to you specifically—and I wanted to help," she said. "I may not be good to go for fieldwork yet, but I can at least help work the case by using my brain."

"But would that really help?" Jacob called from behind them.

"Stuff it, big brother," she said then turned to Spenser. "I'm going stir crazy at home, Sheriff. I need to do something. Anything. Please."

Spenser sighed and tried to balance her thoughts between letting Young help and sending her home. Yes, it was hypocritical of her to demand Young stay in bed to heal while she was back in the office the day after taking her beating. But she was the boss. She wasn't there to be a role model. She was there to do her job and hunt down bad guys and put them away.

But she could use Young's big brain on this. For the last couple of days, she'd been trying to remember where she'd seen the signature on the cable service forms. And for the last couple of days, she'd continued to come up empty. Spenser had even tried getting Jacob to work some magic with his computer, hoping they'd find the signature online somehow. But that proved to be as fruitful as her own endeavors.

"All right," Spenser relented. "But you're not to leave the war room. You're here for your brain and your brain alone. Got it?"

"You are going to be so disappointed," Jacob cracked.

"Stuff it," Spenser and Young said in unison.

"Thank you, Sheriff," Young said. "And yes, I got it. I'm here in mind and not body."

"All right."

Young crutched her way into the conference room and took up her usual position. Jacob slid the donut box over to her and Amanda picked out an old-fashioned chocolate then set it on a napkin and sat back in her seat. She took a bite of her donut then washed it down with a long swallow of coffee. It was a small, simple thing, but Spenser, for one, was glad to have that small touch of normalcy back in the office. It seemed far too long since they'd had that.

"So, you got jumped and then shot at in broad daylight," Young said. "Things have been exciting while I've been away, it seems."

"They've been something," Spenser replied. "That he fired on us like that shows that he's starting to panic. That he's starting to get sloppy."

"Or just more brazen," Young said. "It could be that he's developed a sense of invincibility and he's not afraid."

"If that was the case, he wouldn't have worn his mask or fired on us from a distance," Spenser replied. "He would have just walked up, sans mask, and shot it out with us. It *was* brazen, though."

Young considered it a moment then nodded. "Yeah, I can see that. That makes sense," she said, then after a moment added, "this is getting absolutely nuts."

"Which is why we need to shut him down as soon as possible," Spenser replied. "The more frustrated and desperate he gets, the more dangerous he is."

"Okay, so to that end, what do we have? Where are we at?"

"For now, we're still nowhere. Our UNSUB's buddy and fellow member of the Silver Bullets, Dave Peck, is still in lockup. I've been slow-walking things but I can't drag it out forever," Spenser said. "He's scheduled to be arraigned the day after tomorrow on those possession charges I booked him in on. I keep hoping that as he gets closer to a felony conviction and the real possibility of significant jail time, he'll crack. But he seems intent on playing the martyr. He wants to be known as a casualty of their cause and a victim of government overreach."

"I wish I could say that's going to change and that he'll eventually flip," Young said. "But guys like him are nothing, if not committed to their beliefs. I've seen these clowns doing their thing my entire life. If it's not the Silver Bullets, it's another group like them."

"Most of these groups use episodes like this to fundraise," Jacob said. "Here, take a look."

He tapped a few keys and the monitor on the wall lit up, showing them a GoFundMe page set up by the Silver Bullets ostensibly for Peck's legal expenses. Donations had come in from across the country and totaled more than ten thousand dollars to that point.

"So, if they're raising funds for an attorney to fight these charges, why is he still using a public defender? Young asked.

"Because it's nothing more than a cash grab," Spenser said. "You see it all the time. Peck's legal situation is nothing but a way to grift for the group."

"The guy who set it up is probably going to use the money to buy a car or something," Jacob mused. "But I guarantee that money isn't going to Peck's defense."

"Classy group," Young said. "Anyway, do we have anything else?"

Spenser shook her head. "I went by and spoke with each of the living victims. I got copies of the service records. It looks to me like the same technician serviced each of the houses, but the signature on the form is illegible," Spenser said. "All I got from the forms is the employee ID number, but I spoke to the judge and DA again and they tell me I don't have enough to compel EmComm to turn over their employee lists. So, unless we can magically decipher the chicken scratch that is this guy's signature, we're still dead in the water."

Young reached over, grabbed the copies of the service records, and started to flip through them. Jacob was staring at the GoFundMe page still up on the screen. He was scrutinizing it closely, a strange expression on his face.

"Take a look at the name of the person who organized the GoFundMe," he said.

Spenser's eyes drifted to the name of the organizer and when she saw it, they immediately grew wide with her surprise.

"No," she said in a whisper. "I thought he left the state after…"

Spenser's voice trailed off as the pieces of the puzzle started snapping into place. The picture in her mind was complete and the opacity was gone. She suddenly knew who their UNSUB was and wanted to kick herself for not having seen what was staring her right in the face all this time.

"Oh my God," Young exclaimed.

Spenser quickly turned to see Young staring at the pages in her hand intently.

"What is it?" Spenser asked.

She looked up at Spenser, waving the copies of the service forms she was holding. Her expression morphed from one of surprise to one of near-manic glee.

"I know who this is," she exclaimed. "I know who this technician is, which means I know who our UNSUB is… and I can't believe I didn't think of him sooner."

"So do I," Spenser said. "And I can't believe I didn't either."

CHAPTER THIRTY-TWO

SPENSER STARED THROUGH THE WINDSHIELD OF THE Bronco. They were partially hidden by a tree line at the edge of a field of tall, unkempt grass that stirred in a gentle breeze. On the other side of the grass, about fifty yards from her, was a dirt lot that was filled with cars in various states of repair and decay. There were stacks of old tires, a plethora of parts, and a wide variety of other junk. It looked to Spenser like a DIY junkyard… a graveyard where projects were started and ended up being left to rot unfinished and in pieces.

And in the center of all the debris and half-finished projects was a trailer. It looked to be about thirty years old and, though dingy and dirty, was still in somewhat good repair. The trailer, unlike the various projects that surrounded it, hadn't yet given up hope of being something better. Or at least, it was hanging on and trying to keep itself from getting any worse.

"Isn't Ryker going to murder you for not calling him? I thought he was supposed to be glued to your hip," Young asked.

"He's a civilian and this is a tactical op," Spenser replied. "He can't be here."

"Yeah, he's going to be pissed. I wouldn't want to—"

"How did you know it was him?" Spenser asked.

"Changing the subject?"

"Damn right I am," Spenser said.

"Fine. It was the signature on those forms. Barton Carpenter was my training officer and I saw it on all my eval reports—most of them with scathing commentary about what a piss-poor deputy I was and how I was unfit for duty. So, yeah, I'd know his signature just about anywhere," Young replied. "I just can't believe it took me this long to put it all together. I mean—"

Spenser watched the trailer ahead of them closely, searching for any sign of movement. She saw none. But that didn't mean he wasn't in there hunkered down. The white panel van he'd used to shoot at her and Ryker was parked around the side, barely concealed from sight. It was like he wasn't even trying to hide the fact that he was there and daring them to come in and get him.

"Don't beat yourself up, I should have seen it earlier as well based on physical description alone. And that's not even counting the arrogance—it was all right there, and I just didn't see it," Spenser said. "The last I heard, Carpenter was in Montana. I got a call from a sheriff in some small town out there asking for a reference for Carpenter."

"Did you give one?"

Spenser nodded. "I did. I figured he was better off as somebody else's problem. And I honestly haven't given him a thought since."

Barton Carpenter had been one of the holdovers from the previous regime when Spenser took over as sheriff. He was a Howard Hinton loyalist and had been groomed for the big chair. Carpenter assumed he was the heir apparent for the job so when Mayor Dent and the City Council brought Spenser in, they'd clashed immediately. Aside from being bitter about being passed over for the job, Carpenter had displayed not only his misogyny but an attitude—a mean streak—that didn't belong in her department. He was abusive to not only her but to his fellow deputies. Especially to those he deemed to be weaker or somehow inferior to him. So, Spenser eventually made the decision to fire him.

Spenser shook her head, silently kicking herself for not seeing it sooner. The physical build should have been her first clue. But more than that, the eyes should have been the giveaway. Carpenter had a cold cruelty in his eyes that Spenser had always found chilling when she saw it. He had a presence about him that felt a lot like a thunderstorm that was gathering strength and when it broke, you knew it was going to be dangerous. She'd seen and felt those things in her attacker when she was fighting to save her life. And even then, she still hadn't put it together.

"This is not your fault, Sheriff," Young said. "There is no way you could have known."

"I should have. I really should have," she replied.

"At the risk of overusing those words you threw at me not so long ago, you are a lot of things, but clairvoyant is not one of them."

A wan smile touched Spenser's lips. "You're just going to keep throwing that back in my face, aren't you?"

"Until the end of time. It's a good line," Young said. "And anyway, if you should have known it was him, I should have known it twice over. I trained with the guy. Worked with him for a good, long while before you came on board. If anybody should have known it was him, it should have been me. But I heard he wasn't living in the area anymore either, so he was just out of sight, out of mind. For all of us."

Spenser shook her head. "It was all right there the whole time. Everything I needed to put it all together. And now, Victoria Hall and Lia Rice…"

If she had put it all together earlier, those two women might still be alive. Maybe it was her hubris that kept her from seeing it. Maybe Carpenter was right about her. Maybe she thought because she was a Bureau agent that she was somehow better than everybody else, even if only on a subconscious level. Maybe that arrogance had led her to develop a blind spot.

"You can't do that to yourself, Sheriff," Young said gently. "Their deaths are not on you. There's nothing you could have done with what we had. They're dead for one reason and one reason alone—Barton Carpenter."

Before she could respond, her earpiece crackled to life. "Yeah, I'm here—I mean, Yellow One reporting. Or checking in or whatever."

Spenser and Young shared a look and laughed. "Your brother is hopeless in the field."

"That's why he usually stays in the office."

"Good point," Spenser replied, then keyed open her mic. "Go ahead, Gold One."

"Yeah, Gold One. Sorry," he said. "Anyway, the drone is up, and I've finished the survey of the property. It all looks to be clear. You guys should be safe to approach."

"Copy that," Spenser said. "Red and Blue teams, are you in position?"

"Affirmative. Blue team in position," Deputy Woods, the head of her tac team, replied.

"Red team in position," reported Deputy Berman, Woods' second in command. "Standing by for breach command."

Carpenter's trailer wasn't all that big, making it more dangerous to send multiple teams streaming through the front door. Woods had briefed her on his plan to engage. At Woods' request, Spenser was not part of the op and, much to her chagrin, had to sit back and watch it all unfold. She understood his request. Not only did it make tactical sense since the target was a small trailer, but it also made sense since she wasn't one hundred percent physically capable of leading an assault at the moment. She was still moving pretty slowly from the beating she'd taken.

Spenser understood why Woods had asked her to stand down, but that didn't mean she liked it. Spenser was the one used to leading the charge. On being the first one through the door. She prided herself on never asking somebody to do something she wouldn't do herself. She knew this was different. Since Young was in the same boat, though, she'd had her tag along to help provide overwatch. Two sets of eyes were always better than one.

"Red team ready to breach," Berman's voice crackled through her earpiece.

"Execute breach on my command," Woods replied.

"Still no movement around the property. Still clear," Jacob added.

"You know what gets me?" Young said. "It was that message he left on the bathroom door. You know, the one about hubris and arrogance. I mean, he's one to talk, right? I have never met a more arrogant person than Barton Carpenter."

Spenser nodded as Young's words echoed through her head. She started thinking about the hubris that seemed to be Carpenter's most prominent, perhaps even defining trait.

"Red team, prepare to deploy the flash bangs and breach. Ready to move on my mark," Woods said. "Counting down in five... four..."

Carpenter was a peacock. He liked all eyes to be on him and never failed to put on a show, wherever he was, to ensure he got the attention he craved so badly. Carpenter never did anything small. It was always a production with him. And whenever he did something, it was always for a purpose, always to draw eyes and attention to him.

"Three..."

Spenser's eyes widened as a bolt of fear shot through her heart.

"Oh, God," she gasped.

"Two..."

She fumbled with her mic for a moment before steadying it in her grip and keying it open.

"Abort!" she screamed. "Abort breach. Clear the area. Now! Get the hell out of there!"

Young turned to her. "Sheriff, what's going—"

Before Young could even finish her thought, the trailer in front of them erupted into a ball of blinding light. The sound of the explosion was quickly followed by a sound like a blast of thunder directly overhead. The shockwave of the blast rocked the truck like a powerful earthquake, and when Spenser's eyes cleared, she saw the thick column of inky black smoke rising into the sky. The ground around the trailer was charred and blackened, the stacks of tires and other assorted debris that had been out front scattered and burning.

Spenser jumped out of the Bronco and keyed her mic. "Blue team, red team, report in. Report in. Are you all okay out there?"

Spenser stepped to the front of the tree line and tried to see through the smoke and flames, looking for her people but couldn't see anybody. Young stood right beside Spenser looking every bit as concerned and scared as she did.

"Woods, Berman, somebody, report," Spenser said. "Report, dammit!"

There was a long delay, heightening Spenser's fear and anxiety, but then she heard a crackle over the line. She pressed her hand to her ear.

"Berman? Woods?" she called into her mic.

"Woods," he said. "I'm alive… My entire team is alive, but we've got some wounded. It looks superficial but we're going to need a bus out here."

"Berman checking in. Ditto that. We've got some wounded… some look a little serious," he said. "Get a rush on that bus, Sheriff."

"Copy that."

Young was already on the phone with dispatch, calling for multiple ambulances. The relief that swept through her at hearing that her people were okay was profound. Her eyes welled with tears and her legs buckled, nearly dropping her to the dirt beneath her feet. She managed to stay upright, though just barely.

"How did you know?" Young asked.

"The van partly. He didn't bother trying to hide it. He wanted us to see it. Wanted us to think he was there," Spenser replied. "The other part was that I realized this ending wouldn't have been showy enough for him. It was too… anticlimactic. Having a tac team put him in bracelets and haul him away wouldn't have garnered the type of attention he seeks. I don't think even a shootout would have been enough attention. He wants—no, he needs—something more dramatic. Something people are going to remember."

Young shook her head. "I think killing you would have been memorable."

"It wasn't just about taking me out. He wanted a big body count," Spenser said.

Young frowned. "The man is sick."

"Yes. He is."

The wail of the sirens filled the air in the distance and were drawing closer as the fire department and ambulances raced to the scene. The flames around Carpenter's trailer were starting to die down but the plume of smoke seemed to be getting thicker as it drifted heavenward. Only now could Spenser see her deputies through the haze. She spotted Woods and Berman organizing a triage off to the side of the scene, well away from the fires.

"Come on," Spenser said. "Let's go help get our people squared away."

"Copy that."

They both limped across the field and jumped to help triage the wounded. The ambulances and fire department rolled up a few minutes later and took over the scene. Young sat down on a flat tree stump, a look of weariness and discomfort on her face from overexerting herself. After Spenser directed an EMT over to Young, she looked around. Not seeing who she needed to find, she pulled her phone out of her pocket and dialed the number then pressed the phone to her ear. The call was connected on the first ring.

"Hey, boss," Jacob answered. "I stayed away from the scene because I figured I was going to get in the way and—"

"Where are you?" she asked.

"Right where you told me to position myself. The clearing a quarter mile from the trailer—"

"Good. Stay there, I'm on my way to you," Spenser said as she moved as quickly as she could toward the Bronco. "I need you to do something for me."

CHAPTER THIRTY-THREE

Spenser sat in the Bronco staring at the house across the street. It was a single-level ranch-style home, white with green trim and shutters, with a split-rail fence around the front yard. A large tree that had to be almost a century old stood in the front yard with wide, thick branches. An old tire swing hung from one of them, dangling above the ground and slowly swaying back and forth. It was a nicely maintained home with fresh paint and an American flag hanging in a bracket beside the front door, the red and white fabric rippling in the gentle breeze.

The upper-middle-class neighborhood around her was quiet. A car had passed her by about twenty minutes ago but other than that, it was like a ghost town. No kids out in the front yards playing and not a lot of foot traffic. It looked like the sort of neighborhood that was aging. The kids were all grown and had gone on to build their own lives, coming back for holidays and the like. The parents left behind only planted deeper and deeper roots. Spenser didn't think there was a lot of turnover in that part of town.

The front door of the house stood open, the darkness beyond the threshold ominous, yet compelling. It was an invitation if she dared. And Spenser had no choice but to dare. Not if she wanted this man's reign of terror to finally come to an end. But she would have been lying if she said she wasn't afraid. She would have been foolish if she wasn't. She didn't consider fear a weakness. It was what you chose to do with your fear that defined how you lived your life and who you were as a person. Spenser believed she had mastered her fear, or at least, had learned to use it in a constructive way that didn't leave her paralyzed.

The bleating of her cell phone shattered the silence in the cabin of the Bronco, startling her. Spenser pulled the phone out of her pocket and somehow knew who would be on the other end of the line even before she picked it up. With a flutter in her heart, she connected the call and pressed the phone to her ear.

"Are you going to sit out there all day?" he asked. "Or are you coming inside?"

"Why don't you come out here, Barton? I think it's time we had a talk."

"Nah. You come on in here. I've got something I want to show you."

"What do you want to show me?"

"If I tell you, it'll ruin the surprise," he said in an eerie singsong voice. "Come inside, Spenser Song. Come see what I have for you… and then let's end this once and for all."

The house belonged to Carpenter's parents and had been in the family for more than sixty years. When Spenser had been back at the scene, looking at the bruised and bloodied faces of her deputies, something inside of her had snapped. She'd been filled with a dark rage so powerful it was overwhelming. It had been so strong and so consuming, Spenser had felt smothered. She'd felt like she couldn't breathe. Spenser felt like she was on the verge of a panic attack and just wanted to scream at the top of her lungs.

Watching the EMTs rush around, tending to her deputies, Spenser felt completely powerless. Helpless. She had no idea what to do, but she knew she needed to do something. She felt like she needed to mete out justice not just for Carpenter's victims but for her deputies. For Amanda. And for herself. So, she'd had Jacob find the address for her then swore him to secrecy. She made him promise that he wouldn't tell anybody where she'd gone.

Spenser knew him well enough to know that even sworn to secrecy, it was only a matter of time before Jacob opened his mouth. He just couldn't help himself. Especially when he was worried about her. He'd told her he didn't think she should be going out there alone and implored her to take some backup. But Spenser wasn't going to let this animal hurt any more of her people. He promised not to tell anybody, but she just hoped he'd be able to hold his tongue long enough for her to do what she needed to do.

"All right," Spenser said. "I'm coming in."

"Good. Are you armed?"

"What do you think?"

"I think we're going to have some fun, you and I," he said.

"Yeah, maybe so."

Spenser disconnected the call then dropped her phone on the passenger seat. She got out of the Bronco and slammed the door shut behind her and walked across the street. Her focus was on the doorway, her eyes cutting left and right as she searched for the telltale signs of somebody laying an obvious trap. She saw nothing. Nothing that indicated Carpenter was planning on shooting her from a window or jumping down on top of her from a tree.

She mounted the steps and slowly walked up to the porch. The gaping maw of the open door loomed even larger in front of her. Spenser pulled the Glock from her hip and raised it then drew a deep breath to steady herself.

"Let's get this over with, Spenser," she muttered to herself.

Crouching low and moving swiftly, Spenser darted across the threshold and into a small entryway. The house was dim and cloaked in shadows, adding to the ominous feeling that was pressing down on her.

"I'm in here, Spenser," Carpenter called. "In the living room."

Still moving cautiously, with the barrel of her Glock leading the way, Spenser stepped through the archway and into the living room. Candles sat on every conceivable surface emitting a soft glow and a mélange of aromas. Spenser paused just inside the doorway and took in the scene set out before her.

"Jesus, Carpenter," she said. "You're a monster."

"You shouldn't be surprised," he said. "But tell me, how did you know I rigged my trailer?"

Spenser was unable to take her eyes off what he'd done. Her heart thundered in her chest and her stomach roiled. She knew she needed to keep it together. To stay focused. The only thing more dangerous than a cornered animal was a cornered animal who had absolutely nothing to lose.

"You were too obvious. You left the van out where I could see it, for one thing," Spenser said. "I also knew going out that way—blowing yourself up like that—wasn't flashy enough for you. Not even if you took out some of my deputies. Nobody would remember it six months from now, let alone still be talking about it. Being a narcissist like you are, you needed something grand. Something that will make people remember you."

He grinned wide at her. "Damn, Spenser. Maybe you're a little smarter than I thought after all. Bravo, Sheriff. Bravo," he said, then gestured to the scene in front of him. "I think this guarantees people will be talking about me six months from now. People will remember what I've done here—especially if I take you out in the process."

Spenser's eyes flicked from Carpenter to the man and woman sitting in a pair of recliners in front of him on the other side of the room. Both had ragged slashes across their throats and were soaked in their own blood. As bad as that was, what else had been done to them was even worse. They'd been disemboweled and had their entrails piled in their laps like some ghastly Halloween decoration. Beyond that, the faces of the corpses had been beaten so badly, they were unrecognizable. It was hard to tell they were human at all. A bloody baseball bat lay on the floor beside the recliners which sat in wide pools of blood.

On a credenza against the wall, Spenser noticed a picture of an older man and woman. They were both smiling, holding colorful cocktails, and looked to be having the time of their life on what appeared to be a cruise ship. The physical build of the couple in the picture was roughly the same as the corpses in the recliners which made Spenser's stomach churn.

Carpenter stood behind the recliners cradling a Mossberg 12-gauge shotgun in his arms. He smiled wide at her as she came through the doorway, pure satisfaction etched into his features.

"These were your parents," she said.

He shrugged. "I never really cared much for them. They were always nagging at me. Pick, pick, picking at every little thing I did. Nothing I did was ever good enough for them."

"So, you thought it necessary to kill them? Christ, Carpenter, what sort of screwed up moral compass do you have inside of you?"

He stared hard at her as she spoke, but then his expression abruptly changed. His face darkened. Got tighter. The smile faded and was replaced by a look of pure contempt.

"They nagged me my whole life. But then it got worse after you fired me. So much worse," he said as if she hadn't spoken at all. "I was going to be the sheriff here. That job was mine. Howard had been grooming me to fill his spot for years. But then you came along and screwed it all up. You screwed me out of my rightful job."

"I didn't screw you out of anything. If you were passed over for the job, it was for a reason," Spenser said. "Did you ever stop to think that maybe, just maybe, the mayor and City Council found you so objectionable they felt they had to look outside?"

"They looked outside because they wanted to check all the boxes. Woman. Minority," he said. "Yeah, you check all the boxes people want today. They don't want to offend anybody."

"Keep crying, Carpenter. And keep blaming your shortcomings on everybody but yourself. That's a winning strategy," Spenser said.

"You don't know how hard things have been for me ever since you fired me," he said, his voice hard. "It's been all but impossible to find another job—especially not one in law enforcement. I thought I had that job in Montana but guess what? They hired another woman instead."

A grimace curled his lips as a look of disgust crossed his features. His grip on the Mossberg tightened and his entire body tensed. She knew he was building up to his grand finale, whether it be killing her or suicide by cop. Spenser knew she needed to get him off balance and back on his heels.

"It's so tough to be you," Spenser said. "Poor you."

"You have no idea how true that is. It's impossible for a man like me to get a leg up in this world," he said. "Not with people like you stealing our jobs and our place. People like you need to learn your place. You need to learn to stay in your lane."

"By people like me, I'll assume you mean, intelligent, well-educated, well-spoken individuals who aren't ignorant, sexist pieces of garbage," Spenser said.

Carpenter's face darkened and a sneer showed off his crooked teeth. He had a quicksilver temper, and it didn't usually take much to get under his skin. but his hatred for her seemed so hot, he seemed ready to burst in record time. She had been expecting him to fire another verbal volley at her—Carpenter always liked hearing the sound of his own voice—but instead, he moved faster than she expected.

"Crap," she muttered.

He brought his shotgun to bear, and Spenser watched in horror as flames erupted from the barrel. A moment later, she heard the concussive boom of the shot, but she was already in motion, having thrown herself to the side. As she cut through the air, Spenser squeezed off a pair of shots she knew went wide of the mark. The buckshot from Carpenter's shotgun tore into the wall above Spenser, showering her with plaster, drywall, and bits of wallpaper.

The sound of him racking another round drew her attention and she looked up, realizing she was still fully exposed. Carpenter was grinning as he pivoted and started to bring the barrel toward her once more. Spenser grunted as she quickly rolled out of the way as the roar of the shotgun rang in her ears. The blast tore a massive divot out of the wooden flooring. She scrambled to her feet and ducked behind the wall as Carpenter fired another shot that tore a chunk out of the archway.

"You can't hide from me, Spenser."

Her heart was beating wildly, and fear-fueled adrenaline coursed through her veins. But Spenser tried to push through it. She leaned out, raised her weapon, and took aim. Carpenter was gone, though. Ice formed in her belly and spread outward to all her limbs. He was smart to have drawn her in since he had the advantage in the house. And Spenser felt like such a fool. Her hubris and a possibly fatal sense of herself had led her to think she could get the drop on him. That she could bring this situation to an end all on her own.

Spenser pushed her fear and her doubt out of her mind. She didn't have time for it. She gritted her teeth and was just about to step back into the living room to find him when she heard the squeak of a floorboard behind her. Moving on instinct, Spenser threw herself to the side. She was quick but not quick enough as the butt of the Mossberg clipped the side of the head. Her head ringing, she went sprawling and hit the hardwood floor with a hard grunt.

Spenser's vision blurred and her head rang as Carpenter stepped forward and brought his weapon to bear. Spenser quickly rolled over and squeezed off a shot, Carpenter howling in pain as her round tore through his thigh, sending a spray of blood onto the wall behind him. He dropped to a knee and the Mossberg hit the floor with a loud clatter as he grabbed at his wounded leg.

"I'm going to kill you!" he roared.

Spenser was already getting to her feet and started to bring her weapon up. Carpenter was in motion and threw a wild haymaker as he leaped up, catching Spenser in the side of the head, spinning her around like a top. Panic flowed through her veins as she lost her grip on her gun and it went flying, hitting the ground somewhere behind her. Carpenter was already on her and delivered a vicious punch to her stomach, driving the wind out of her lungs.

Spenser doubled over, gasping for air, when Carpenter brought his knee up. She grunted as it connected with her face. Spenser heard the crunch of her nose, and the coppery taste of her blood immediately filled her mouth. She let out a yelp of pain as he yanked her up by her hair and slammed the back of her head into the wall. She felt lightheaded and her vision wavered as he wrapped his massive hands around her throat.

"I'm going to kill you, Spenser Song. I'm going to choke the damn life out of you," he grunted then gave her a malicious grin. "But before I kill you, I think I should have a little fun with you first. What do you think, baby?"

Struggling for air and fighting to breathe, fighting to stay alive, Spenser pistoned her foot out with as much force as she could muster. It caught Carpenter square in the groin. His eyes widened comically and his mouth fell open, a low groan drifting from somewhere deep in his throat. His grip on her neck loosened and Spenser took advantage of the temporary reprieve, wriggling out of his grasp and squeezing away from him. Drawing in deep breaths, she darted out of his reach, doing her best to keep as much distance between them as she could.

"I'm going to kill you," he wheezed.

"You keep saying that," Spenser croaked. "And yet, here I am. Still."

Carpenter pulled a knife out of the sheath on his belt, the same he'd used on her the last time he attacked her. She stared at the blade, trying to suppress a shudder as she remembered how her blood had stained it dark the last time she'd seen it. Spenser cut her eyes away from the knife and frantically looked around the foyer, searching for her Glock. There. Fifteen feet away. Too far. The Mossberg, however, was near the toe of her boot. If she could just somehow get to it...

"Yeah, you remember this, don't you?" he sneered and waved the knife at her.

"I remember you failing to kill me with it, yeah," she replied.

"Not this time."

"We'll see."

Carpenter moved again quickly—quicker than a man his size should be able to move—and closed the distance between them seemingly in the blink of an eye. He brought the blade down with a murderous gleam in his eye, but Spenser pivoted and darted to the left. The blade embedded itself nearly to the hilt into the wall where she'd just been standing. Not giving him time to yank it out of the wall, Spenser quickly snatched up the Mossberg. Holding it by the barrel, swung it like a baseball bat with all her might, a howl of pent-up rage bursting from her mouth.

The butt of the shotgun crashed into the side of Carpenter's head with a slapping sound like a bat hitting wet meat. Limp and boneless, he dropped to the floor and lay there motionless. Spenser's field of vision wavered and was narrowing quickly. The sound of sirens filled the air, but they sounded distant. Far away. It was like she was hearing them from a tunnel on the other side of the world. She fought to stay in the moment. Fought like hell to keep from passing out.

On unsteady legs, Spenser stumbled over to Carpenter and rolled him onto his belly. It was a Herculean feat, but she managed it somehow. She knew her time among the conscious was fading as quickly as her strength. Spenser fell to her knees and pulled out her cuffs. She fumbled with them, nearly dropping them several times before she finally got him hooked up, tightening the bracelets as much as she could. To hell with whether she cut off circulation to his hands.

Spenser didn't know if Carpenter was simply unconscious, if he was alive, or if he was dead. And at that moment, Spenser didn't care. She wanted to make sure that if he was alive, he wasn't going anywhere. She wanted him to know that he wasn't going to get the ending he was after. Wanted him to know that nobody was going to be talking to him six minutes from now, let alone six months from now. She wanted him to know that he would be forgotten soon enough.

But most of all, Spenser wanted him to know that she'd won. That she'd beaten him. She wanted him to live with that indignity of having lost to somebody he considered so vastly inferior to him. And she wanted him to know it was she who'd put him in an eight-by-eight concrete cell for the rest of his miserable life.

SHADOWS OF THE FALLS

Spenser slumped back against the wall and let out a heavy sigh. She closed her eyes and, as the sirens approached, finally gave in to the rapidly encroaching darkness.

CHAPTER THIRTY-FOUR

THE FIRST THING SPENSER BECAME AWARE OF WAS THE darkness that surrounded her. A dim light burned somewhere behind her, but the rest of the room was left thick with shadow. The next thing she became aware of was the pain that radiated from every corner of her body. Spenser had taken some beatings in her day, but not one of them had ever left her feeling quite as beat up and haggard as she did right then. She felt like she'd been put through a meat grinder. Even blinking hurt.

She looked down and groaned when she saw the array of tubes sticking out of her arms. She glanced over and saw the tubes and wires were attached to a battery of machines that stood beside her bed tracking every function of her body.

"You're in the hospital," Ryker's voice sounded from her right.

"No, I'm in hell."

Spenser groaned and winced in pain as she turned her head to see Ryker sitting in a chair beside her bed. He reached out and gingerly took her hand. He looked tired. Like he'd been there all night. Or longer.

"How long have I been here?" Spenser asked.

"Two days," he said. "Almost three."

"Seriously?"

He nodded. "Seriously. Carpenter gave you one hell of a beating, Spenser. He could have killed you. Almost did, actually."

"Yeah, he said he was going to. He was wrong."

"Yes, he was. And I'm grateful for it," Ryker said, then quickly added, "we all are."

Spenser offered him a smile and softly squeezed his hand. Even a gesture that small, though, sent sharp spikes of pain shooting through her body, making her wince. She fumbled with the controller and finally got her bed to raise her to a sitting position. Spenser grimaced but rode the waves of pain that battered her until they faded. Ryker poured a glass of water from the pitcher on the table then helped her to take a drink.

"Thank you," she said. "I hate being in a hospital."

"I know you do. But I have to say, it was kind of nice having you unconscious and unable to fight us about admitting you to the hospital," he said. "Even in your condition, I have no doubt you probably would have tried to say you were fine."

"I hate you."

"That's the drugs talking."

"I'm on drugs?"

"A lot of them."

"They're not working," Spenser said. "I feel like hammered horsecrap."

"You kind of look like it, too."

"Did I mention how much I hate you?"

Ryker laughed softly. "Yeah, you mentioned it."

"Where's my dog?"

"This is a hospital. They said she wasn't allowed to visit."

"I hate them, too."

"That's justifiable. I hate them for that, too," he said. "For my money, there is no better medicine than the love of a dog."

"For once, I agree with you."

He smiled and they sat in a companionable silence for a couple of moments. Spenser just looked into his eyes and felt her heart flutter as he held her hand. The air between them crackled with an energy that made Spenser feel warm inside and filled her with emotions she hadn't felt in a very long time. And she had to admit, it was a nice feeling.

Spenser looked away and the moment passed, bursting that bubble of emotion that had enveloped them. She held onto his hand, though, unwilling to give it up completely.

"What happened to Carpenter?" she asked.

"Believe it or not, he was in worse shape than you," Ryker replied. "You put a beating on him for the ages. It was a classic case of David and Goliath."

"Where is he?"

"He's in a room a couple of floors up under very heavy guard," he said. "I think it's a bit of overkill but Young insisted on having three on the door at all times."

"Three? I'm going to need to talk to her about deploying her resources more efficiently. I thought I taught her better than that," Spenser said.

"You're not going to be talking to her for a while, I'm afraid. You are strictly forbidden from being anywhere near the department building until you're healed. Doctor's orders."

"You mean Marley's orders."

"She's a doctor, so, what she says, goes," Ryker replied. "But don't worry. The department's in good shape. She's still gimpy, but Young has taken command and seems to be doing a good job with everything. She seems to be coming into her own. I can see now why you pushed for her to be your second."

"What has Young told you about the case against Carpenter?"

"Spense, you need to rest—"

"I'm not going to be able to rest until we fully close the book on him," Spenser said. "I need to know about the case."

Ryker sighed and seemed to be debating with himself whether to indulge her or not. But then he offered her a smile, perhaps realizing the futility of trying to deter her when she had her mind set on something. He'd known her long enough to know it was easier to give her what she wanted so she could move on than play the back-and-forth game with her.

"Come on, Ryker. I know Young and know she would have told you what was going on so you could pass it along to me in the event I woke up while she wasn't here," Spenser said.

He laughed softly. "You're pretty wise."

"I trained my protégé well."

"Alright, fine," he said. "But after I tell you, can we move on to better, more restful, and less stress-inducing things?"

"Scout's honor."

"I'm skeptical you were ever a Scout, but I'm willing to overlook it. This time, anyway."

"That's very kind of you."

"So they've got Carpenter cold on the two counts of murder. His parents, obviously," he said. "They're also building the case against him for the murders of Victoria Hall and Lia Rice as well as the rapes of all the others."

"Do they have a case? What did Young say the DA is saying?"

He shrugged but she could see the glimmer of doubt flashing in his eyes. The idea of building a case against him was the one thing that had nagged at Spenser from the start. They didn't have much to build a case with. The surviving victims could ID him by his eyes and the tattoo on his forearm. But any halfway decent defense attorney could tear that to shreds in court. Outside of getting him to confess, there was only one way they were going to be able to tie Carpenter to the series of rapes and murders—the tokens he took from each scene.

"Has Carpenter said anything yet?" she asked.

"I believe Young said the only word he's spoken since you cuffed him was, 'lawyer.'"

"That figures."

"What about the tokens he took from his victims?" Spenser pressed. "Have they found them yet? Those would be definitive proof he committed those crimes."

"Not yet," he replied. "And Young says it's possible those tokens were in the trailer that blew up. She isn't sure they'll ever be recovered, but she's got your techs out there sifting through everything at the site with a fine-toothed comb."

Spenser felt like a lead weight dropped into her belly and she gritted her teeth in frustration. She pressed her head back into the pillows and growled to herself.

"C'mon, they've got him cold on two counts of murder. He's going away and he's never getting out," Ryker said. "Isn't that enough?"

"It's not. It's not even close to being enough," she said. "What about justice for all his other victims? Women who have to live with what he did to them for the rest of their lives. It's great that he's going away for killing his parents, don't get me wrong. But I want justice for all the other women whose lives he's shattered, too."

"I understand that. And I want that, too. Everybody does," he said. "But we can't always get the justice we want. Sometimes, we have to settle for the justice we're able to get. It's a sad reality, but sometimes, that's all there is."

"Yeah, I know," she said softly. "I just hate that. Those women deserve more. They all deserve better. They deserve to watch that bastard fry."

Ryker chuckled softly. "We're in Washington, not Florida. We don't fry people here," he said. "Though, it certainly would solve a lot of problems."

Spenser's mind raced. She turned the case over and over in her mind, trying to see it from all angles, trying to find a solution to the problem. And that's when it hit her.

"A narcissist like Carpenter isn't going to let go of his tokens. They're souvenirs. He's going to want to keep them, even if he's in prison. Just knowing they're out there is enough to get him off," Spenser mused. "He might even get somebody on the outside to bring them to him. Those tokens are out there, Ryker. I know they are."

"Okay, but where?"

"His parents' house. I'll bet he stashed them there."

"They've been through the place already—"

"But I guarantee they weren't looking for a hidey-hole," Spenser said. "I need my phone. I need to call Amanda—"

"You're not getting your phone. Also doctor's orders. She said no police business for at least a week. Maybe two."

"That's not going to work for me."

"Marley said she will keep you sedated the entire time you're here if she has to," Ryker said.

"She can't do that."

"She controls your meds, so I'm pretty sure she can," he replied. "I'll tell you what. I will pass on your message to Amanda. I will make sure she has the techs go back out to the house and look for his tokens. Will that satisfy you and help you relax?"

Spenser sighed. "Not really. But I guess it'll have to do."

"Good," he said. "And Spense, you've got a lot of great people around you. You need to learn to start trusting them and loosen your hold on things. You don't have to do everything yourself. I know it's hard but learn to lean on your team."

"And where did you come by this wisdom, Mr. Lone Wolf?"

"A friend taught me the value of leaning on others. Of learning to trust people," he said with a soft laugh and pointed look.

Spenser grimaced. "Point taken."

"You should get some rest," Ryker said.

"So should you."

"Yeah, I'll head out once you drift off."

She closed her eyes for a minute, feeling wrung out and exhausted all of a sudden. As she focused on her breathing, she felt her body start to relax. Spenser felt like she was drifting. Floating. Though she longed for justice for all his victims, maybe knowing that Carpenter was going away forever relieved some of her tension, and maybe, something more.

"Hey," she said. "Thank you. For everything."

"You're welcome."

Spenser smiled and felt herself slipping away. For the first time in what seemed like forever, Spenser gave herself over to the dark, warm embrace of sleep without the shadow of guilt darkening her soul but with a free and light heart.

EPILOGUE

Two weeks after the incident at the Carpenter family home, Spenser was finally released and sent home. Of course, with how closely Ryker had been hovering over her, she still kind of felt like she was in the hospital—though, with fewer needle pricks. Not that she minded him hovering over her. Spenser enjoyed being around and spending time with him. She just hated feeling like an invalid. She hated feeling like she needed somebody to take care of her.

Over her stay at the hospital, she'd been in constant communication with Young. Ryker had been right about her taking command and doing a good job as the acting sheriff. She was still healing herself, but that hadn't stopped her from doing her duties—an argument Spenser tried to make on her own behalf, but Marley wasn't having it. And when Spenser threatened to sign herself out against medical advice, Marley again advised her that she would incapacitate her by keeping her in a constant state of sedation. She wasn't kidding.

So, Spenser had contented herself with keeping an eye on the office from afar. She'd been gratified to learn that her hunch had panned out. Young had sent Arbery and his team back into the Carpenter family home and practically tore the place down to the studs. But they'd eventually found a hidden compartment in the wall behind a cabinet in the garage that was loaded with tokens. More tokens than they had victims, which meant that Carpenter had been at it for far longer than they believed and had claimed many more victims than they knew.

They had no way of knowing who or where these other victims were. And according to Young, he wasn't talking. He refused to give them anything, preferring to keep his thoughts and memories to himself. Spenser had no doubt that reliving those terrible things he did was sustaining him. They didn't need him, though. They had his fingerprints on the tokens in their active cases, each one another nail in his coffin. Carpenter should have been thankful Washington state didn't have the death penalty because he would be a prime candidate for it.

Carpenter was healing and suffered no permanent damage. He had been discharged a few days before she had and was booked in then held down at the office until King County had been able to send a few deputies to escort him back up to a proper cell in Seattle where he would wait to stand trial. From what she'd heard, even his most ardent supporters down at the office had turned their backs on him, shocked and disgusted with what they learned he truly was. Apparently, nobody liked a monster. Or at least, nobody liked the species of monster he turned out to be. Knowing how alone and isolated he must feel made Spenser smile.

Spenser pushed all thoughts of work aside as she lay on the bed in her room staring up at the ceiling, a gentle smile curving the corners of her mouth as she thought about her time staying in Ryker's place. He had gone to pick up some dinner from the Jade

Panda, of course, and left her there to rest. Annabelle lay beside her, the dog's enormous body pressed close to her own. She'd been beside herself when Spenser came home from the hospital and hadn't left her side since. She idly stroked Annabelle's head as she mentally took stock of the last few weeks.

With the threat that had been looming over her officially over, Spenser had moved back into her cabin. She had to admit, it felt a little bittersweet. Even though neither of them was anywhere near ready for that level of commitment—hell, they still weren't admitting they were even dating—Spenser had started getting used to coming home from work to Ryker. She had started to enjoy that feeling of domesticity in cooking dinner and washing dishes together. Enjoyed hanging out with the dogs and going for walks. She'd come to enjoy everything about it. A lot.

But Spenser knew that sort of situation wasn't something you fell into like that. Living together was the result of both parties wanting to advance their relationship and move it to the next level. Although they both acknowledged—if only to themselves—that there was something more between them, they were a long way off from being ready to play house. And forcing that issue or jumping into it before they were ready was a recipe for disaster for two people with as much combined baggage as they had.

Still, Spenser wouldn't lie and say it wasn't sometimes nice to think about or that just the idea of it brought a smile to her lips. They were a long way from taking that particular fork in the road, but Spenser still sometimes liked to think that maybe one day they'd get there.

"One day, huh?" she asked.

Annabelle let out a hefty, contented sigh as if telling her she was just as happy right there as anywhere else in the world at the moment. The shrill chirping of her phone shattered the stillness in the cabin. Spenser looked around and groaned. She'd left her phone in the kitchen. Thinking it might be Ryker, she slid out of bed, still moving somewhat gingerly. She was ninety-nine percent healed, but there were still times when a flash of pain would grip her body with such intensity, it would nearly drop her. Marley said those should eventually heal in time. Spenser hoped it would be sooner rather than later.

SHADOWS OF THE FALLS

With the big dog at her side, Spenser shuffled down the hallway and into the kitchen. She grabbed the phone that sat on the center island before it could stop ringing and connected the call. She pressed the phone to her ear as she leaned back against the island.

"Shrimp lo mein for me," she said, her voice filled with her smile. "And char siu pork."

"Clearly, you were expecting somebody else."

Spenser grimaced like she'd just bitten into the sourest lemon ever grown. As much as she'd like to forget it, Spenser would have recognized the man's voice anywhere.

"Clark Harris," she said. "What can I do for you?"

"That's ASAC Harris, Sheriff Song."

"Well, as you're so fond of reminding me every single time we speak, I'm no longer part of the Bureau. So, I'm embracing that. Leaning into it, as you might say," Spenser said. "And in that spirit, I no longer have to use Bureau titles or honors since you're no longer part of my chain of command and I'm not beholden to you. For anything."

Her voice was cold and tight and the message in her words clear. Even a dolt like Clark Harris should be able to pick up the subtext in her words. He was silent on the other end of the line for a long moment, no doubt seething. He was used to deference from her. Used to her adhering to all the Bureau conventions and protocols even though she was no longer party to them. Spenser had given him the respect his title granted him even after she'd left the Bureau because that sort of deference toward superiors had been ingrained in her at Quantico. Hell, it had been ingrained in her throughout her entire life.

It was a trait Spenser didn't like and she made a conscious decision to deprogram herself. She vowed to herself to only give respect to those who'd earned it. And Clark Harris, ASAC of the New York Field Office and her one-time superior officer, had most definitely not earned it. In fact, he used to show her, on a daily basis, how much he didn't deserve her deference or respect. Therefore, she decided, he would no longer receive it.

Something had changed in Spenser during her stay in the hospital. Maybe it was coming somewhat close to dying at the hands of Barton Carpenter, or more likely, it was because he forced her to take a close look at herself, to take an account of her faults and flaws—of which, there were many—but something inside of her had shifted. Carpenter had been right when he called her out for her hubris. As she lay in the hospital all those days with nothing to do but marinate in the toxic stew sloshing around in her head, Spenser was forced to take a closer look at herself. And she didn't exactly care for the reflection looking back at her.

It was a tough pill to swallow, but in some ways, he had been right about her. Without realizing it, Spenser had believed she was on a different level than most people. She did believe she was the smartest person in every room she walked into. It was something that made her good at her job. But it was also something that led her to not being able to trust anybody around her. Spenser realized she was holding onto everything so tightly and tried to do everything because, on some deeper level, she didn't believe anybody else could do as good of a job as she could.

Along with that realization came a determination to do better. To be better. To learn to trust those around her. Ryker was right about her being surrounded by good people. Smart people. People eager and willing to do a good job. She just needed to loosen the reins a bit. She needed to let them run and show her what they were capable of. Spenser only needed to look as far as Amanda Young to prove what was possible when she learned to trust. Not everybody was going to flourish the way she had, but that didn't mean they couldn't flourish and thrive in their own ways.

"So, Clark," Spenser pressed. "What do you want?"

"It has come to my attention that you are still poking around your husband's case," he said. "It has further come to my attention that your old partner, Derrick Ricci, has contacted you. In fact, I have it on good authority that he's contacted you several times."

"Yes, he has. So, what?"

"And what was the substance of your conversations?"

"They are none of your business," she said. "As a private citizen not being investigated for any crime, I'm not obligated to disclose the substance of private conversations. Besides, I'm sure you can get the audio of the call since they're recorded and there is no expectation of privacy in jail."

It would cost her nothing to tell him what Derrick said. After all, he didn't say anything other than beg her to testify on his behalf. But she didn't like Harris. So, she decided to be a pain in his backside simply because she could.

"We don't need to be antagonistic with each other, Spenser."

"I believe we do. After all, we find ourselves standing on opposite sides of a great divide."

"And what divide is that?"

"You want my husband's case to just go away," she said. "And I want the truth to come out. I want justice for my husband—and for myself, by the way. I was shot in that attack as well—"

"We want justice, too. Same as you."

"Then why aren't you looking for the real shooter?" Spenser fired back. "Derrick Ricci is guilty of a good many things. But he did not shoot me, and he did not kill my husband. I want the man who did in prison for the rest of his life and will not accept anything less."

There was a long pause on the other end of the line and Spenser could practically see Harris' face turning beet red as she recalled it did when he was upset and frustrated. Derrick Ricci was a stain on the fabric of the Bureau. He's tarnished their image. And if there was one thing the Bureau as an institution cared about more than anything, it was their image.

From their perspective, piling all the charges on to Ricci and then throwing him into some hellish supermax prison for the rest of his days would send the right message—nobody was above the law, and the Bureau, in its war on criminals, would hunt down and prosecute anybody who breaks the law. Even one of their own.

From the Bureau's perspective, it would be good PR. It would be the right message to send out to the public. But it wouldn't be the truth.

"Spenser, I'm calling to ask you once again to stand down," Harris said.

"No."

"We are moving forward with Ricci's prosecution for your husband's murder along with a slew of other crimes. He's going to prison for the rest of his life one way or the other," Harris said.

"Do what you have to do," Spenser replied. "And I'll do what I have to do."

"Meaning?"

"Meaning, while you idiots are patting each other on the backs, drinking your scotch and smoking your cigars as you congratulate yourselves on gaining a conviction, I will continue to hunt down the man who actually pulled the trigger that night," Spenser growled.

"I would advise you against that."

"And I would advise you to take your advice and shove it straight up your—"

"I'm aware that you have been using Bureau personnel to gain access to information that you, as a civilian and no longer a Bureau agent, are not entitled to," he said smugly.

Spenser's belly clenched and she frowned. She should have known that he would be keeping tabs on her and the moves she was making. This case was personal to him since he very likely stood to gain from a successful prosecution of Derrick Ricci. Spenser had no doubt he would move another rung up that ladder for successfully rooting out a corrupt murderer within the Bureau. She should have covered her tracks better.

"I have no idea what you're talking about," she said.

"Yes. You do," he said. "I could have you thrown in jail for obstruction right now."

"Good luck making that case stick."

"This case is no longer in your hands, Spenser. You are not employed by the Federal Bureau of Investigations, and therefore, possessing classified Bureau materials is a crime," he said. "If I learn that you are still engaging in this practice of compromising actual agents to gain access to such materials, I will have you prosecuted to the full extent of the law. Am I understood?"

"I bet the public would be interested to know how the Bureau is railroading a man for a crime he didn't commit while letting the one who did commit that crime walk free simply as a matter of optics," Spenser said. "I bet the public would like to know you're offering up a sacrificial lamb simply for better public relations points. Yeah, I bet people would like to know all that. Don't you?"

"I would advise you against a course of action like that. As a former agent, you know just how difficult the Bureau can make life for you."

"So, the Bureau is threatening me, a private citizen, for wanting to uncover the truth about my husband's murder and put the real killer behind bars?"

"Some truths are best left undiscovered."

"No. They're not. Not from where I'm standing."

"I always respected you, Spenser. Please don't make us do something I would rather not do," he said. "We are going to prosecute Ricci. That train has left the station and there's no calling it back. I don't want to see that same train run over you."

Spenser gritted her teeth and felt her face growing hot as the anger flowed through her veins. She was gripping the phone so tightly, she was surprised she hadn't crushed it like a beer can and quickly had to force herself to loosen her grip. Spenser closed her eyes and silently counted to five. It didn't help calm her down.

"Clark, do what you have to do," she said, her voice low and tight. "And like I said, I'm going to do what I have to do. The truth will come out. One way or another, it will come out."

Spenser disconnected the call and dropped the phone onto the kitchen island. Annabelle looked up at her with those soulful brown eyes of hers and a concerned expression on that big doggy face. Spenser fished a treat out of the jar and gave it to the big dog.

"Looks like we're going to war with the Bureau, girl," she said. "This should be a lot of fun."

AUTHOR'S NOTE

Thank you for joining Spenser Song on another exciting adventure in Sweetwater Falls! Your support for this series has been nothing short of amazing. So, as we wrap up this adventure, I'm sure you're already curious about what awaits Spenser next. Get ready for, *'The Lies in the Falls'*, where we will see the town celebrating Founders Day and embracing the festive season. But amidst the celebrations, Spenser finds herself drawn into a gripping hunt when a prominent figure mysteriously vanishes. Tangled family secrets, political pressures, and a startling discovery lead her on a search for truth and to an unexpected, chilling culprit. Brace yourself for a riveting holiday mystery where nothing is as it seems, and danger lurks beneath the glittering Christmas cheer!

Your feedback is invaluable to me, and let me just say that I am all ears. I want to know what delighted you and where I can improve so that I can continue to craft the best reading experience for you. As an independent writer, I rely on your support to keep writing and delivering pulse-pounding and entertaining reading experiences like this one. Please consider leaving a review to let me know your thoughts on this book. I'm looking forward to you reuniting with Spenser and Ryker in the enchanting world of Sweetwater Falls in the next addition!

And if you haven't caught wind of it yet, let me introduce you to something special: *'Watching Her,'* the latest gem in my Blake Wilder series. Your reception of this book has meant the world to me and your support not only warms my heart but also helps spread the word that this is a story not to be missed! In it, a familiar case lands on Blake's lap, and she could have never imagined the horrors that would follow. A serial killer with a chillingly familiar pattern resurfaces, and it will take all her wit and power to ensure that the culprit never sees the light of day again. As the case and the body count mount, it becomes apparent that he's not just a step ahead of Blake: he's a shadow in the darkness, a relentless tormentor who's watching her every move.

Thank you again for your continued support. It is because of YOU that I have the motivation to keep going and keep delivering the stories you love.

By the way, if you find any typos or want to reach out to me, feel free to email me at egray@ellegraybooks.com

Yours truly,
Elle Gray

CONNECT WITH ELLE GRAY

Loved the book? Don't miss out on future reads! Join my newsletter and receive updates on my latest releases, insider content, and exclusive promos. Plus, as a thank you for joining, you'll get a FREE copy of my book Deadly Pursuit!

Deadly Pursuit follows the story of Paxton Arrington, a police officer in Seattle who uncovers corruption within his own precinct. With his career and reputation on the line, he enlists the help of his FBI friend Blake Wilder to bring down the corrupt Strike Team. But the stakes are high, and Paxton must decide whether he's willing to risk everything to do the right thing.

Claiming your freebie is easy! Visit
https://dl.bookfunnel.com/513mluk159
and sign up with your email!

Want more ways to stay connected? Follow me on Facebook and Instagram or sign up for text notifications by texting "blake" to 844-552-1368. Thanks for your support and happy reading!

ALSO BY
ELLE GRAY

Blake Wilder FBI Mystery Thrillers

Book One - The 7 She Saw
Book Two - A Perfect Wife
Book Three - Her Perfect Crime
Book Four - The Chosen Girls
Book Five - The Secret She Kept
Book Six - The Lost Girls
Book Seven - The Lost Sister
Book Eight - The Missing Woman
Book Nine - Night at the Asylum
Book Ten - A Time to Die
Book Eleven - The House on the Hill
Book Twelve - The Missing Girls
Book Thirteen - No More Lies
Book Fourteen - The Unlucky Girl
Book Fifteen - The Heist
Book Sixteen - The Hit List
Book Seventeen - The Missing Daughter
Book Eighteen - The Silent Threat
Book Nineteen - A Code to Kill
Book Twenty - Watching Her

A Pax Arrington Mystery
Free Prequel - Deadly Pursuit
Book One - I See You
Book Two - Her Last Call
Book Three - Woman In The Water
Book Four - A Wife's Secret

Storyville FBI Mystery Thrillers
Book One - The Chosen Girl
Book Two - The Murder in the Mist
Book Three - Whispers of the Dead

A Sweetwater Falls Mystery
Book One - New Girl in the Falls
Book Two - Missing in the Falls
Book Three - The Girls in the Falls
Book Four - Memories of the Falls
Book Five - Shadows of the Falls

ALSO BY
ELLE GRAY | K.S. GRAY

Olivia Knight FBI Mystery Thrillers
Book One - New Girl in Town
Book Two - The Murders on Beacon Hill
Book Three - The Woman Behind the Door
Book Four - Love, Lies, and Suicide
Book Five - Murder on the Astoria
Book Six - The Locked Box
Book Seven - The Good Daughter
Book Eight - The Perfect Getaway
Book Nine - Behind Closed Doors
Book Ten - Fatal Games
Book Eleven - Into the Night

ALSO BY
ELLE GRAY | JAMES HOLT

The Florida Girl FBI Mystery Thrillers
Book One - The Florida Girl
Book Two - Resort to Kill
Book Three - The Runaway
Book Four - The Ransom

Made in United States
Troutdale, OR
03/11/2025